CRITICAL PRAISE FOR MELANIE TEM!

WINNER OF THE BRAM STOKER AWARD!
WINNER OF THE WORLD FANTASY AWARD!

"Her writing is a cry from the very heart of darkness."
—Dan Simmons

"Put aside V. C. Andrews and John Saul. Melanie Tem knows intimately the terrors that haunt families."
—*Locus*

"The power of her writing is extraordinary. Melanie Tem is one hell of a writer."
—*SFX*

"A master at conveying visceral terror."
—*Rocky Mountain News*

"Melanie Tem has an uncanny knack for probing everyday families, finding their deepest fears and turning them into waking nightmares of real or perceived horror."
—*Fangoria*

Tem is "an author of lyrical precision. [Her] words speak with valuable authenticity."
—*Cemetery Dance*

JUST A LITTLE TEMPTATION . . .

"Bingo!" Reluctantly, Tommy looked over his shoulder. Dropping with a nasty thud a leather-bound book lettered in gold, Tobias held up three bills, too crisp to flutter. "Three c-notes. Not bad, huh?"

"Cool," Tommy said.

"Probably forget which book she put 'em in. Probably forgot she even put 'em in a book. They were in the Shakespeare sonnets." He threw his head back and spread the hand with the money in it over his heart. " 'Thou art more lovely than a summer's day.' " When he dropped the pose, he kept his hand over his heart. "Probably doesn't even remember she had this cash. Won't even miss it."

Tommy couldn't quite get a handle on his feeling that this wasn't right. All he could think to say was a vague "I don't know—"

Tobias shrugged. "Suit yourself. All I can tell you is I had a lady friend once who took money from her grandmother and she says the cops wouldn't even take a report because it was family. So it's not really stealing, right?"

Other *Leisure* books by Melanie Tem:

SLAIN IN THE SPIRIT
THE TIDES

THE DECEIVER

MELANIE TEM

LEISURE BOOKS NEW YORK CITY

For Roberta—thanks for all the stories.
And for Steve, who knows the importance of details.

A LEISURE BOOK®

May 2003

Published by

Dorchester Publishing Co., Inc.
276 Fifth Avenue
New York, NY 10001

ISBN 0-8439-5097-8

The name "Leisure Books" and the stylized "L" with design are
trademarks of Dorchester Publishing Co., Inc.

Printed in the United States of America.

Visit us on the web at www.dorchesterpub.com.

ACKNOWLEDGMENTS

For research assistance, my thanks to Marsha Schultheis, Betty Brower, Roberta Robertson, David Coy, Dr. Dale Lervick, and Deirdre Cunningham, Budscape Curator, George Eastman House.

THE DECEIVER

And the Lord said unto Satan, "Where hast thou been?"

Then Satan answered the Lord, and said, "Round the earth, roaming about."

—*Job 1:7*

Chapter One

Stereopticon
(1894)

Exquisite dusk, layered pink and blue, sheered through the tall parlor windows like the illumination depicted in a chromo, which was never quite identical to that in the painting the chromo reproduced, which itself had been subtly or wholly altered from the ambient light in the original scene. Filtered by the lace under-curtains and given resolution by the frame of heavy maroon velvet drapes layered and tasseled above them and on each side, the light was just now fading, both early evening and early autumnal.

This particular time of day and year, this moment

in Harry Harkness's life, had an aura of shimmering importance and complexity. That which ordinarily presented itself as flat and simple now suggested a moral dimension. The house felt simultaneously eternal and ephemeral. Whatever was suspended in either memory or anticipation had a certain vivid cast, too, as though especially real and especially fleeting.

Harry was alone in his house, a rare circumstance that caused him great unease. He'd been busying himself with viewing and arranging new stereo cards and making observations to himself about them. This was not, though, in the nature of a distraction but was itself a primary activity, one to which his attention and energy turned whenever possible.

"The Yukon Territory," he said aloud. "Look at that." The muscles in his forearm twitched reflexively as if to pass the stereopticon to Martha, but she wasn't in her pink velvet chair under the fringed pink lampshade this evening because she was at an abortionist's disposing of their third child.

Harry raised the stereopticon and widened his eyes to take in the bright, busy scene at its other end, which did not quite fill his field of vision. The impression that it was both closer to and more remote from him than he knew it to be was slightly thrilling, thrilling enough. He'd exchanged a card of the Chicago Fire for this one, trading as he often did with Mr. Pruitt over on Chestnut Street; despite the pleasure the Yukon card gave him, Harry would have regretted what he'd given up for it if he hadn't, rather secretively, kept back another Fire picture just like the one he'd traded away.

He now carefully removed the Yukon card from its slot and regarded it, as it were, in its natural state, a thick rectangular paper board like an oversized postcard. Indeed, he'd heard of but not yet seen actual postcards—marked with address lines and meant to be mailed—that were also stereo cards, and he had an almost painful desire to add one to his collection, which, though it was growing and diversifying nicely, still had numerous gaps.

The principle behind the stereopticon was deceptively simple. A scene was reproduced once on the left end of a card and once on the right, separated by a thin line. Each and in tandem, they were utterly one-dimensional. At first he'd thought the two images were precisely identical, the stereoptic effect somehow produced when both eyes saw them independently and simultaneously through the viewer. But then he'd begun noticing tiny variances that must be what somehow triggered the illusion of three-dimensionality. In matters of physicality as well as other aspects of life, Harry was often unclear about cause and effect.

He peered at the Yukon card again now—the very blue sky across the top third; might the blue swath representing sky be slightly thinner in the right-hand scene? Small brown figures along a blue-white stream; on the left, weren't their shadows darker, sharper? Whatever the specifics, it was an optical illusion in which he was happily complicit.

Both frustrated and gratified by the persistent mystery of the phenomenon, he slid the card into its sheath and then into the narrow pasteboard box with the other cards; likely he'd want to look at it again this evening, but the ritual of taking the cards out of their envelopes and putting them back in was part of the pleasure. "The Chicago Fire," he commented as he lifted the viewer. "Look at that."

"The work of the Enemy!" All but hearing the thundering indignation of his brother Clyde, Harry grinned, though it also made him flinch like a guilty child.

Clyde had no objection to other modern worldly amusements. Not infrequently, for instance, he would spend an entire Saturday with one of the girls, going from one movie theater to another for the fifteen-minute features or staying for the continuous show whose slogan he would then chant annoyingly for the rest of the weekend: "After Breakfast Go to Proctor's/After Proctor's Go to Bed." He was a great fan of the new Sunday comic "The Yellow Kid," the first one anybody'd ever seen in color, and he lustily sang along with the nickel-in-the-slot jukebox at Henshaw's, dancing with his nieces or any other young girl, reluctant or otherwise, who strayed within reach.

But for some reason, he'd judged the stereopticon—a term Harry preferred as more grandiloquent than the common "stereoscope"—to be the Devil's spyglass, and he railed against it, at the dinner table and to Harry in private and twice from the pulpit; stereo cards had seemed a flimsy pretext for fire and brimstone, but Clyde's public passion had been convincing enough to make Harry, in the congregation, briefly entertain the possibility that he'd missed something about his hobby, though not convincing enough to make him give it up.

His enjoyment was heightened by the knowledge that generations to come would do as he and Martha and numerous of their friends now did, collecting and trading stereo cards, viewing and discussing them. He could only wonder what scenes would be depicted in his grandchildren's day, or even in the twentieth century, less than seven years away, well within his lifetime but in some senses an unfathomable distance that could and must be bridged by small tàngible things such as the stereopticon.

"There are Christian cards," he'd said to tempt his brother. "Scenes of Jesus. Scenes of the Cross." Surely, if there were such cards—he'd personally never come across them, but he saw no reason there couldn't be—the pastime would shift, in Clyde's cosmology, from the province of the Devil to the Kingdom of God.

But his brother had not been mollified. "Blasphemy!" he'd howled, raising both fists in a manner Harry first took to be personally threatening but then recognized as more theological than that, a

7

threat against Satan, an entreaty to the Lord. "Heresy! Illusion only! Trick and deception! Why, my brother, do you willingly put yourself and your precious family at the mercy of the Devil's lies?"

On the skirted table at his knee, Harry had set a box of the new confection called Cracker Jacks, and now he took a handful. Martha found Cracker Jacks an abomination, declaring she preferred the new breakfast cereal and sometime snack Shredded Wheat for both flavor and healthfulness. Harry suspected that his having Cracker Jacks tonight, while partaking without her of what had become their customary evening pastime, might be a gesture of defiance or even retribution. If so, it was pitiable, Cracker Jacks in return for the killing of his unborn child.

"I would not be the first to do it," she'd insisted.

Harry himself knew the wives of two former business associates had done the same thing, both, he believed, at their husbands' urging. His maternal grandmother, who'd died of something else when he was small, had reputedly tried to do it on a bedpost; Harry had never quite been able to choreograph that incident in his imagination, nor decide which of his many aunts and uncles had been its object. He had read that one-third of all pregnancies in the country were now being terminated, a skyrocketing trend that had led to recent laws against it; he could not be sure whether this shocking statistic was accurate, but it had stayed with

8

him. An irrelevance, though; this would have been *his* child.

"Two children are enough."

This had been weeks ago, when she'd still been deciding, still attempting to enlist his support, and she'd been weeping. Once she'd made up her mind, she had met his every gaze, fiercely dry-eyed. Harry tried to take some responsibility for the fact that the delay had increased the risk to her.

"The girls are nearly grown, twelve and eleven years old," she'd argued, when she hadn't yet lapsed into grim, determined silence. "I'm not strong enough for another pregnancy."

The state of his wife's health, like so much else about her, was a mystery to Harry. He knew she suffered from neurasthenia, but he did not think of her as sickly; her impression in his mind, usually in the back of his mind, was strong and vivid, though he could not have said in what ways. She did purchase great quantities of Baker's Stomach Bitters whenever the salesman came to the door, consuming them like candy. Each of the last three summers she'd taken a hot-springs rest cure. So many women of their acquaintance complained of the same discomforts and applied the same remedies that Harry had scarcely taken notice of the condition until she'd held it out as justification for not wanting their child.

"And you can scarcely support the family as it is." Even if this were wholly or partially true, which

9

Harry was not prepared to admit, to his mind it was another irrelevancy.

Harry believed himself to be the only person who knew Martha was with child, let alone what she'd determined to do about it. She'd claimed no more sickness or fainting spells than usual. She'd still been corseting herself, which could not have been good for the baby. Perhaps all this time she'd been trying to kill it herself. Harry winced at the thought, then chafed over what he'd say to Clyde and the girls if Martha didn't come home soon and he had to explain why she was out unaccompanied so late.

The girls had tired of stereopticon viewing a year or more ago; this allowed their father a mild smugness, persuaded as he was that their preferred entertainments, moving pictures and vaudeville, would not stand the test of time. He suspected they'd been influenced, too, by their uncle's disapproval. Going against Clyde's charismatic morality was hard enough for an adult, too much to expect of a youngster. Did his daughters regard him as a pawn of Satan, then?

Unaware of their mother's whereabouts and intentions—for that matter, unaware of his—they were playing croquet in the twilit back yard. Through the film of lace at the windows Harry could see them, and their muffled sounds were like baubles winking through layers of cloth. As though he'd been struck by a new thought, Harry said to himself that these were his children, taken rather for granted until the precious detail of them had

10

been raised by the one he would not have, the one who might at this moment already be gone, or might still be living.

Harry was vague as to the tools and techniques of an abortionist's trade. From his boyhood he remembered circulars advertising "infallible French female pills," and he knew about aloes, iron, paregoric, but he understood these substances to be effective only in the earliest months. He and Martha did not speak of such things, of course, but he thought she was quite far along in her pregnancy, so perhaps the abortionist would tell her the thing couldn't be done now. Before he could stop himself, a terrible hope had descended on him, swept away then by thoughts of knives and suction.

Hastily he positioned the stereopticon over his eyes again, but he hadn't put a new card in and the blank white space was unnerving. He jerked the instrument back down.

Viewed this way, as if through a lens that brought them at once closer to and farther away from him than he knew them to be, his daughters cut figures quite different from each other. Helen moved in the lacy dusk with the ease of a child, hair and skirts flowing freely, body lithe. Elizabeth, called Libby, had about her a stiff pride altogether unfamiliar to her father, and heartbreaking. At this age, his sisters had indeed been grown. Harry, though, subscribed to the modern notion that young people between the ages of twelve and twenty were neither children nor adults but some

11

other thing entirely. So he did not like Libby's new grown-up appearance, affected only these past two or three weeks with her mother's consent and assistance, not to say urging. She was looking very much like her mother, Harry thought fondly, and had lately acquired her mother's habit of pulling a wrap more snugly around her even inside or when the weather wasn't really cold.

Popping another handful of Cracker Jacks into his mouth, Harry spread his other hand on his shirt front. His growing corpulence pleased him, and even the accompanying dyspepsia, for they bespoke material success. Martha was wrong; belated indignation seethed. He could have supported a third child somehow, whether his current financial situation indicated so or not.

After a moment, he sighed again heavily and began cleaning his fingers with the moistened handkerchief ready for the purpose. It wouldn't do to transfer sticky sugar syrup to the stereo cards. On the other, dimmer side of the window, Libby bent at the waist at the elegant angle the corset required, lowered her head with her neck straining in a womanly fashion to counter the weight of her newly pinned-up hair, positioned the croquet mallet among the layers of the long skirt she was not quite accustomed to, and tapped the wooden ball. It rolled languidly, delicately, for a few inches and stopped without going through the wicket. The candle in the socket on the side of the wicket flickered, but there hadn't been enough force in Libby's ladylike shot to snuff it out.

Martha had gone alone on the train to Detroit. Many aspects of this had surprised Harry, once he'd no longer been surprised by her decision itself: He'd have thought there'd be abortionists closer to home; this was not, after all, an especially provincial town. And how had she found one in the city? He'd have expected her to go with someone, if not him then her sister or a friend. He'd have expected her to ask him for money. And he'd thought she'd be home by now, although he realized he had no idea of the time of her appointment, the length of the procedure or recovery period, or the train schedule.

From his breast pocket he pulled his watch. 5:37. It would be the same time in Detroit, since the railroads had established a standard time, over considerable public protest; there was talk of making it a law, but that seemed unlikely. Harry had approved of this measure in principle, as a sign of benevolent progress, and this evening he felt more secure knowing it was 5:37 in Detroit and here and all points between, not five thirty-eight and -nine and -forty.

Another figure approached Libby and Helen where they stood in the gloaming near to the window but not so near that their father could have touched them even had he been so inclined. Libby was leaning on her croquet mallet like a lady posed with a parasol; her grace and aplomb shocked him.

Helen cavorted like the child she still was, whacking the ball and racing after it; something about her playfulness, seen this way, was shocking, too. Unsure who the newcomer was except that it was a man, Harry didn't know whether his mild alarm was justified. He was viewing the scene through several layers of different substances—lace, glass, twilight—and each layer added its own alteration; for a second or two he tried hard to determine what color Helen's croquet ball really was. He wished for another version of the scene—his daughters, the green croquet ball, the blue-gray light, the tasseled maroon frame created by the draperies, the man—so he could compare them or view them simultaneously for further dimension. Then he saw that the man was Clyde, and wondered why he hadn't realized that at once.

As the scene through the window grew darker, the scene on its surface, reflected from the scene in which he sat, grew brighter and more textured. Somewhat self-consciously, he tried to dodge the reflection, layered in ways the original was not, in order to watch his daughters. He had the uncomfortable feeling that he'd already missed something. Perhaps Libby had made some small womanly motion in her animated conversation with her Uncle Clyde that Harry, simply by virtue of being her father, had never seen her make. Perhaps Helen had sent her croquet ball straight through a wicket. Or perhaps it was only that the evening had fallen in one more gauzy layer. Not knowing, Harry fretted.

14

He'd thought he'd been paying close attention.

Clyde reached toward Libby; for some reason, seeing rather than hearing him laugh sent a shiver down Harry's spine. Libby moved away, out of her father's line of vision. Then he saw Clyde break into song, a hymn or one of the silly popular songs to which he brought equal enthusiasm. Harry swore his brother sang more than he spoke, rather like a vaude performer. The telephone rang.

The telephone seemed to be catching on; Harry hadn't thought it would. He supposed that in time one would become inured to its ring, but now his heart was pounding from startlement. Carefully so as not to dislodge the stereopticon or cards from the bench, but hastily in order to quell the ringing, he got to his feet and stepped around the corner, through the dining room, just into the foyer.

The size and shape of the telephone were reminiscent of a human forearm with a fist, punching up out of the clothed side table. Touching the instrument seemed a terribly, wonderfully intimate thing to do—grasping it, lifting it to his ear and mouth. "Yes," he said, and cleared his throat. "Hello."

"Mr. Harkness?" the hello girl inquired.

"Yes," he repeated. "This is Harry Harkness." He thought it was Mr. Pruitt's oldest daughter, who'd informed him not long ago that the correct term for a telephone operator nowadays was Central. Such impudence was what came of young women in coarse public positions. He'd have addressed her by name now or made a point of calling her a "hello girl" if he'd been sure who she was, but the telephone wire made its own alterations in the human voice it carried. Though he did not share the technological trepidation of Martha and others, Harry was a bit unnerved to be thus hailed in his own house by a disembodied voice whose owner he could not see, name, or visualize.

"I have a call for you," the hello girl announced cheerily, and before he could assent or refuse—though he would almost certainly have assented—there was a daunting, purposeful clicking on the line.

"Mr. Harkness?" A man's voice this time. For a moment Harry thought he might recognize it, then didn't.

He drew himself up. "Yes," he said again, somewhat reluctantly but, at the same time, eager to receive the message, if for no other reason than to relieve the tension of its imminence. He heard Clyde come into the house, singing "Abide with Me," excessive ardor as usual marring his otherwise reliable baritone. It was such a melancholy song. "Fast comes the eventide . . . the darkness deepens . . . change and decay in all around I see . . . the Tempter's pow'r." Clyde seemed to find such sentiments uplifting, but Harry shuddered.

"Your wife will be on the six twenty-five train from Detroit," the caller informed him breathlessly. Harry's own panic spurted, drawn up by the panic in the other man's voice. "You must meet her."

"Why? Has something happened?" That wasn't quite what he'd meant to ask, for of course *something* had happened.

The man said, as if in reply, "I'm sorry," and broke the connection.

Seized with a frantic aversion to encountering the strained, perky voice of the hello girl again, Harry quickly put the handset down onto the table. Someone who did not already know its function would not guess it from seeing the handset passively sitting there like the stalk of a black plant. He laid both palms on his belly, which was growling and would soon begin to ache. He looked at his watch. 6:01. There was no time to ready a buggy; he'd walk to the station.

Clyde loomed in the archway between the foyer and the dining room. In one hand he was grasping the stereopticon the way one would a cudgel or a sorcerer's wand, in the other the long box of stereo cards. Harry caught his breath and took a step forward. Clyde raised his hands above his head and declaimed, "I will rid this household of evil! In the name of Jesus Christ Our Lord, I will strike a blow for righteousness!" In his wake, dimly silhouetted against the bay window, Helen and Libby waited to see what would happen next.

"Yes." Harry advanced, causing Clyde to retreat, which caused the girls to scurry backward. He raised his voice nearly to match his brother's. "Do it, Clyde. Destroy it all. Dismantle the stereoscope,

17

tear up the cards, burn them. Do it now. There's no time to lose."

Clyde stared at him for a moment, unsure whether or what he'd won, and Libby asked softly, "Papa?"

The foyer was almost dark now, and he reached to turn on the Tiffany lamp on the table beside the telephone. The red, blue, and yellow trapezoids of illumination, which had come white from the bulb, glowed in layers on the marble floor, on the gold flocked wallpaper and the two chromos between the stairway windows and the little oval wreath framed in gilt that Martha had woven before they were married from the hair of her deceased mother, glowed on the skin of his own hand moving under the shade.

"Join us, brother," Clyde entreated hopefully. "Cast your lot with the Lord against the forces of darkness."

"I regret that I have another obligation. But I trust you." He clapped his brother on the shoulder. "The soul of this household is in good hands."

"The Devil stands behind you at this very instant," Clyde intoned, and Harry nearly turned to look. "Can't you smell him?"

"Oh, Papa, I can," Libby breathed, but Harry smelled nothing other than the various scents of the house itself and of the girls, meant to disguise by layering over.

"The Devil," Harry mocked recklessly, "works in mysterious ways."

18

Clyde strode past him and out the front door with the Devil's spyglass and its accoutrements held firmly away from his body as if their evil were a contagion. Helen giggled nervously at his heels. Hands crossed at her corseted waist, bustle making her seem to be leaning slightly forward, brow furrowed, Libby asked again, "Papa?"

He smelled a faint acrid odor, maybe like something sweet burning, but distant and explainable if he turned his attention to it, which he would not because he must hurry to meet Martha's train. Harry told Libby, "Your mother is going to have a baby," which he could regard as not entirely untrue.

Libby's head with her heaped-up hair moved in what might have been a nod. "Where is Mama? It's getting late."

"She went to the city to see a doctor. I'm going now to meet her train."

"May I come with you?"

"You're too young."

"Too young to meet a train?" Libby gave a sharp laugh and adjusted her shawl, spreading it and then tucking it snugly around her shoulders. "Papa, she told me where she was going."

The array of possible meanings made this last statement virtually meaningless. It could imply that Martha had told her daughter the same lie about seeing a doctor as Harry had, or a different one, to excuse her absence. Or Libby might know her mother had gone to an abortionist—might, in fact, have been entrusted with more information than Harry.

"Stay here," he instructed her. "I need you to stay here. Prepare the bed for her in the downstairs bedroom." Libby's eyes widened and she made as if to question or object, but Harry's watch now said 6:18 and it would take him longer than seven minutes to reach the train station. As he hastened through the long house to leave by the back door, he heard Clyde and Helen on the front porch, singing and praying.

Harry ran as much of the way as he could and puffed onto the platform at 6:25. He was reassured—foolishly, he knew—that the train was precisely on time. When he first glimpsed his wife emerging from the car, he thought she looked no different from when he'd last seen her—last night, because he'd deliberately stayed in bed until after she'd left this morning; he did not know whether to feel relieved or mocked by her unchanged appearance. But she stumbled on the steps, and before he got to her he heard the short, hard spurts of her breathing.

He didn't know what to ask: "Is it done? Is the baby dead? Are you all right? Will our lives ever be the same? What would our lives have been if this had not happened? What, exactly, has happened? What shall I say has happened?"

In the awkward circle of his arm, Martha flinched and moaned. He saw how pale she was, how tightly her eyes were closed, how her lips trembled. It took a long time to get her home, and Harry kept thinking he should call for a cab, should call Clyde to come with the buggy, should summon Libby to help, but he saw no telephones and no one who might act as messenger.

What he said when he got her into the house was, "Something's gone wrong with the baby. Call Dr. Holton."

And later, when the house glittered with Martha's cries of fever and pain and with the cries of the infant, born too early and too small but strong enough to live, what he decided to say was, "More than anything else, she wanted this baby."

And, finally—in fact it was not final, but he intended it to be, an irrefutable message sent down through the generations, a three-dimensional illusion: "Martha died in childbirth. She gave her life for the life of our child."

Chapter Two

Aunt Libby's Grave
(1916, 1942)

Libby glided from the sitting room to the bedroom. She sat in both, slept in both and on the dusty floor of the roughly pentagonal central hall off which they and three other rooms opened like petals. No matter how unclear the functions of things were, it was important to have names for them.

She crept from the bedroom to the study. Papa brought her books and she did indeed study them, her mind's alchemy transforming the information into her mind's own thing.

She sped from the study to the nursery, which was empty. It had in it pale lovely light and motes of dust like old lace. It was not really a nursery; she only called it that to gather in one place her desolation and resolve. Another room might gather tedium, or joy.

Pulling her pink sweater more tightly around her, she sang so they would hear her—in the rest of the house, moving behind walls; in the wide world, drifting from window to window; in days gone by and days to come.

Aunt Maureen was poised to tell a story—the story that Cecelia guessed now, too late, was the reason they'd come to the cemetery. Cecelia didn't want to hear it. She had a strong sense of danger, a physical feeling of dread.

But she liked her Aunt Maureen. She'd always liked her, and now that her mother had died, taking with her any hope that they could be close or that Cecelia would ever be brave enough to ask her why they weren't, her desire for Aunt Maureen to like her had intensified into a childish yearning.

That was why she'd taken the long train ride from Denver to Detroit to visit—hoping for guidance, maybe; hoping for approval, or just for contact. That was why she'd not had to feign interest in the news of Aunt Maureen and Uncle Everett's grown children, her cousins whom she knew little and liked less, although it had been necessary to conceal her jealousy as their mother talked fondly, worriedly, proudly, knowingly about them. It was why she'd found herself fretting at odd moments about whether she was carrying on a conversation sufficiently polite, about how the things she told of her life were sounding to Aunt Maureen, about whether there was cat hair on her clothes since assuredly no fur-bearing animal had ever set foot in Aunt Maureen's house.

Wanting to please Aunt Maureen was also the main, though perhaps not the only, reason she'd acquiesced to come here and stand on this hill in this bright cold autumn afternoon and look at grave markers neatly embedded in the family plot. Dark gray metal rectangles with raised inscriptions she assumed to be bronze were all partially obscured now by leaves skittering in a breeze she couldn't yet feel but would soon enough. Aunt Maureen pointed out those for Cecelia's grandparents, Harry Harkness, whom she remembered with a dim affection, and Martha Harkness, who had died young in childbirth. Those for Elizabeth and Frances Harkness were next in line, separated from the rows for the next family by a blank space which Cecelia found a trifle unsettling.

She couldn't refuse to listen to the story Aunt Maureen had to tell her, nor even let her attention wander for fear her aunt would notice and disapprove. But apprehension made her pulse skitter like the leaves.

"When your Aunt Libby died," Aunt Maureen declared, "I was the only one at her funeral. I stood right here, where we're standing now, and I watched the funeral procession come up that hill.

There was just the hearse and the undertaker, and I was the only mourner at the graveside."

"Why didn't my mother come? Aunt Libby was her sister, too."

"Dad said Helen and Libby were close when they were girls, but once they were grown they didn't get along." Aunt Maureen shook her head briskly, as though dismissing the squabbles of her two much-older sisters. But something about the set of her shoulders or the cast of her glance piqued Cecelia's attention.

Maureen was a tiny woman, even shorter than Cecelia's mother had been, considerably thinner, and equally formidable. Cecelia thought she remembered Aunt Libby, the eldest of the Harkness girls, being taller and lean, gaunt to Maureen's wiriness and the stocky sturdiness of her mother, Helen. But Aunt Libby had died when Cecelia was no more than three years old, so she hardly remembered her. The images she had of her mother shifted from time to time, she'd discovered, depending on the context of her own life from which she viewed them, on her state of mind, on what other information she had. She thought about her mother a good deal and, of course, remembered her vividly, but what she remembered changed. It wasn't as if she'd forgotten what her mother had looked like, but as if she'd never exactly known.

"It was a chilly fall day like this," Aunt Maureen continued, and as though to illustrate pulled her navy blue sweater tight around her and crossed her arms over it.

Cecelia caught her breath. Her mother used to make a habitual gesture like that. It had been a bright pink sweater with embroidery on the collar, and she'd pull it snug around her just like that and cross her arms, tucking her hands in. The memory had been buried until this moment and had the feel of very early childhood; it pierced and hummed like an arrow that had hit its mark, as though it meant something.

The air wasn't moving, but in it was the anticipation of chill golden wind and sleet. The gray-gold sun through layers of hardwood leaves, compressed this late in a Michigan October, had a metallic sheen, a wet-metal taste. Cecelia fumbled for a comment so Aunt Maureen wouldn't think she wasn't interested. In truth, she wasn't particularly interested in Aunt Libby's death and funeral, but she didn't want Aunt Maureen to stop talking to her.

"I stood up here on this very hill and I watched Libby's funeral come toward me—" Cecelia looked where she was pointing, at the winding dirt road below them and beyond. There, in fact, she caught sight of an oncoming funeral procession, a boxy black hearse, one other dark car nearly as tall at the hump as it was long, and—oddly, she thought, though she couldn't quite have said why it was odd—several pedestrians.

The road was apparently much farther below

them than she'd realized, for the figures stayed tiny, their movements blurred by distance and perspective. She blinked, glanced at her aunt beside her, looked back. The sad little parade of miniatures was no closer, although it was still in forward motion.

Uncle Clyde's flesh was mostly pale pink, darker pink in some places Libby could not think about, and smooth, hairless. If he'd been hirsute, darker-skinned, or covered with warts, she'd have found his body no more or less revolting.

When she was little and Uncle Clyde would come to get her, she'd sometimes open his shirt and feel around for his nipples, like little stones in the ocean of his soft smooth flesh. Then he'd whisper to her, or say out loud if he was sure they were alone, "You like this, too, don't you, sweetie? You *like* your Uncle Clyde."

Libby did like how his nipples felt under her fingertips. They gave her something to fasten her thoughts onto. Sometimes, too, she'd imagine that she could slit him open by tracing a line from one of those hard pinkish-brown dots to the other, and his pink heart would tumble out into her hand. That never happened.

All the women in the family knew about Uncle Clyde. As girls grew up, they learned what to say about him. "Oh, that's just Clyde," Grandma said nervously the single time Libby—thirteen years old, scrubbing clothes on the washboard in the big black tub—told her about the kisses he stole from her in the pantry, which was not the worst she had to tell. Her little sister Helen was peeling potatoes on the back porch, out of sight but not out of earshot, and Maureen, crawling, was under everybody's feet, with Mama eight months dead.

"Clyde is a good man," she was instructed sternly. "Clyde is a man of God," and Libby, observing, could see that this was true. Uncle Clyde performed many acts of charity. He was a good citizen, a good son and brother, a good neighbor. Everybody loved Uncle Clyde. For a little while, she tried on, like somebody else's frock, a feeling of being chosen.

"He does it to me, too," Helen informed her from the other edge of the billowing sheet as they changed his bed the next Monday morning. "Maureen's next, you know," and that was when, for the first time in her life but by no means the last, Libby was aware of making up her mind to do something hard, something she was afraid to do. She would tell her father, Helen's father, too, and Maureen's, a man newly bereft of his wife, and Uncle Clyde's brother. She would tell. Frightened as she was, full of dread as she was, her resolution buoyed her, made her feel grown up and strong, gave her something better to fasten her thoughts onto.

Walking home from school the next day, worrying about telling, worrying about the English exam on Friday and about the ink stain on her skirt, wishing she hadn't started wearing a corset but knowing it would be disloyal to Mama if she went back to childish clothing now, she smelled something funny. Ever since she was little she didn't like going past that big old tree in front of the grocery store. It had a knob on it that looked for all the world like somebody hiding, waiting to jump out and grab her. This time when she hurried past it, there was an odor, vaguely bitter, wrongly sweet, and then a man was walking beside her.

Libby did her best to edge away. The man said in a pleasant voice, "I won't hurt you, Libby," which made her even more afraid.

"How do you know my name?"

He was nicely dressed. His hands were in his pockets. That bittersweet smell seemed to be coming from him, although it was so faint she couldn't be sure. "You know," he said in a friendly, threatening tone, "if you tell your father what you've been doing with Uncle Clyde you'll cause a great deal of trouble in the family. Your father is suffering already because of your mother's death and the way she died."

Tears hurt Libby's throat at the mention of her mother. Confused, she found herself puzzling over how this stranger knew about that, rather than, she realized later, the greater mystery of how he could know about Uncle Clyde and that she'd decided to tell. Maybe he was a family friend. Maybe he'd been at the funeral. She thought his voice did sound familiar.

"Your father cries at night." From the angle of

his voice he might have been looking gently down at her, although she could hardly see him beside her. "Did you know that, Libby?" The thought of Papa's sorrow was worse than her own. "If you tell him, you will only give him more to cry about."

Libby didn't know what to think. She stayed silent.

"You don't *have* to tell. You're almost grown up now. Uncle Clyde won't bother you anymore. He doesn't like grown-up women."

"My sisters—"

"Helen can take care of herself. She's growing up, too. And you don't know he'll start with Maureen. You don't know that." He patted her shoulder. "You're a good girl, Libby. I trust you to do the right thing."

He was gone, the after-image of too-bright light fading away, and Libby was left to ponder, fist to her lips, whether what he'd said was wholly or partially true or not true at all.

Aunt Maureen didn't seem especially aware of the procession below them. "Can you imagine?" Her voice was crisp and controlled; Cecelia had never heard it otherwise. But she was hugging herself. "You'd think Libby had lived on this earth an entire lifetime and never made a difference to anybody."

"She made a difference to Frances," Cecelia protested. A cousin fully a generation older, Aunt Libby's only child, Frances had died a long time ago, Cecelia thought from complications of morbid obesity. Cecelia had hardly known her; it was difficult to comprehend what connection there'd ever been between them, other than the blood ties, mostly abstract, of their mothers' sisterhood. "Anyway, do you think that's possible? Not to make a difference to *anybody?*"

Aunt Maureen shot her a look. Cecelia didn't want to seem rude, but she did want to understand what Aunt Maureen was saying. Such questions—whether or not people made a difference as they passed through this world; how to tell whether it was or was not taking place in one's own life—had lately come to be of considerable importance to her.

Approaching thirty years old, she was feeling less and less substantial. She and Ray, whom she supposed she would marry when he came home from the war, had seemed scarcely to touch even when they were seeing each other every Saturday night, and her weekly letters to him now might have been written to anyone; if he did not come home, perish the thought, she would mourn what might have been between them more than what was, and she feared she might live to mourn that anyway. Her job with the insurance company, though she was skilled at it, sustained her in no way other than financial. No one with whom she came into contact in the course of a day was likely to remember her once their specific business with each other was done, nor would she remember them. Certainly, if she were to die today, none of them would come to her funeral.

Aunt Maureen, gazing off over the gilt vista through which Cecelia was still watching the funeral procession move like a model train through a toy landscape, proceeded deliberately. At this point, Cecelia dimly understood that the story was in some way hers, too, if only because she was here, in this place and time, with this purposeful woman who had something to tell her.

The story became more and more hers, too, because it wasn't given to her all of a piece. She had to work for it, put forth something of herself to receive it; she could not simply listen passively. As parts of the tale emerged, tales unto themselves, Cecelia was required to interpret, to fill in spaces, to arrange and rearrange incidents and the interstices among incidents so they made sense and then, given more, made sense again.

Later, she would not be sure what Aunt Maureen had actually told her or in what order, what context. Now and then throughout her long life, images and information from that day would present themselves to her—the light's particular glint; the yearning (and it was to be the last of it, really) for Aunt Maureen to tell her what she knew, give her what she had, love her; the chill of unease as imagination played over what might be underground in this place, what the embedded grave markers might be taken to signify. Each time these things would seem to mean something slightly different, something cumulative or stripped down or newly nuanced.

On the train ride home, for instance, she would

puzzle over the relative position of the embroidered pink sweater in her own life, the movement of it and the truncation of movement as its wearer repeatedly pulled it snug. The realization would descend on her, stopping her breath for a moment, that it must not have been Helen she remembered doing that but Libby.

William Bradley was earnest, decent, rather dull-witted. He loved her, he insisted gamely; he could love her. Libby did not believe that, though it was kind of him to say so, and it would not have persuaded her if she had. "I can't marry you," she said to him. "I'm crazy. Everybody knows that. Don't you know that?"

"I have a duty to our child." The words were resolute, but clearly he was appalled to be saying "our" to her about anything, let alone a child, and already grateful that he would not be bound to say it much longer.

"I'll do what's right," Libby promised. "Send money."

"Kill the child."

It was not, of course, William Bradley who suggested such a thing. There was an actual voice but no visible source for it, and, more than hearing it, Libby felt the voice in her hollow bones. There was a bittersweet fragrance, too, that clung to the skin between the bones of her fingers as they stretched around the baby's tiny neck. She clenched her fists in refusal. "No."

"What sort of life will this child have?" She had to admit it was a reasonable question. "You sent young Mr. Bradley away. You're crazy. You said so yourself. You barely managed to raise Frances, and look at her."

"I won't do it."

"It would be easier on everybody. On you, too."

"No." Libby took a deep, steadying, bittersweet breath, and freed her hands from her baby's throat to push his voice and his insinuating odor away.

On that melancholy golden October afternoon in 1942—soon to be gray and doleful November, another season altogether—Aunt Maureen asserted, as though satisfied that she'd worked it all out in her head, that Frances had died soon after Libby because she hadn't known how to live without her mother. "A grown woman, you'd have thought she was an orphan," which prompted Cecelia to ask about Frances's father. Who was he? What had happened to him? It amazed her that she'd apparently never wondered about him before; she thought that could not be true, but she had no memory either of her own curiosity in this regard or of any answers forthcoming or withheld.

It also caused her to think about her own father, but her thoughts, having nothing much to snag onto, didn't stay long with him. Cecelia believed her relationship with her father to be uncomplicated. Easily, they loved each other. She supposed they could be considered neither close nor distant.

He mourned her mother now, as did she, but simply, cleanly.

"I don't know," Aunt Maureen said evenly. "As far as I could ever tell, nobody in the family knew who Frances's father was. Including Frances. Papa didn't know."

The funeral procession below them gave the overall impression of coming closer, while its component parts—dark figures except for one swatch of pink; dark motion—appeared no bigger or clearer than ever. Distracted by this contradictory perspective, Cecelia at first merely nodded in response to the last statement. Then, suddenly disoriented among the tangles of the family tree, she chanced a quick look at her aunt. Aunt Maureen was watching her, and, when Cecelia's glance swung her way, she nodded emphatically.

"But I believe it was Uncle Clyde. Our father's brother. I believe he was Frances's father. Libby said some things to me, nothing definite, but they added up. Libby and Helen always behaved strangely when his name came up, and he never came to our house, although I heard he used to live there. Libby was fourteen when Frances was born."

Cecelia pulled her gaze away, not wanting to stare. For a while when she was the age Aunt Maureen was now, she would find herself flashing back to this moment, this secret told first and smallest among many, as a point at which her life had veered off one course and onto another. Eventually, though, she would cease thinking of life in terms of courses and veerings at all.

"Our mother had died when I was born."

Self-consciously, Cecelia waited for some sort of signal as to what her reaction ought to be. This she'd known already, presumably from her mother, although she remembered no time or place she'd been told, no specific conversation, no gift or complaint or instructive intent personally to her.

It was the first time, though, that Aunt Maureen, the infant in question, had spoken of it to her, and maybe she should offer reassurance or condolence. There was no hint of a request for such a thing; if anything, Aunt Maureen looked angry, though Cecelia couldn't think why. "It wasn't uncommon in those days for women to die in childbirth," Cecelia offered, almost eagerly.

"That's not exactly what happened." Aunt Maureen allowed her sweater to fall loose, then pulled it around her again. "I don't think that's quite what happened, but it doesn't matter now. What matters is that Libby raised both Frances and me. We grew up more like sisters than aunt and niece. Papa worked a lot to support us and most of the rest of his time he spent looking for a suitable stepmother, which he never found. Helen went off and had adventures. And misadventures." Aunt Maureen gave a quick smile, then repeated, "Libby raised us."

Without peering at her or making any otherwise obvious scrutiny, Cecelia tried to decipher the edge that had come into Aunt Maureen's voice and manner. Perhaps it was nothing more than a natural reaction to the mention of a difficult childhood; certainly it would have been odder if she'd maintained her characteristic matter-of-factness. Cecelia ventured, "My mother never talked much about her past. I do know she always thought you were Grandpa's favorite. Even all those years he lived with us, she thought he really looked forward to your visits." Cecelia had thought so, too, but left responsibility with her mother.

Aunt Maureen snorted. "When it came to our parents, things were not always what they appeared to be. Our family had a few secrets."

Cecelia waited. When her aunt didn't go on, she said, by way of encouragement without giving the appearance of prying, "Mama almost never told me any stories about her life." It was a sorrowful thing to admit.

"I'll tell you."

There was something ominous about the pledge. Hastily, Cecelia asked, "Was Aunt Libby a good mother?" It was, truly, something she wanted to know, but the fact that it was also a diversionary tactic made her feel dishonest. Perhaps, then, self-justification was the source of her upsurge of interest in Aunt Maureen's childhood. "What was it like," she asked, too eagerly, "growing up with your sister for a mother and your cousin for a sister and your father never home? Was it confusing? Was it awful?"

"Libby," said Aunt Maureen grimly, "did the best she could. She could have said no."

In the silence that followed, the funeral ascended the hill, though the perspective was still skewed. The hearse in the lead had its headlights on. Two figures, the one in pink and one of the handful of dark-dressed ones, had broken away from the formal procession, leaving it paltry indeed. As Aunt Maureen resumed talking, Cecelia watched them against the mown gold and brown cemetery grass. Shadows fell everywhere, and in the thin low light theirs were indistinguishable. They seemed, she saw with something like shock, to be cavorting, and they were holding hands.

Libby said, "Papa," and couldn't believe what she was about to do. How could she tell him? How could she tell him? How could she speak of such things to her father?

Maybe she would not. Maybe she didn't have to. Almost, she looked away and pretended she hadn't spoken. Most likely, her father wouldn't have pressed, wouldn't have even noticed or would have been glad for one less worry.

But she thought of Helen, and her fists clenched in her lap. She thought of Maureen, who wouldn't even remember their mother; Maureen, whom Mama had said to take care of. She made herself say again, "Papa. I have to talk to you."

He was on his way out, not an unusual circumstance; tonight he was going to a motion picture with Betty Pruitt, who was only a few years older than Libby herself. He'd buttoned and belted his big gray coat neatly over his rotund belly, and was fitting his gray hat over his bald spot, rolling the rim just so, the tiny maroon feather slightly off to the right. He glanced down at her. "Not now, Libby. I'm late."

"When? I *have* to talk to you."

"*Later.*"

Later, then, very late, she was waiting for him when he came home. She'd fallen asleep at the kitchen table. She woke up, abruptly and fully, at the click of the door and his quiet despairing sigh before he came in and saw her there. "Papa. Please. I have to tell you something."

When he took off his hat, his head was so bare she had to look away. When he took off his coat, she saw that his shoulders were shaking. "I'm exhausted, Libby. Not tonight."

He was already out of the room, and she was hearing his dogged, hasty footsteps rounding the corner of the living room toward the stairs, when she said, just loud enough for him to hear if he would, "Uncle Clyde touches me." The footsteps didn't stop immediately, but they did stop. "He touches Helen, too. Next he'll start on Maureen because we'll be too old."

Her father came back, a large sad man, and Libby was so sorry and ashamed, but her little sister Maureen hadn't done anything wrong, had she? If Uncle Clyde started on her, would it be her fault?

It would be Libby's fault if she didn't tell.

Her sad father with his sad footsteps and uncovered head came back into the kitchen, and Libby could hardly breathe in the face of his sadness, to which she was adding. He pulled out the chair opposite her, scraping its two back legs across the old wooden floor, and heavily lowered himself into it. She locked her gaze on him and said what she had to say, every dirty word.

Cecelia took a breath and said, although she knew Aunt Maureen had no need of permission or encouragement, "I know only a handful of things about our family's history. I'd like to know more."

Later, at various times in her life when secrets from the past seemed especially vital or especially irrelevant to her, she would consider with a certain wonderment what she had thus invited. Sometimes almost idly, occasionally with an urgency that was utterly impractical, she would wonder what difference it might have made in the lives of her children and grandchildren if she hadn't invited Aunt Maureen to tell her this story, or if she'd pressed for more.

Aunt Maureen began by fixing things in place: "The year was 1916." For the same reason, Cecelia's attention was momentarily occupied by the fact that she herself would be born the same year.

Contemplating time before her birth or after her death always evoked in her a disquieting sense of continuity and insignificance, of being one small bead on an infinitely long and infinitely splitting string. She felt much the same way when she looked up at stars on a clear night, lay flat in a mountain meadow, or on the one occasion when she walked along an ocean beach. It was somehow the same feeling, too, that made her back away from cliff rims—for fear not of falling but of jumping.

Aunt Maureen had gone on, oblivious to or, more likely, contemptuous of Cecelia's momentary inattention. "Libby had another child. I was at the Normal, away from home for the first time, and no one had told me of her condition for fear of disturbing my studies, I suppose, or out of shame, or for some other reason. She and the baby came on the bus. I didn't know she was coming. I understood right away what she wanted."

For a moment or two, Cecelia puzzled as if over a riddle. Then, stymied, she shook her head and asked, as she knew she was intended to do, "What did she want?"

"Why," said Aunt Maureen, as if it were the most obvious thing in the world, "she thought I should just give up everything and raise her child. I was young. Your Uncle Everett and I were already engaged. Here she was, a middle-aged woman alone with a grown child and not well. She never came right out and asked, and I never came right out and refused, but we both understood what was going on between us. Forever after, it was between us."

The wind had picked up. The navy blue sweater

was obviously providing as much warmth as it was going to, and Aunt Maureen's hands were hidden under her upper arms. Cecelia's cheeks, stiff from the cold, were wet already from the wet wind, although rain wasn't actually falling yet. The mass of clouds descending overhead like a lid didn't yet cover the entire sky, and the gold light skimming in under its edges and through its gradually closing fissures glinted like ore in granite.

"So then what happened to the baby?" All sorts of possibilities flashed through her mind, among them that in this world was a cousin utterly unknown to her and that there was an infant's grave among the others in this hillside plot somewhere.

But Aunt Maureen wasn't ready yet to recount that part of the tale. "The father," she said deliberately, "was a business associate of our father's, a man named William Bradley, a decent man I'd always thought, a good deal younger than Libby. As a matter of fact, at one time I'd considered setting my cap for him myself."

Restraining herself from glancing sharply in her aunt's direction to assess regret, Cecelia listened for it instead and heard none. "And he wouldn't marry her," she supplied.

Aunt Maureen tsked. "My sister refused to marry him. William Bradley tried to do the honorable thing by her, and Libby sent him packing. But then, she wasn't well."

The funeral now appeared to have reached what, presumably, was the edge of the Harkness family plot, although boundaries were blurred and Cecelia was still confused about the position of the procession relative to herself and Aunt Maureen. The figures were not only undersized and shadowless but also translucent; the gold light glimmered through them, and the gray light, and the suggestion of objects which, when the figures moved, were revealed as not there.

With a shock it came to Cecelia that somehow she'd been regarding this as a re-enactment of Aunt Libby's funeral, and that, because of the motorized vehicles, it could not be. Apparently some aspect of her mind especially suggestible to this ethereal time and place had accepted that a funeral from more than two decades ago should reappear to her, and only a detail which in fact was irrelevant had made her decide otherwise. That she'd so readily made such a ghostly association gave her gooseflesh, and she found herself pulling her jacket snugly around her in the manner of the Harkness women and tucking her icy hands under her arms.

The hearse and the other black car stopped. Hearing no cessation of engine noise, Cecelia realized she had not been hearing engines in the first place, nor any other sound from the funeral. Silently, small figures disembarked from the two vehicles, and, together with the straggling pedestrians, formed a little graveside crowd. Six in black coats and black hats lifted a casket from the back of the hearse. The wood of it caught thin sunlight and briefly glowed; fleetingly, metal glinted like the edges of the sky.

The two individuals who had split off from the rest, one pink- and one black-clad, were some distance away now, though it was hard to tell just where they were in relation to anything else. They danced, floated. Cecelia didn't know whether to watch them or the group at the grave, where the casket—dull and self-contained, catching no light now—was being lowered. She didn't know whether she could watch either without losing track of what Aunt Maureen was telling her. Recurring throughout the rest of her life, then, would be the suspicion that on that late-autumn afternoon, in a part of the country which otherwise would prove to have no special significance for her, she might have missed something important.

Doubtless because Cecelia had not asked, Aunt Maureen informed her rather testily, "Libby had always been moody and high-strung. Within a few months after the birth of her second daughter, she had a full-fledged breakdown."

At the time, Cecelia thought she had no memory of this, which would have made sense considering her young age when it happened. But later, telling some of the story to Ray, who didn't seem especially interested, two clear images came to her that might be attached to that time and place: laughter, song, wails echoing, traveling from room to room she couldn't see; and a sign she gradually grew able to read after it had been read to her numerous times. Its black letters were painted unevenly on a cut board, nailed to a door jamb well above her head, then, as she grew, not so high: STOP. DO NOT GO PAST HERE.

Again she asked Aunt Maureen, a bit breathlessly by this time, "What happened to the baby?"

"Libby gave her to Helen," Aunt Maureen replied without hesitation. "Helen raised her as her own."

For a split second, Cecelia thought she was being told she had a cousin/sister about whom she hadn't known, and she felt as much eagerness as trepidation. But then the events of the story abruptly aligned themselves for her, and she stared at her aunt. "Aunt Libby was my *mother*?"

"Libby gave you birth," Aunt Maureen said firmly. "Helen was your mother."

Chills sped through her, and she pulled her jacket snug. "My father was William Bradley?"

"Your father is Emil Parmalee." Aunt Maureen reached out from under her taut dark sweater, and her hand came startlingly around Cecelia's exposed wrist. "This doesn't change anything, Cecelia. I just thought you had a right to know."

There would be times—moments, decades— when this insistent, imposed interpretation would ring true: Her understanding of who she was had not, in fact, been changed by what she'd heard and seen that day in the cemetery on the cusp of the seasons. What she knew about herself remained known, and she'd found out nothing new that mattered in any sustained way.

45

There would also, though, be reeling moments and decades of cumulative vertigo—such as when Ray and the children were all, for their various reasons, busy leaving her—when it would seem that some fundamental thing had been shaken that day, some profound and still-hidden depth plumbed. Not until Ray had left for good would she think of searching for William Bradley, and then all the trails would turn out to be cold. Not until she was old herself would she come back to Michigan—this time in hot and humid July—to stand again at Libby's grave. Finding no markers for Aunt Maureen, Uncle Everett, or their two sons also gone by then, Cecelia would conclude that they, like the rest of her own family, must be buried somewhere else, and would muse with acute but indeterminate emotion on the complexities of human connection.

Libby would wake up in the night or, worse, in the middle of the day, alone, and she would bring with her out of fitful sleep that faint bittersweet odor. Sometimes there would be a voice and sometimes not.

"Libby, Libby, you don't have to stay here."

"I'm not well. Papa says if I won't stay here he'll have to put me in the state hospital."

"You can get out. There are windows in every room."

"They don't open. Papa nailed them shut from the outside." She'd gone with him from window to window, she on the inside and he on the outside, glass between then. He was too portly to be climbing so high and working so hard. But she'd stayed with him, and in their companionship had been solace and strength.

"Glass breaks."

"This is the third floor."

"I will catch you."

Libby was distressed that she even considered it, but there was no question that her resolve was greater than her suggestibility. "No," she said, and kept saying so.

Then she was freed and the signs were taken down. She had not known there were *signs*, and the discovery of them gave her a peculiar little thrill as rapid-fire fantasies rocked her of who might have read the warnings, whom they might have been posted for, who might or might not have heeded them. Otherwise, though, her life didn't change much.

Over the years, she took care of her father and he took care of her. Always she kept a place in her house for Frances to come home to, and Frances required a larger and larger place. She welcomed her sisters and their families on their annual visits, and was only a little sorry to see them off. Once in a while, taking a tiny stitch in another intricate quilt design, she would flinch as the needle, suddenly, pierced her heart with longing for her younger daughter and worry for her elder.

"Take your daughter back. She's yours. Helen isn't her real mother."

Having held her breath against him as long as she could, Libby took a heady gasp of him. "Could I?"

"Sure. I'll help you. She's your child." But it wasn't right, and Libby refused. "At least tell her," he urged, exasperated. "Tell her who you are." But Libby, tempted, refused.

"What do you want with me?"

He leaned over her as if to kiss her, but still it was only his insinuating voice that touched her, and the odor of him, and his intense body heat. "You know what I want, Libby. You want it, too."

She did. "Surely there are other girls. Younger. Prettier." To her horror, she was envisioning Frances for him, offering her daughter to him in her mind.

He said, "Frances is fine enough," and Libby caught her breath, although she ought not to have been surprised. "A fine girl. But I want *you.*"

"Who's that?" she demanded with a laugh, then waited anxiously for him to tell her. Was she Uncle Clyde's girl? Frances's crazy mother? The woman who had given away her child?

"Yes, darling. I'm afraid you are all those things."

Or was she—perilous thought—the woman who, more than once in her life, had made a hard, right choice?

Hastily, he murmured, "Be mine, Libby, and I'll show you who you are."

"No," she said.

*   *   *

48

They talked about other things until Uncle Everett
came for them. Cecelia said a little about Ray. Aunt
Maureen told about how close Libby and Frances
had been—unhealthily close, she declared, which
was the impression Cecelia already had had; during
the months Libby was locked for her own safety in
her suite at the back and top of the house, Aunt
Maureen said with a shake of the head, Frances had
even stayed in there with her for days at a time.
Cecelia said it was getting really cold; Aunt Maureen predicted the first snow out of those heavy
clouds.

Disappointingly, the two of them seemed to Cecelia no closer than ever. Wistfully she wondered
whether Aunt Maureen would come to her wedding. As it turned out, Aunt Maureen and Uncle
Everett would agree to take care of their grandchildren that weekend, but they would send a quilt
that had been in the family for a long time; a note
pinned to it said Aunt Maureen wasn't certain
which of her sisters had made it, but she thought
Cecelia should have it either way.

As they wended their way to the road where Uncle Everett waited with the car, Cecelia caught sight
once more of the two figures spun loose from the
miniature funeral procession, which otherwise was
lost now in the thickening mist and twilight gloom.
The one in pink stood still. The one in black moved
away until she couldn't see it at all anymore. A peculiar fragrance, not quite autumnal—vaguely bitter, wrongly sweet—lingered in her nose and on the
cold skin of her hands as they drove away.

Chapter Three

The Tulip Festival
(1929)

In May of 1929, the little Michigan town was re-splendent with tulips. Normally a pleasant but un-remarkable place, now it fairly dazzled with color—full-bodied reds and yellows, mostly, but also pink, silvery white, purple so deep it was nearly black.

To someone observing from outside and, say, a little above, the overall impression would have been of town-with-tulips: waves of color. Streets and trees and houses vivified by association. Here and there a single bloom standing out like a sequin. Designs formal or free-form or accidental depend-ing on the aesthetics and skill of particular gardeners and on the interplay between one garden and its neighbors or with another across town. Such harmonics were almost never intended; usually, in fact, the tulip growers had done everything they could think of to make their beds distinctive from the others, so as to catch the eye and the blue ribbon of the Tulip Festival judges, given the rather limited range of materials they had to work with, tulip bulbs and amended soil, rocks and little white wooden fences, maybe a fountain or a garden gnome.

Though their ancestors had all come here from somewhere else, most who were townspeople now had never lived outside the county. Twenty-one of the twenty-four men who'd fought in the Great War had come home, a few all of a piece; World War II would claim five, Korea two, Vietnam four altogether—two killed, one missing in action, and one vanished, presumably to Canada. Almost without exception, young people in May of 1929 were staying put; this would be the last generation of which that could be said.

What the townspeople knew that spring, and knew intimately, were individual tulips in individual plots, and exactly the original winterbound inspiration and sustained practical effort required to get and keep them there, just so. Some added a historical perspective, that 1929 was the best year ever for tulips; no one could prove that wasn't so.

The tulips that year even had a fragrance, which ordinarily tulips do not. Not sweet like lilacs' or roses', not astringent like that of marigolds or Queen Anne's lace, the odor was experienced by some as indescribably delicious and by others as unpleasant to the point of disgust; there were those whose response shifted from pleasure to revulsion and back in the span of one day or one hour, or even within the same inhalation. Townspeople kept demanding of each other, as though the ready and repeated explanation didn't quite suffice, "What's that smell? Do you smell that?" and even those who weren't gardeners would answer self-importantly, if a trifle uncertainly, "Must be the tulips. Sure is a good year for tulips."

Like much else across the country, then, tulips were thriving in the spring of 1929. Some people liked to call it a miracle. Some held that such abundance was only to be expected, even predicted, a result of scientific progress and right living. Some had been uneasy all along and experienced a chilling epiphany when, the night before the annual Tulip Festival, somebody snipped off the heads of every tulip in town.

Cecelia Parmalee and Lurleen Simpson, both twelve, were finishing sixth grade and next year would go to the junior-senior high school up on the hill. The excitement in the air that spring was making them even giddier than they'd have been normally.

As they did their schoolwork together on Cecelia's kitchen table, those evenings when they couldn't bear to shut the window even though tulip-smelling breezes kept blowing their papers around, something about fractions or adverbs and adjectives would strike them as emblematic of the tragedy of life of which they felt themselves—with equal parts dread and hope—on the brink, and they'd collapse into self-perpetuating sobs; after the massacre of the flowers, Cecelia toyed with the notion that they'd been prescient, though she never spoke of it that way to Lurleen.

Sitting on Lurleen's front stoop shelling peas for her mother and styling each other's hair, both of them just dying for the crimping irons that were forbidden them, they'd get started giggling, and when the laughter started to subside, one or the other would say something—often just part of a sentence not even entirely comprehensible, or a code phrase they couldn't have translated—and they'd be off again, eyes watering and stomachs aching, the hilarity intensified by having to suppress it because Lurleen's mother would say it was unladylike and it did make it harder to get the peas out of the pods. In the decimation of the tulips, awful as it was, Cecelia couldn't help also seeing something comic, and for months afterward, she would occasionally be seized by spasms of amusement that to everyone else, including Lurleen, seemed utterly without explanation, even perverse, even worrisome as to her sanity and moral character.

Both girls had been nominated for Junior Tulip Princess, along with Dottie Frasier and Alice Benemann. Dottie's chances they confidently assessed as nil—imagining her in a fancy princess gown with a crown on her cropped head was one of the things that could render them helpless with mirth—and mousy Alice seemed unlikely. So it came down to the two of them, best friends and, not for the first or last time, adversaries.

In the way of twelve-year-old girls, Cecelia and Lurleen that spring were convinced, out of a dramatic dreariness, that their lives would never be any different from what they had been so far. Simultaneously, they were sure that everything was about to change forever, maybe because of the tulips, although to fevered adolescent sensibility the putative instrument of transformation could have been anything: the weather, the stock market, the alignment of stars, a few bars of ragtime, a coveted hairstyle, the nubby powder-blue fabric Cecelia's Aunt Maureen had brought her to make a summer frock, an unusual permeating odor, or the astonishing fact of thousands of decapitated tulips.

Lurleen and Cecelia had been best friends for a year or so by then. For Cecelia, this had the makings of one of the most important relationships of her life. Lurleen, though, had her eye on what she thought of as the wider world.

Not that she planned on leaving town; on the contrary, she was set on getting for herself everything the town had to offer, which, really, was quite a lot. After years of lessons from the local piano teacher who'd played professionally in vaudeville,

Lurleen was sought after for programs at church, at school, at the grange; she played entertainingly, but with no real passion, and passion was not what was called for. She did just well enough at her studies to attract just the right kind of attention. She'd already had boyfriends, whom her parents didn't know about; Cecelia had teased her once about turning into a baby vamp, but had stopped saying it when Lurleen had seemed to think it a compliment. That spring, she'd taken to using Cecelia as an excuse to get out of the house so she could meet Albert Hazen down by the creek, and on a few of those occasions Cecelia had been fooled, too, had waited a long time before she figured out Lurleen wasn't coming to her house after all. There was never any apology, and Cecelia felt a bit silly that her feelings were hurt. Albert Hazen was fifteen, and everybody knew his mother was making a small fortune on the stock market, whatever that was.

It made Cecelia nervous how much Lurleen wanted to be Junior Tulip Princess. "You're going to win," Lurleen told her again and again, and across her scalp Cecelia felt the nail of the forefinger around which her damp hair was being curled.

"Oh, applesauce. You don't know that. I bet they haven't even decided yet."

"Liza heard them talking. You win."

The little buzz of excitement in the pit of Cecelia's stomach made her mad. Lurleen's older sister Liza had been predicting the end of the world every

New Year's Day Cecelia could remember. Obviously, she couldn't be trusted, so Cecelia didn't know why Lurleen believed what she'd said about Tulip Princess, unless for some reason she wanted to believe her.

"I've met somebody new," Lurleen told her, more in the way of a boast than of a confidence. Cecelia couldn't tell if she was changing the subject or not.

Despite herself, Cecelia was curious. "Who is he?"

Behind her, Lurleen gave a coy little shriek. "That's for me to know and you to find out."

Cecelia scowled and refused to give Lurleen the satisfaction of asking more.

"I'll tell you this much. He's older, and he's not from here, and he's very rich and *very* handsome."

"That's nice," said Cecelia, with studied nonchalance.

Lurleen tugged impatiently on Cecelia's hair. "Don't you like *anybody* yet?"

"Sure I do." Cecelia defended herself, although the truth was she didn't exactly know what all the fuss was about.

"If I don't win I'll die," Lurleen suddenly declared in the same flat, emphatic tone her sister annually employed to forecast doomsday.

Cecelia was surprised to hear herself snap back, "Well, me too." It wasn't true, but this was some sort of competition now.

"I was talking to this boy about it. He says why

take chances. Why not make it happen."

Cecelia was interested. The fact that advice on something so intimate to the town as the Tulip Festival was coming from a stranger, and a boy, gave it an air of, if not quite authority, at least novelty worth listening to. "How?"

After a pause, Lurleen said, and Cecelia could hear the grin in her voice, "Dottie's easy. If the judges knew she was queer, that'd take care of her."

A prickle traveled across Cecelia's back just under her shoulder blades. "You told him Dottie was queer?"

"He knew. He said it first."

Cecelia didn't see how this could be true, unless there was a connection between Dottie Frasier and this boy that Lurleen didn't know about or hadn't told her. More likely, Lurleen was lying. Cecelia fidgeted, which caused Lurleen to pull her hair, a quick, sharp pain like a warning. "Ouch. What about Alice?"

"Did you know Alice is allergic to strawberries? I mean, *really* allergic. She could end up in the hospital. It'd be a shame if she got too sick to be in the Festival."

Later in her life, looking back on this moment and on others that followed it, Cecelia would wonder, skeptical of her young self, whether she'd have taken the same moral stand if her own personal stakes had been higher, if she'd cared as much about Junior Tulip Princess as Lurleen did. As it was, it didn't cost her much, beyond a pang of acute adolescent self-consciousness, to object, "I don't know, Lurleen. I don't think that's right."

"Well, if I can't be Princess, nobody should. That's what *he* says." In tears now, Lurleen pushed Cecelia's half-curled head away with such force and venom that both girls almost fell off the steps.

Cecelia announced in a mean tone that she was going home, and she didn't see Lurleen again until the Friday of the Tulip Festival when all the tulips in town were discovered to have had their heads cut off. Then, best friends again brought together by shock and sorrow and heady drama, the girls cried in each other's arms, and Lurleen whispered, as if it were a gift, that her new love, whom Cecelia had practically forgotten about, had left town. Always after that, Cecelia would suspect the mysterious older, rich, and handsome boy of having been a product of Lurleen's overheated imagination, and that more than anything would sour her relationship with Lurleen.

The fragile, riotous beauty of the 1929 tulips was almost more than Harry Harkness, Cecelia's grandfather, could bear, harder to bear, even, than their destruction turned out to be. There was something secretive in the air that year, right from the beginning, and Harry knew about secrets. Five festivals in a row, his tulips had taken ribbons, three times the blue, but not once during the 1929 season had he been confident.

Experience having taught him not to underestimate the competition or to take anything for granted, every day Harry strolled around town. Often he ran out of steam and had to sit a while, and sometimes these intelligence missions took up more of a day than did the gardening itself, but since the first fall plantings, indeed since fall plantings two and three years ago which were maturing this spring, he'd been keeping close tabs on every other garden and gardener in town. No doubt about it, it was a very good year for tulips, and Harry was worried.

But his Lucretias and Cordelias, new bulb varieties from Eastman, surely deserved to carry the day. Though he was a newcomer, having lived here with his daughter only eleven years, he knew the contest judges well enough to be more or less assured that they were not, at heart, unreasonable people, or their tastes fundamentally unnatural. Because nobody had ever seen anything like these new tulips, it wouldn't have been surprising if they'd seemed unreal. But instead they were hyper-real, more tulipy than ordinary tulips, meta-tulips. And extraordinarily beautiful.

Harry had a habit of examining them, which was, though he didn't say so to himself, really a sort of communion and a sneaky way of tempting fate: kneeling or crouching with considerable arthritic discomfort, he'd steady a stem with his left hand and position his right at the base of the bloom, palm up, index and middle fingers spread on either side. The hollow sphere, open at the top and slightly elongated, quivered temptingly in the cup of his hand. His hand shook, too, from a welling up of emotion that might be anticipation or fear, or from appreciation of how one single action of his could change the course of history, or maybe just from age. At dawn or dusk, the Cordelias looked black, but in broad daylight the real purple of them tinged his flesh purple, and the peachy, pearly Lucretias glowed in any light, or, he swore, in no light at all on a moonless night.

From the moment in March when his fingertips had identified his first soft quarter-inch shoots, three of them in the north end of the bed and one toward the middle, Harry had been loathe to leave his tulips, even when he knew they were well-watered and properly fed and free of weeds. It was not that he had any real premonition of their untimely end, but, having lived a life long and full, he knew, among other things, how it was to be vulnerable both to good and to evil, both to beauty and to pain. The tulips threatened to break his heart that year, long-weakened seams giving way and it wouldn't be his fault but the tulips'. Or, Harry sometimes thought with equal trepidation, their vigor and valor would finally heal old wounds, and he'd be forced to reconsider certain things long since settled, rightly or wrongly, in his mind.

From the first setting on of the buds in April, Harry had had the feeling something was going to happen, if not something altogether new, then a new twist on something old. It wasn't the first time in his life he'd experienced this vague sort of clairvoyance, and more times than not it had proved bogus. Still, he'd been right often enough; after his wife Martha's death, thirty-five years ago this fall, for instance, he'd remembered having premonitions, but even if he'd paid attention to them he'd have been powerless. He stayed with his tulips every minute he could, so as not to miss whatever was going to happen, whether or not he could change it.

Helen had given up trying to get him to come in at a reasonable hour and just brought him his supper out there, or sent Cecelia with it when she could get the girl's attention. Helen had a lot to put up with, not least him. His youngest daughter, Maureen, who was coming from Ohio in June, would have something to say about that; Maureen did have opinions. But by then the Tulip Festival would be over, one way or another.

Harry tried not to indulge the speculation that his eldest girl Libby, dead since long before he'd discovered tulips, would have been out there with him. The indisputable fact that Libby had been not quite right in the head didn't diminish her father's sharp sense of lost companionship.

He tried to think about Martha, as he often tried to do, out of an indistinct sort of husbandly duty. Her image was as falsely three-dimensional as the picture at the end of a stereoscope, dependent for any reality on the eye of the beholder, not to mention the beholder's willingness to participate in illusion. Dead maybe eight minutes less than

Maureen had been alive, Martha might or might not have liked tulips, might or might not have approved of his obsession with them. Harry could ascribe to her any characteristic he liked, a habit by now of long standing.

The tulips unnerved him, obsessed him. Something about their perfect teardrop shapes made him yearn to clench his fist and flatten them, one by one. More than once, as the Festival weekend approached, he had to wrest his fingers away and wipe his hand on his pants to get rid of the physical temptation to do something awful, something that would jeopardize his soul.

One bright noon in early May, Harry was in his garden. There wasn't much real work to be done—a few weeds to pull, a section of fence to straighten—and so he was just sitting there on a kitchen chair at the border of the beds, booted feet in the grass, hands absently rubbing thighs, belly rumbling and mildly aching. Although the sun wasn't too hot, the air was heavy with humidity unlikely to be expelled as rain; Harry was uncomfortable and ought to go inside, but he didn't want to leave his tulips.

"Sure is a good year for tulips, isn't it?" passersby would call out to him by way of greeting, and he'd lift his hand to them. Or, sizing him up, "Your garden looks great, Harry," and he'd be the one to make the prescribed observation, "Sure is a good year for tulips."

Though the flowerbeds were edged with purely

decorative fences, the yard wasn't fenced at all, and the higher the tulip excitement rose all over town the more people came by to view his tulips. So Harry didn't think much about it when a young girl was suddenly at his elbow saying, "Sure is a good year for tulips, isn't it?"

He hadn't seen or heard her until she was right beside him, but it wouldn't be the first time he'd dozed off in the sun. He didn't know who she was exactly, but she was vaguely familiar, and he figured her for one of his granddaughter Cecelia's little friends.

She said to him sweetly, "Your tulips look great, Mr. Harkness."

He was amused and touched that she'd care about tulips; he wished Cecelia did. This girl even had about her a concentration of the unusual fragrance that was permeating the whole town this spring, which made him wonder, with an odd strong tingle of hope and unease, if she might actually have been tending tulips somewhere herself.

"Thanks," he said, and found himself patting her small, graceful hand where it rested companionably on his shoulder. Easy intimacy wasn't like him, and he hastily withdrew his hand.

"I like the pink ones," she confided. When Harry had ordered the Lucretias, he'd been thinking of Cecelia, for surely all young girls liked pink. But she'd never taken more than minimally polite interest. Now, as this girl moved past him to kneel beside a particularly nice grouping of the frothy globes, Harry's vision sheened with pink-tinted tears. She made a pretty picture, there among his tulips; he pressed his itching palms against the rough fabric of his trousers and leaned eagerly forward as far as his girth would allow.

He saw her left hand slide down to steady a stem at ground level, and his breath caught. When her right index and middle fingers spread delicately to take between them the perfect hollow head of a Lucretia, he knew very well what she was about to do, but he didn't stop her. The truth was, he didn't want to stop her.

For an excruciatingly long moment, the flower quivered on the collar formed by her pale hand, a head ready for impaling, and then she closed her small fist hard. Pink petals oozed out between her knuckles. There was no sound, but there was the unmistakable and terribly satisfying sensation of something having imploded.

"See?" she called to him softly. "It's easy." She raised her hand to him; it was speckled pink.

Harry made a noise and shut his eyes, held his sides. When he could bring himself to look again, both the girl and the single ravaged tulip, a harbinger, were gone.

From then on, Harry concentrated fiercely on the upcoming contest. Those last days, he'd sit on his chair in the center of the precise concentric circles in which he'd planted his bed, keeping watch, keeping vigil. His visits to other gardens around town took on an intensity approaching frenzy, and, when he judged he could get away with it, he'd lower himself and take other people's tulip heads between index and middle fingers, only just barely restraining himself from squeezing. Old knees aching, old heart beating so wildly it must be for the tulips, he'd stay in his garden or someone else's until the sun went down and sometimes long after.

The night before the Tulip Festival, a Thursday, Harry finally went in about midnight. All the tulips in town had looked wonderful under the misty moon. Agitated, he doubted he would sleep, but for quite a while he did.

Emil Parmalee, Cecelia's father and Harry's son-in-law, was up and down all night, which was not unusual. He'd retired well before nine o'clock, in the faint hope of getting some early sleep; this habit forced everyone else in his household to whisper and tiptoe, and usually to no avail, for worry about life in general and Cecelia in particular rose like a dust devil the minute he started to relax. Then, half a dozen times during the night, he'd just be drifting off, trying not to let his determination to lose consciousness prevent him from losing consciousness, and something would startle him awake—a dog barking that might signal a stranger in the yard, a cough (was it his daughter? was she sick?), a noise he didn't hear anymore once he was wide awake. Then, when finally he did doze, he was disturbed by his wife coming to bed or getting up, by a shift in the quality of night air through the open window, by his own dreams.

Since it never seemed to Emil that he slept soundly enough for dreams, he speculated fretfully that these might be something else—visions, say, visions of the future. Cecelia grew up overnight and moved to South America and he never saw her again. Cecelia told him calmly he wasn't her real father. He woke up and realized he'd never had a daughter except in his dreams. Those were coherent enough for him to grasp and more or less dismiss; countless others wouldn't quite declare themselves, snippets and suggestions, sly hints and undercurrents that kept him in a state of perpetual anxiety, waking or sleeping.

That Friday morning, when the decimation of the tulips was discovered, Emil would swear he hadn't seen or heard a thing and he hadn't slept more than an hour all told. He made the same insomniac claim virtually every morning, though, with such grim pride that his wife was skeptical. Besides, she considered it unlikely that anybody could survive for long on that little sleep.

Sometime that summer or fall, Helen took to saying privately to Cecelia, "When you're awake and everybody else is asleep, it always seems longer than it really is, you know?" She'd smile conspiratorially and shake her head. "Men. If their sleep is the least bit disturbed, they didn't sleep all night. If they have a head cold, they take to their beds and you'd think they were dying. It's a good thing it's not up to men to have babies or human beings would have been extinct a long time ago!" Sometimes Helen would wink.

At first Cecelia didn't know what was expected of her when her mother voiced such comments, and just hearing them made her feel disloyal to her father. But, as 1929 went along, the exclusionary female rite became established as part of her initiation to womanhood. She'd nod and smile back, feeling complicit and superior as she came to understand that her father in particular and men in general could not quite, poor things, be trusted or taken seriously.

So it was that a fact which Emil considered central to his identity, his essential sleeplessness, was denied by the people closest to him. Before the year was out, this fundamental rejection itself would become a central, even defining, fact of his life.

In truth, the abrupt onset of fatherhood nearly thirteen years ago had all but ended for Emil any chance of ever getting a good night's sleep again. His daughter had entered his life on a warm winter midnight, unnamed and squalling, in a basket like eggs on the arm of his wife's sister Libby, whom he'd never seen before. The sisters had argued till the middle of the next morning when Libby, eyes glazed with madness and sorrow and determination and fatigue, had hurried away to catch the bus home, and sometime during that incredible conversation the baby had fallen peacefully asleep in Emil's arms. From then on he'd been afraid to put her down.

She'd been more than two years old when he'd finally built a bed for her and almost four before she'd had her own room; she was a restless sleeper, but neither Helen nor Emil could bear to miss more time with her than they already had. Helen could sleep through anything, a talent Emil regarded with extreme suspicion even as he envied it; he still checked on his child several times a night and heard her stir in between. Any sleep he did manage to get was troubled by the conviction that despite his best efforts he missed things—nightmares that didn't quite wake the child, moments when her breathing stopped and then started again, secrets she wouldn't share with her father.

Emil knew this excessive paternal vigilance was neither necessary nor good. It was wearing him down, and his love for his daughter, great as it was, was thickly plaited with resentment. But over the years he'd become more or less used to the gritty nervousness of chronic sleep deprivation, and it seemed, though he knew it shouldn't, proof of how much he was willing to sacrifice for the sake of his child.

He'd learned to use the time. In the wee hours of the morning he could do quiet household repairs. He listened to the short-wave radio on the back porch, calculating what time it was somewhere else where somebody was awake. He worked in the barn before it got hot, or shoveled snow in the half-light the snow itself created. Lately, undistracted by anybody else's opinion or caution or advice, he figured with pencil and paper more stocks to buy on margin, sometimes hardly able to wait till Helen woke up to show her how they could make money.

These last few weeks when he couldn't sleep he'd mostly prowled around town looking at tulips. Emil found all flowers boring, garden vegetables only slightly less so (though vegetables on his plate he rather liked), and the annual mob mentality of the Tulip Festival caused him positively to detest tulips. Usually he could just ignore the whole thing. For a couple of years he'd gone fishing, leaving before the worst of the craziness started and coming home Monday morning when it was all over. Once the national Elks convention had fortuitously fallen on that very weekend, in Chicago; the only convention he'd ever attended, it had been a damn sight better than tulips, anyway. Last year he'd stayed in bed for the three days, claiming a headache which in fact got worse the more he needed it; he hadn't slept any more than usual, and he certainly hadn't rested, but for the most part people had left him alone about tulips.

He'd thought about spending the Tulip Festival weekend this year holed up in a certain blind pig north of town. He'd paid the joint only a handful of visits, each time for one brown plaid, which was all he could handle, but he'd heard that behind the back panels of the tobacco-shop facade were cots where drinkers could hide out, and maybe a man on the run from tulips could take refuge there, too.

69

But that was before the DeKing woman in Detroit was shot and killed by deputy sheriffs raiding her house for moonshine, a story that caused some men of Emil's acquaintance to consume more rotgut with more defiant abandon, but that he found distinctly sobering. It was also before his daughter had been nominated for Junior Tulip Princess. Because of that, he couldn't ignore the Tulip Festival this year. He had to pay attention, for Cecelia's sake, another enormous sacrifice in the name of fatherhood.

That night as Emil tossed and turned, or lay rigid trying not to wake up Helen (reminding himself bitterly that Helen could sleep through anything; self-righteously hoping his insomnia did at last wake her up so she couldn't say it wasn't real), his chronic agitation suddenly grew intolerable. As he peripatetically wandered the neighborhood in his nightclothes, trying blearily to assess tulips although he knew nothing about them, lightheaded from their odor and from sleeplessness and worry, everything he was worried about abruptly resolved itself into a dilemma with two blessedly clear horns: If tomorrow Cecelia was not crowned Junior Tulip Princess, she'd be humiliated and broken-hearted, and he, her father who loved her, couldn't allow that. If she did win the title—which by rights she should; there was no question she was the prettiest girl in town—he could just see her, radiant up on the stage bedecked with real and tissue-paper tulips, riding in the parade on the tulip-shaped float among tulips with tulips in her arms, waving to the admiring crowd of which he'd be only a part; crown on her head, she'd have taken her first big step toward leaving him for good, and her father who loved her couldn't bear that, either.

Dew dampening his slippers as dawn closed in, Emil ambled among other people's tulips and pondered what to do. It was such a relief to have something specific to worry about, and to know that a course of action was about to be revealed to him, that his anxiety was starting to feel more and more like eagerness. The bittersweet odor of the tulips thickened in the darkness just before dawn. Birdsong carried instructions.

On each of his several passes by his own house, Emil noted that his daughter's bedroom window was dark, but that didn't necessarily mean she was asleep. Her nocturnal restlessness shamed him just because he was her father.

The sky was clear, the sunrise like a petal. Good weather today. In '27 it had drizzled the whole weekend, and there'd been years so hot the tulips had wilted before the parade was over, but never had a Tulip Festival been called off for weather or any other reason. Emil hated knowing that. He hated knowing anything about tulips.

Irritable and very tired, he glanced behind him. Tulip heads lay on the ground like plucked eyes. Tulip stems stood straight and bare. Horror and horrible satisfaction almost bowled him over in the seconds before comprehension dawned, and then

71

Emil hurried home to rouse his family. As he'd suspected, Cecelia was already awake, but she didn't know what had happened to the tulips until her father, who loved her, took her face in his hands and told her.

There was a vehement debate among the townspeople over whether to go on with the Tulip Festival without tulips. Obviously there could be no garden judging; though the judges had been more than familiar with every tulip in town, and mourned them now individually as well as collectively and symbolically, all three had taken seriously their mandate not to make a final judgment until the last possible moment, and had counted on those Friday morning presentations. The parade could have gone on with only artificial tulips, crepe paper and fabric and painted wood, and the choices for Tulip Princess and Junior Tulip Princess had, in fact, already been made, but, by general if not unanimous consensus as to what constituted good taste, both the parade and the pageant were canceled. They did go ahead with the pancake breakfast, and had a good, if somber, turnout. Most people spent the rest of the weekend cleaning up and looking for clues.

The perpetrator was never identified. There were numerous suspects and theories, all with some plausibility but none entirely satisfactory. Some people were sure they'd had a brush with nothing less than evil.

By autumn, Lurleen Simpson's and Dottie Frasier's fathers had lost their jobs; Lurleen's shot himself in the woods on the opening day of doe season, but he didn't die and his medical expenses further impoverished his family. Cecelia's father, having lost in the crash more money than he'd thought he even had, put in vegetables where her grandfather's tulips had been; he wasn't much of a gardener, but he could hold lettuce and tomatoes and yellow squash in his hands.

Early in 1930, Albert Hazen showed up in town again. Lurleen was afraid to meet him alone this time, so Cecelia went with her. He really was handsome, and he had a way of looking at you when he talked that made anything he said seem true.

The three of them went for a walk down along the creek. It was a cold, blustery day, snow falling onto iced-over water and snowed-over trees. They stumbled upon an encampment, two or three families with children, all of whom Lurleen and Cecelia knew; a year ago Cecelia would have thought this faintly embarrassing, but now the tents and the campfire and the dirty, ragged children made her wonder if Lurleen's sister had finally been right about the end of the world.

When Albert told them his mother had disappeared one night after she'd lost all the family's money in the stock market, Lurleen started to cry. "And somebody cut all the heads off the tulips!" she wailed, and threw herself into his arms.

Over her head, Albert caught and held Cecelia's gaze, though she wanted to look away. "Tulips don't matter anymore," he declared, and, because he said so, Cecelia thought then that it must be true. But throughout her life, she would find herself thinking about tulips whenever there were moral choices to be made.

The 1930 Tulip Festival was not a celebration of plenitude but testimony to human resilience in the face of adversity. The tulips themselves were ordinary, gardeners having been short on both inspiration and wherewithal. Some people commented on the pervasive odorlessness; some were afraid to; and some refused to believe that, even in the best of times, tulips had ever had a fragrance.

Chapter Four

On the Steps Somewhere
(1937, 1996)

On a lovely midnight the spring before she was to
graduate from college—amid banks of rhododendron she knew to be scarlet and pink though they
looked only gray and paler gray, causing her to
speculate somewhat dreamily whether it was the
reflected quality of moonlight that leeched or the
radiance of sunlight that imparted false color—Cecelia Parmalee found herself back in Johnny Cory's
arms, where she'd never expected to be again.

He still smelled delicious, like vanilla extract. He
was crying, as he often had, not entirely out of sadness and not for her. The moonlight made his tri-

angular face look even more pointed at temples and chin. An unaccustomed purposefulness under-girded his movements, steadying them, giving them cumulative direction, as though everything he did—every step he took beside her along the romantic winding campus paths, every hug he stopped to give her or to accept, every wave and whorl and clasp of his expressive hands—were part of a grand design.

For her part, Cecelia was honored that he had chosen her. And there was something else that thrilled her: Just the other afternoon, the group of girls she ran around with had been playing with the Ouija board, and under Cecelia's fingertips, no matter who else was touching it at the same time, the pointer had sped urgently from one letter to another spelling out long messages: JOHN WILL DIE. JOHN WILL LIVE. DOESN'T MATTER WHAT YOU DO. DOESN'T MATTER. DOESN'T MAT-TER. At the time, Cecelia couldn't think of who John might be.

Johnny Cory held her tight. She hadn't seen him in the more than four years since, heartbroken but sure of herself, she'd told him she couldn't be his wife. She'd heard about him, though, from people who knew them both, some who didn't realize Ce-celia Parmalee and Johnny Cory, a decidedly un-likely couple, had ever crossed each other's paths, much less been engaged to be married.

She'd heard, for instance, that on a certain Sun-day afternoon, in the Memorial Park south of town, he'd climbed atop a headstone and serenaded with heartfelt love songs the picnicking families within earshot of his reedy, sweet singing voice. She'd heard he was smoking opium for pains in his head and asthmador cigarettes for breathlessness, thus purposely rendering even more peculiar his already peculiar manner of experiencing the world. She'd heard he'd gone off to Alaska and hadn't heard he'd come back.

But tonight here he'd been, tossing pebbles at her window until she'd looked out and seen him and hurried down the back stairs to meet him. The family with whom she boarded would have been scandalized, might well have asked her to leave, and out of deceptiveness more than deference Cecelia carried her saddle shoes in her hand. She thought of her father, checking on her half a dozen times every night she could remember, and felt a little silly, a little guilty, wondering if there was any way he could know she was sneaking out. But she knew she was doing nothing wrong. This was Johnny Cory. The rules did not apply.

"Johnny?"

"Celia. You look lovely." He executed a graceful, ridiculous little series of dance steps, climaxing with a kiss on her forehead. "Your light was on. You were awake so late at night? Were you thinking of me?"

"I was studying. I was not expecting company."

"I'm not company."

"Why are you here, Johnny?"

"Ah, the eternal question. And I believe I have discovered an answer." Here he was, embracing her almost joyfully again, weeping again into her hair. And she was so glad he had come, moved to tears herself that he had chosen her, though it would be quite some time before she understood what it was he'd chosen her to do.

He'd come to her to say good-bye. His body, which suggested frailty even though to all appearances it was perfectly sturdy, quivered now with fear and excitement. Tonight, he told her, he was going to kill himself for love. Not, though, for love of her. She was glad of that, and at the same time a trifle jealous.

There had been many reasons not to marry Johnny Cory. The unlikelihood of his ever being able to support a wife and family, for one thing. The flightiness of his intelligence and the peculiarity of his overall view of life, both mightily attractive to a fifteen- and sixteen-year-old girl but which would not have stood either of them in good stead had he attempted to be husband and father.

And, of course, there'd been his obsession with Jimmy Herringer, which he'd never tried to conceal. In fact, it had always seemed to Cecelia that he'd flaunted it, held it out for the world to mock or admire as it chose—much to the dismay of simple, handsome, somewhat loutish Jimmy Herringer himself, who'd seemed not so much inspiration as excuse, the hapless object upon which Johnny's passion had chanced to alight.

"I love you enormously," Johnny had written to Cecelia. "I love you more than I can say," which was saying something.

Although they'd lived not two miles apart and had been seeing each other nearly every day, although they'd talked and talked for hours when they were together, they'd been fond of writing to each other, too. Cecelia had a hatbox full of his one-word missives and lengthy epistles, poems and essays on the nature of love itself and the nature of their love for each other, monographs on life and death. And of hers, for she'd painstakingly copied everything she'd ever written to Johnny Cory, whether she'd sent it to him or not, suspecting she would want to keep all of it always, already guessing she could not keep him.

"I love you more than I love myself." Chilled and impressed, Cecelia had not doubted either the sincerity of this declaration or the truth of the more beautiful, more dangerous qualifier that had followed: "But then there is this other."

She never could quite regard Johnny as homosexual. At the time, she'd hardly have had words for such a thing. Many years later, when the possibility of someone being gay would more readily occur to her, and even after she'd settled on ways of understanding most other things about him or made peace with not understanding, Johnny would, in this way among many others, continue to confound her.

After all, there'd been secret kisses between

them, and kisses for God and all the world to see, not a few of them open-mouthed. There'd been daring and rather exuberant fondling. There'd been breathless remonstrances each to the other that they must wait until they were married and that marriage must wait until after college, and there'd been the giddy and largely unacknowledged possibility that they would not be able to wait. There'd been, for instance, the rainy afternoon on the swing on his parents' screened porch, his little sisters noisy in the kitchen on the other side of the open door instead of chaperoning them as assigned. Unthinkingly or to test and tease, Cecelia had worn a cardigan buttoned fashionably down the back, with the dictated strand of false pearls. Johnny had tugged on the pearls with some force and whispered, only half-playful, "I want in! I want *in!*"

This incident remained vivid in her memory, partly because the small prolonged sexual frustration had aroused in her a new sort of eroticism she would never after that entirely lose. Also she was mildly obsessed by the fact that Johnny had been undeniably aroused, too. The meaning of his trousers pressing hard against her thigh became less and less ambiguous over the years.

She'd immersed herself in their love. The feeling of immersion would come back to her for the rest of her life whenever she thought of him, and she'd think of him for the rest of her life. *"Je suis engagée,"* she'd announced, inaccurately but plainly, to her French teacher, who'd replied sternly, *"Tu es trop jeune,"* but had not inquired to whom she was engaged, as though the fact that it was Johnny Cory made no difference.

Fancying herself already his wife, his soulmate, lifelong companion to this young man so unlike anybody else she'd ever known, she'd inscribed book flyleaves with "Cecelia Elizabeth Cory" and filled whole notebook pages with "C.E.C." She'd gazed at the star sapphire engagement ring—no run-of-the-mill diamond for them—until she almost could imagine losing herself in the winking on and off of its star, and later she'd wish, a little aghast at herself, that she hadn't given the ring back to him.

But she'd left him after all. A practicality she hadn't known was in her had won out over romanticism and loyalty, and once she'd made the agonizing decision she hadn't wavered, though she'd had many regrets.

What made up her mind was a poem. She'd kept the poem, lettered on a half-sheet of plain white paper and bound with five others between flimsy cardboard covers, decorated with colored-pencil designs and tied with lavender ribbon. Johnny had given her the booklet for her seventeenth birthday, as though he hadn't foreseen what effect that poem would have on her, or as though he had.
It was called "Pledge":

I want to die at thirty-one,
A half-grown friend with battles won,

No chance to brood on things begun,
  On the steps somewhere.

The little poem had stopped her cold. Maybe it was the truncated, echoing rhythm of that last line. Maybe it was the numbers. She'd calculated rapidly and repeatedly: If she and Johnny married after they finished college and started a family right away, the plan they'd agreed on, the oldest child would be no more than ten years old when their father died at age thirty-one.

So it was plain that she couldn't marry him, couldn't have children with him, and, then, couldn't stay with him a day longer. Sobbing, she'd pressed the sapphire ring into his hand without even looking to see if at this moment, in this light, a star was blinking in it. He'd cried, too, but not entirely out of sadness and not wholly for her.

Cecelia had gone to college. She had met other young men, for none of whom she felt anything like the inundating love she'd felt for Johnny Cory, but whom she judged to be steady, sensible, decent, and some of whom she did, because the word had so many vastly different meanings it might as well not be the same word, love. So hard had it become for her to imagine how she ever could have entangled her life with Johnny's that before long she didn't even consider herself to have had a close call.

Tonight, among the redolent banks of rhododendron, he drew back slightly, put a knuckle under her chin to tilt back her head, and kissed her sweetly on the lips. He turned his flushed, pointy face to the side a little but put no real distance between them to confide, "I'm going to die tonight, Celia. I wanted you to be the first to know."

"Why?" she breathed. She wasn't surprised, either that he had come to her or by what he had come to say. It was all just like the Johnny Cory she had loved and left.

"Because I knew you'd understand."

And she did understand, in some fundamental way, but she craved details. "Why are you going to die? Why tonight?"

"It's the only thing I can do for him."

"Jimmy."

"This afternoon he pointed a shotgun at my head, and I could see in the liquid fire of his eyes how much he wished he could pull the trigger."

She drew in her breath. "He did that?"

He waved away the outrage she wasn't even sure she felt. "I don't fault him. I have made his life miserable these last five and a half years. My love, the very best thing I have, has made his life miserable."

He shook his head wonderingly, and his tragic smile sent a rush of tenderness through her. "Oh," she whispered. "Johnny."

"He doesn't love me. He'll never love me. He wants me out of his life forever, and he's right that I cannot stay out of his life so long as I'm alive. Dying is the only thing I can do for him, but it's wonderful, isn't it? To be able to do something so profound and meaningful for the one you love? It's enough." He hugged her fiercely. "Oh, Celia, isn't love grand?"

They'd come by then to the footbridge across the ravine, where lovers often spooned and sparked on the thirteenth plank. Designating that board the Thirteenth Plank allowed things to happen that might not have happened otherwise, as if by magic, and sometimes pranksters stole the plank so courting couples had to stand one foot on the Twelfth and one on the Fourteenth, which was not the same.

Cecelia and Johnny were not like any of the other people they'd met, singly and in couples on this bittersweet spring night. The fragrance of rhododendron was heavenly, quite unlike the tulips her grandfather was devoted to, which were the only other flowers she'd paid much attention to. The stream below them was like sapphires, sometimes merely lustrous, sometimes sparkling with perfect four-point stars, sometimes so subdued as to be all but invisible. The immensity and fragility of the gift Johnny was giving her made Cecelia feel she might swoon. "What will you do?" she whispered, in his arms again.

"I have a pocketful of Seconal. I don't sleep anyway. I don't want to sleep. I want to die. I will curl up on the floorboards of his automobile and simply drift away, and when he comes out of the saloon where he plays cards with his chums every night he'll find me, and he'll know what I've done for him. For love of him. For the rest of his life, he'll know." Johnny's gray eyes caught moonlight and sparkled.

"I'll miss you," she told him, and her voice broke. It was not precisely true, though, even when she said it. She hadn't seen him in more than four years and hadn't expected ever to see him again. What she felt keenly, facing his death, was not so much impending personal loss as inevitable, exquisite tragedy, the frisson of anticipation one feels as the death scenes of *Romeo and Juliet* inexorably approach, knowing that one's heart will be broken and that one would feel cheated if it weren't.

"I've been so unhappy."

"I know."

"In all my life I've never been happy. I think that happiness is not intended for me. I believe my purpose lies elsewhere."

Weren't you happy with me? she wanted to ask, a bit insulted, but she didn't. She reminded herself that Johnny Cory wasn't like anybody else, which was why she'd so loved him in the first place, and she had no right to expect him to be.

"This is my chance to fulfill my purpose," Johnny all but sang. He had swung her out to arm's length to tell her of his unhappiness, and now he drew her close again to proclaim, "Oh, Celia, Celia, I have loved you so much!"

"I love you, too," she answered, and, because love could mean so many different things, she was telling the truth.

He left her then. His final kiss was sweet and sustained, but his attention, she could tell, was no longer on her in the least. He smelled like vanilla extract, sweet and bitter. She didn't try to hold him. She watched him run away, knees and elbows poking out sideways like a child's, and listened to a few of his footsteps on the bridge. But he veered off the paved path into the dense, shrubby ravine, where perhaps there was a shortcut, down and then up, or a way of getting lost altogether. In order to follow his trajectory then, Cecelia would have had to lean far out over the bridge railing or even hoist herself up onto it, or clamber down into the ravine, or otherwise put herself at risk, and she was not, then or later, willing to do that for Johnny Cory.

Johnny didn't die that night, never mind that he did everything right: He found Jimmy's black Ford parked outside the Silver Slipper and double-checked to be sure it was the right automobile, giggling to think how ludicrous it would be to die in a stranger's car by mistake. On the front seat he placed the final draft of the letter that in flowery iambic pentameter simultaneously expressed tremulous gratitude for this opportunity to demonstrate his undying love and went to great lengths to exonerate Jimmy from all responsibility. Then, curling up on the back floorboards out of immediate sight but not hard to find when the time was right, he swallowed his hoarded sleeping pills with whiskey purchased earlier in the evening from the Silver

Slipper itself under Jimmy's baleful, unsuspecting eye.

But the thing turned tawdry. Jimmy came out of the saloon well before it closed, having other plans for the rest of the evening with his female companion. If he'd stayed later, as he usually did, Johnny would have been farther along on his path to oblivion; as it was, he'd managed to reach only ordinary unconsciousness. Jimmy was drunk on beer and cannabis, so the young woman insisted on driving; because she was short, Jimmy, laughing uproariously, fumbled on the floor of the backseat for a pillow she could sit on and came upon Johnny, whom she'd never seen before. If Jimmy had been sober or unaccompanied, if the girl had been taller or hadn't known how to drive, if Jimmy hadn't kept a pillow in the car, no one would have looked in the back at least until morning and things would have turned out right.

Johnny didn't respond to Jimmy's embarrassed curses, pleas, and prods. With the young woman behind the wheel and Jimmy resentfully crouched on the floor beside this boy who loved him, they drove him to the hospital and left him there to have his stomach pumped. Jimmy visited him once to repeat that he wanted him out of his life.

Johnny sent Cecelia a note telling her all this, with flowers. She went to the hospital, but he'd been discharged, and she made no further effort to find him. It would be sixty years before she'd see him again.

*   *   *

That night in 1937 when Johnny came to tell her good-bye, Cecelia was twenty years old and a romantic. Since no one was privy to what Johnny told her or what she said in return, she was not asked to defend herself, but if had she been, she'd have said confidently that she was only receiving, at most bearing witness, not really making a choice for the choice was his.

As the years went by, she thought about Johnny a good deal and took pride in her love for him. Her behavior that night would seem to her, in fact, to be among her finest moments, a rare pure act, the veritable distillation and personification of selfless love. Anyone who'd known her with Johnny gradually went out of her life, and she came to regard the girl who'd been in love with him as a face in a cameo, her own almost impossibly fine-featured profile in a pale oval, set off and set apart by the clutter of other things she knew and was learning about herself.

She finished college with honors and found a respectable job. When some of those steady young men came back from World War II, she married one of them, who turned out to have undercurrents and undertows of his own. They had a boy right away, then twin boys, then a girl; in 1949, when the eldest of the four was not yet in school, Cecelia was pregnant again and unable to keep her mind on much else.

Stories of concentration camps, which had been

seeping into the public awareness since before the end of the war, now began to take on more substance and detail. During her four pregnancies, a virtually seamless blanket of years, she was beset by terrible images that flashed into her wakeful mind with force enough to jar her, for a fiercely split second, away from the diapers she was stretching through the wringer, the scraped knee she was painting with mercurochrome, Ray's fingers sliding with exquisite slowness from the pulse point under her ear to the pulse point at her wrist, the phone that didn't ring, the car that didn't turn into the unlit gravel driveway.

What if she had to choose one of the twins to be gassed, in the slim hope that the other would be spared? She'd stare at the little boys with such awful intensity that one of them, usually Dennis, would start to whine or outright cry and the other, most often Dean, would scamper self-protectively out of her reach. What if her baby were to be pulled from her womb and thrown into a pit squirming with scores of other babies, unless she sacrificed herself? She'd clutch at her belly. What if it didn't matter who your parents were, or your children?

On a night she waited up for Ray, or a morning when she'd awakened to find him still not home, sometimes her outrage and hurt would be sliced through with a sense of proportion: It could be worse. He could have been picked up by the SS today. There were women in this world whose husbands didn't come home because they'd been sent to Dachau.

During the early '50s the focus of these fantasies shifted, casting her less often as the helpless victim and giving rise to emotion more complex and addictive than sheer vicarious terror. She was never Hitler or even Eva Braun, but almost always now she imagined scenarios in which she was faced with an excruciating moral decision.

Helping Karen and Dennis decorate the big picture window at Halloween, for a moment the orange construction paper pumpkins and black yarn cats would be yellow Stars of David, and she'd be agonizing over whether or not to open her hand and expose them for what they were. Gluing onto the black pages of the photo album the little black tabs to hold the pictures in, she'd be struck by sharp fear that she was keeping a record of the wrong things, the wrong events, the wrong people.

Hurrying out her back door to collect tomatoes for a summer salad, fleetingly she'd fancy herself on her way to deliver food to the Jewish family hidden under a nonexistent false floor in the shed. Would she have had the courage really to do that? With five small children of her own, would it have been the right thing to do? Sometimes she'd imagine men in brown uniforms goose-stepping across the field; sometimes her lips would move as she played out the conversations, defiant or submissive or deceptive, she might have with them.

Gradually the Holocaust, which after all was several times removed from her no matter how pressing and intimate it seemed, became no less chilling but less obsessive, less tantalizing, somehow less useful. It wasn't that the images went out of her mind but rather that they settled in, so that when she stumbled upon them she was less shocked than vindicated.

For some years then, Cecelia hardly thought of her life as having any moral dimension at all, except in reaction to other people's choices: Ray was involved with one woman after another. Philip cheated on a math test. Dennis called another little boy "nigger." Karen kept shutting the cat in the closet.

Then, one afternoon in May of 1956, about an hour before the schoolbus would stop out front, Cecelia was rummaging through a file cabinet looking for Philip's immunization records for Boy Scout Camp that summer when she came upon a folder labeled JOHNNY CORY. Just glimpsing his name made her eyes mist over. A faint, bittersweet odor drifted up from the old papers; remembering how Johnny used to smell like vanilla extract, she inhaled this subtler, sharper odor and wondered if it could be vanilla, aged.

There were letters from him, creased like windowpanes, though not nearly as many as she'd thought she'd kept. The lavender ribbon binding the booklet of poems had paled; in some places, especially around the bow, it was downright gray. In his high school graduation photo, the blunt hairline across his wide forehead emphasized the triangularity of his face; she found she remembered the photo better than his face itself.

One at a time, she picked up and read the papers and laid them face down in a reverse stack on the desk. Her fingertips began to feel powdery; she rubbed them together, wiped them on her house-dress, touched her tongue to them so she could separate the sheets. Five or six pages down, somehow removed from the little booklet, was the fateful poem with its heart-stopping final line that both called eternally for more and said all there was to say: "On the steps somewhere."

Something was wrong. She raised her eyes to the window, thinking. Her memories of her time with Johnny Cory had changed since she'd last regarded them. She sat back hard in her chair. She'd done something wrong. Guilt swelled in the pit of her stomach. She'd done something reprehensible and irremediable.

Was it that she should have tried to stop him from committing suicide?

The possibility had never occurred to her before. Now she couldn't fathom why it had not. It seemed obvious and irrefutable that she should have tried to talk him out of it. She should have called the police. She should have gone to the saloon herself and warned Jimmy Herringer of what was about to be done in his name.

Somewhat frantically, she reminded herself that it had turned out all right, Johnny hadn't died. But the outcome seemed completely beside the point; it was no thanks to her that he hadn't and, in fact, she was stunned to recall her own impatience and disappointment when she'd received his missive confessing failure.

Glancing at the clock, she put the papers tidily back into their folder and the folder into the proper place in the file cabinet, and rushed to the corner to meet the schoolbus. It was a few minutes late. Bedlam was immediate: Ginger was crying when she got off the bus because somebody'd put gum in her hair; Cecelia assessed the damage rapidly and concluded the sticky mass would have to be cut out, but didn't say so yet to Ginger.

The first-grade teacher had sent home a note requesting a conference about Ginger's problems getting along with others; Ginger said nothing bad had happened in school today. Philip had trouble with his math homework, and told her he'd finished it when he hadn't. Dennis reported—without much reaction; just as a matter of interest, on the level of the air raid drill they'd had that afternoon and the stray dog that had wandered onto the playground— that a black classmate had called him a honky. Ray phoned to say he'd be working late again, but she didn't hear the noise of the factory lunch room in the background. Cecelia didn't think about Johnny Cory any more that day.

But what she came to regard as her own cowardice, on the footbridge with Johnny that youthful night among the bittersweet rhododendron, swelled now at certain moments of her life like background music signalling significance, alerting her to *pay attention here.* Trying to make something honorable out of staying with Ray by declaring it was all right for him to go with other women as long as he didn't lie to her, she could not stop thinking Johnny's words: "But then there is this other"; when Ray found a way of cheating on her anyway, and when, finally, he quit coming home altogether, her self-castigating "I should have known; I'm such a fool; I should have known" was about Johnny, too. Years later, when hormones and other chemical imbalances hit Ginger like a mudslide, and Cecelia lay awake nights worrying about how to balance freedom and limits, Johnny's farewell kiss was on her lips.

During the Red scare of the late '50s, when more than a few of their friends were building fallout shelters and the kids were taught to dive under their school desks as if that would protect them from an atom bomb, she was often put in mind of Johnny: pointlessly aroused on his front porch swing, pirouetting at the very edge of the bridge, curled up as if for protection on the floorboards of Jimmy's car. A decade later, she marched against the war, supported one son's flight to Canada and with greater effort another's enlistment, was not nearly as shocked as she might have been by free love and drugs—and still ended up failing her daughter Karen anyway, much as she'd failed Johnny.

Somehow she lost the poem. She had no memory of taking it out of the JOHNNY CORY folder, but when, sometime in 1973 or '74, she next looked for it, it wasn't there. At the time she was not unduly distressed, believing she remembered it precisely.

But when, another few years later, she tried almost idly to write it out, she found to her dismay that she'd forgotten the adjective in the second line. What kind of friend had he wanted to be when he died? And had he, in fact, died at thirty-one?

Thus began a rather long period of intermittent detective work. A search strategy would occur to her and she'd pursue it until the trail went cold, and then, weeks or years later, another possibility would surface, which she'd follow as far as she could.

Information for her hometown and the surrounding area had no listing for John Cory or, a longer shot, James Herringer. Johnny's parents had long since died; his sisters had married, each more than once that she knew of, presumably changing their last names each time. He hadn't gone to her high school or college, so reunion committees and alumni associations had no information about him; when she thought to call his high school, the secretary didn't know his name and couldn't give her a phone number for any member of the class of '34.

Then, in the summer of 1996, came a letter-size

envelope from a classmate of Cecelia's. Real gladness made Cecelia's heart leap when she saw the return address; this was someone she'd always liked and never been close to, and after their sixtieth high school class reunion two years ago, she'd just about given up. Now here was a letter from her, surely a friendly overture at last.

But the envelope contained only a poorly photocopied newspaper clipping with a handwritten note inked in the blank space at the left margin: "Thought you might be interested—D." Cecelia could justify no more expansive a reply than "Thanks"; this was apparently nothing more than a thoughtful gesture, not to be construed as an invitation to anything more.

Putting on her glasses so she could read past the headline, Cecelia gazed at the blurry photo for a second or two before checking the caption, a game and a test, and then was quite taken aback by the byline "John H. Cory" underneath. The people she'd seen at reunions had all looked more or less like their younger selves; even those she might not have been quite able to place if she'd met them on the street had something familiar about them. But she never would have recognized this full-faced, necktied man—glasses, mustache precisely the width of his nostrils, gray hair swept back from unremarkable forehead, double chin. Maybe in person, she thought anxiously, or maybe if she heard his voice, he wouldn't seem so thoroughly a stranger.

Johnny was, apparently, a sometime columnist for the local paper. This column was an opinion piece about a pending city council vote concerning downtown parking, written emphatically in admirably clear prose but assuming, in order for its ethical position to make sense, a commonalty of information and experience among his readers that Cecelia didn't have. She skimmed. Italics following the column gave a phone number and e-mail address at the paper where readers could reach John Cory with comments.

Nodding happily, Cecelia went right to her computer and entered Johnny's e-mail address in her address book. "Dear Johnny," she began, wondering affectionately whether anybody called him that anymore. She explained how she'd found him, made a teasing-admiring reference to his small fame. Not sure he'd know who she was—and hoping there weren't two John H. Corys in the area and Dottie hadn't got the wrong one—she reminded him first of how they'd known each other as teenagers, then told him she'd been thinking about him lately because of trying to reconstruct his poem; what was that adjective in the second line? She did not say that he—or, more precisely, a single moment of her life in relation to him—had been on her mind off and on for almost sixty years as symbol and signal of moral choice. She signed the message "Cecelia Parmalee Melchior" and clicked "Send," briefly marveling that she scarcely even marveled at electronic messaging anymore.

His reply was waiting when she checked her e-mail the next morning. "Dear Celia, How nice to have our friendship renewed, I hope. This is a business address, though, and I'd like to tell you my story." His home phone number on the screen stirred in her both satisfaction and unease. He did add, "I remember the poem you mention, but no specifics. Feel free to plug in any adjective you like." This made her even more uneasy; that poem, of all things, shouldn't be a collaboration.

She called him that evening as soon as the rates went down. Very sure the man who answered was somebody else, she said not, "Johnny, hello" or "Is this Johnny Cory?" but "May I speak to John Cory, please?" Even when he greeted her by name as if they'd spoken yesterday, even after they'd been talking for a while, there was nothing about the timbre of his voice or the patterns of his speech to recall the boy she'd listened to all those years ago.

"Let me tell you my story," he repeated almost the first thing, and she, wanting to hear it, didn't object, though she did think it would have been more polite of him at least to inquire about hers.

He told her about freelance writing, which he hastened to say he didn't consider a love or a calling but which he rather enjoyed, and various other jobs he'd held to pay the rent. He detailed extensive travel, and with a studied laugh, from which she gathered he'd said precisely this before, observed that he liked the "I" countries best: Ireland, Israel, India, Iceland, Italy; he'd save Iran and Iraq for another life. He'd had a lot of bad relationships, he confessed, *really* bad relationships, but he was in a good one now; when he described his current companion, though, Cecelia thought the man sounded terribly difficult. She was tempted to mention Ray, but Johnny didn't ask. He didn't ask about children or work, either, and left no openings for her to say anything else about her life.

So she was feeling sad and impatient that this was going to be a one-sided friendship, and trying to remember if it always had been, and speculating on whether it might be worth it anyway, when abruptly Johnny exclaimed, "Hey! How about this?" and launched into a poem. Assuming it to be another of his, Cecelia rolled her eyes and waited for him to finish. But as he came to the last faux nihilist stanza, she realized it was hers, from the same period as his "Pledge." Moved to tears by his having memorized it, she recited the last lines with him:

So I don't need anyone
Not even God

and added in a rush, "My God, we were young then, weren't we?"

"And obsessed by the Big Questions." He chuckled.

Encouraged, perhaps wrongly, she blurted, "Should I have tried to stop you that night you

99

came to tell me you were going to kill yourself for love of Jimmy Herringer?"

"I don't know," he said, without hesitation, as though he'd been ruminating about it, too.

She tried again, as if this would be her only chance for blessing or curse, at least from him. "Are you glad you didn't die?"

But he said again, readily, "I don't know," and she had to settle for that.

Chapter Five

Woman on the Corner
(1954)

"What's her name?" Cecelia always asked sooner or later. She didn't know why she did that. It was bad enough to have to be saying to herself as she went about the daily business of raising five kids, "My husband is unfaithful. My husband goes with other women. And I've said it's all right." Thinking a name to pair him with was worse, but if she didn't have a name she made one up.

Ray had been cheating on her since before they were married. The first one she'd found out about was a girl named Dee he'd picked up at a beer joint on base, and she knew seventeen others by name;

the list she'd made waiting up for him not long ago—he never did come home that night, just went right on to work and called her from there to say he'd be home for supper—was still in her desk drawer, and bitterly she thought she'd better update it soon before she got too far behind. She knew there'd been others, in between the ones on the list and at the same time, since there was no earthly reason to suppose that God's gift to women Ray Melchior would have confined himself to one mistress at a time or put up with any dry spells.

It was an old story, and it galled her to think what a typical wronged wife she'd been; like most who weren't suspicious by nature, she'd been a slow learner. For an embarrassingly long time she'd thought he really was working late. She'd called the hospitals so regularly that the nurses must have come to recognize her by name or by voice or by her sordid situation; even after she'd known Ray wouldn't be in any emergency room, she'd still called whenever he wasn't home by the middle of the night, her part of the sick little routine. In fact, thinking how awful she'd feel if this time he really had been in an accident, she'd called last night, the whole list of numbers she almost knew by heart, the questions and answers she did.

Losing sleep over your kids was part of the job description; by the time she was grown her father had hardly been sleeping at all, a model she'd probably emulate though hopefully in a less extreme form. She hadn't expected to stay up nights won-

dering where her husband was. Like every other
wronged wife, she'd cried. She'd raged. She'd ag-
onized over what it was she wasn't doing to please
him. She'd schemed how to prevent him from
meeting girls, for a while even going to work with
him, to the gas station, to the store for cigarettes.
She'd figured how she could leave him; if she'd
done it early on, when they'd had just Philip, or
even after the twins were born, she might have
been able to pull it off, but there wasn't much time
between pregnancies and once the girls came along
it just hadn't seemed possible to raise five children
on her own. And kids needed their father; he wasn't
a bad father. And, anyway, it would have broken
Ray's heart.

That contradiction shook her every time she encountered it, and whenever she wrestled with the
truths of her marriage she ran right into it, and
wrestling with her marriage was virtually a full-
time occupation. For a long time his apologies and
making-up sweetness had repeatedly convinced
her, in the face of all evidence to the contrary, that
he would change his philandering ways. Then, for
a long time, she'd refused to believe that he was
ever sorry, that he loved her at all, that he cared in
the least about his family.

But the devil of it was that it was all true, his
betrayals *and* his love, his uncontrolled desire for
other women *and* his commitment to her and the
children. "This is what I've always dreamed of, a
home and a family," he'd told her once, miserably.

"But there's a part of me that doesn't give a damn about my dreams."

So four summers ago, Cecelia had decided she could stand it if it was out in the open. She was pregnant with Ginger at the time and he'd been seeing Anna Mary Stevenson, whom he'd met because her little girl Brenda played with Karen, both three years old. It was their neighbor Mrs. Farris who'd told Cecelia about that one, and at first she hadn't believed it, not because she'd been naive enough by then to think they wouldn't do such a thing but because she couldn't see when they'd have had a chance.

"Are you and Brenda's mother having an affair?"

"What I do is my own business."

"Are you sleeping with my husband?" Karen and Brenda had been chasing each other screaming around the back yard, and Cecelia could only hope they wouldn't hear, or they wouldn't understand if they did hear, or they wouldn't remember if they did understand. Anna Mary had plenty of time to answer before Brenda fell and cut her chin on the step, but she didn't.

"Let's be honest with each other," Cecelia had insisted—pleaded—that afternoon to Ray. He'd come home early, probably hoping to see Anna Mary, but she'd whisked Brenda off to take care of her chin though she could have doctored it perfectly well at Cecelia's house. "Maybe you can't help that you need other women, or maybe you won't, but don't lie to me anymore. Tell me where you really are. Tell me their names. Tell me when something starts and when it's over." *Then it wouldn't be cheating,* she went on to herself—not out loud to him, though, for fear of giving him ammunition; *it would be an understanding between us.* Instead of shame, there'd be a kind of nobility to the whole thing, an admirable resilience and flexibility.

The proposition had been so daring, so adventurous that, giddy, she'd thrown back her head and guffawed, her pulse racing fast enough to make her light-headed. Ray'd been gratifyingly astonished, more than a little sheepish and skeptical, but he'd agreed. And why wouldn't he, when she was giving him license to have his cake and eat it, too?

As if in gratitude or celebration, or maybe in reaction to the sudden shift in the way they regarded each other—an unaccustomed angle, an exciting new friction—they'd made love right there and then. It had been spectacular, the source of many a sexual fantasy since then and for years to come. She'd beaten his back and buttocks with fists and open palms, and he'd yelled; it had all been part of her climax and, a split second later, of his.

She had no interest in meeting his other women, though once or twice he suggested it, a kinky or mean-spirited or careless exaggeration of the honesty she'd proposed. She didn't care anything about who they were, whether they were married and had children, whether they liked roses. Except when she was feeling especially matronly, she hardly thought about what they looked like.

But she wanted their *names*. She collected their names like butterflies pinned to a cork board. "Dolores," he'd say, ducking his head in embarrassment, but also in a kind of pride. His pride didn't keep Cecelia from feeling briefly triumphant. "Trixie. Jane."

Things hadn't lasted long with Anna Mary Stevenson; by the time the girls were in preschool, he'd lost interest in her. Cecelia didn't much care why, any more than she cared why he'd taken up with her in the first place. Juggling baby Ginger—Ray's baby—she went out of her way to nod and wave to Anna Mary across the playground. The other woman looked more and more haggard, as if she might be seriously ill. Then Brenda's grandmother started picking her up after preschool while her father came alone to evening events. Cecelia had tried to make sure her concern was genuine, though she had allowed herself spite enough to also wonder if what Anna Mary Stevenson was suffering from was a broken heart.

Among the preschool parents there was speculation, minimal and almost offhand, about drink, about diet pills and sleeping pills and nerve pills, about cancer and any other wasting disease that came to mind. Then one of the other mothers commented how sad it was for little Brenda and her brother that their mommy had deserted the family, but Cecelia would have known if Ray had had anything to do with that.

Then the school year ended, and the Melchiors wouldn't have had any contact with the Stevensons over the summer anyway. Once the girls had been in first grade and in school full days, they hadn't played back and forth anymore. Karen mentioned Brenda once in a while, but they weren't friends. By now Cecelia hadn't seen Anna Mary for years and had scarcely thought of her, other names having superseded hers on the list.

For a while—years—the plan had seemed to be working. "Don't wait up for me tonight. I'm going out," he'd tell her civilly, and she'd nod, jealous and unhappy but at least not worried about him, not a fool.

Sometimes she didn't even mind. On those evenings she'd plan a family outing that Ray wouldn't like or a supper he'd turn his nose up at, and be glad he wouldn't be home to complain. Or she'd look forward to the book she could immerse herself in once the kids were in bed and she was alone.

They got so they could even plan around his extramarital activities. "Are you busy Thursday night," she'd inquire, "or could we have dinner with the Werners?"

"Wednesday would be better," he'd reply, and she'd tell Twyla Werner Wednesday.

"Don't forget Dean has a game Saturday," she'd remind him.

He'd say, "Oh, that's right. I'll change my plans. I'll be there," and he would.

So Cecelia had been rather proud of herself and, by extension, of Ray. They'd weathered a problem, could even be said to have solved it, that had destroyed many another marriage, and theirs seemed better for it. They were having fun together again. They handled the kids as partners. Their sex life was wonderful; there was no other word for it. She'd found herself tempted to tell people about it—her father, her friend Lurleen in a letter—but knew how it would sound to outsiders and so regretfully restrained herself. All in all, though, this phase of the Melchior marriage had been a good one. And it had been months since he'd told her about a woman; she was chagrined to discover she was hoping he'd finally changed his ways.

A few weeks ago he'd mentioned that he'd be working late for a while, and she'd reminded herself that she had no reason to doubt him anymore. She'd been ashamed of her own suspiciousness when he'd explained the phone number on the scrap of napkin in his pants pocket was some guy who might buy the truck. He could have all the affairs he wanted. He had no reason to sneak around.

But just now, she'd seen them.

Tonight she'd hired the girl across the street to stay with the kids so she could go see *Rear Window*. Reaching this agreement with Ray had given her first the idea and then the courage to go out by herself now and then, and she'd come to enjoy it considerably, much more, she thought in some amusement, than she'd have enjoyed affairs of her own. By not telling Ray, she even managed to imbue these outings with a slight clandestine quality, which, though not exactly real, gave them a pleasant little frisson.

As had become her habit, she'd bought a large buttered popcorn, Milk Duds, and a Coke with lots of ice, and hunkered down in the back row with her knees up against the seat in front of her. This was not the same out-of-this-world experience as *Gone with the Wind* had been; she'd seen that one four times, all three hours of it. But the show was wonderfully terrifying, and when the credits rolled and the house lights came up she had a buoyant feeling of accomplishment and release.

Whistling music from both *Rear Window* and *Gone with the Wind*, making a medley, she let herself be carried along by the crowd until she was outside in the spring evening, cool in a much nicer way than the theater had been. As she crossed the parking lot she broke into the silly, happy lyrics of "Mr. Sandman," which the radio played dozens of times a day; on the surface, its mood was the polar opposite of the movie's, but her enjoyment of them seemed to come from the same source. On the way to her car, she skipped, and the up-and-down "bum-bum-bum"s of the melody made her laugh out loud.

It always took a few seconds to get the key into

109

the lock, and while she fiddled with it she was gazing without particular thought across the top of the car when she saw her husband with a woman whose name she had not been given. Cecelia froze.

Apparently they'd also just come out of the movie. Apparently they'd been in the same dark theater she'd been in, eaten popcorn, watched Jimmy Stewart, and she'd never known they were there.

Pretending to be scared, the woman half-hid her face in Ray's shoulder. Ray hugged her close, pretending to comfort her. Their trajectory kept them turned away from Cecelia, so she and her car were effectively concealed from them, though she hadn't planned it that way. Wouldn't have planned it that way, in fact; would have stepped right out in front of them if she could have moved fast enough, or driven. They stopped two rows over at what must have been the woman's car, a turquoise-and-white late-model Chevy Bellaire.

Cecelia stared. Later, the profundity of her shock, the way it seeped through her to numb her mind and make her fingers and toes tingle, would seem preposterous, as in retrospect all this came to look utterly, squalidly predictable. But in that long ringing moment she barely comprehended what she was witnessing, and certainly did not believe it.

Ray and the woman embraced and kissed. He had his hand on the back of her head. Knees glimmering, she got in behind the wheel. Ray opened and shut the driver's door for her and went around to the other side. The shutting of the passenger door was obscured by the revving of the engine. The Bellaire pulled out of the lot, in no hurry, and turned right onto 64th.

Cecelia must have got herself into her own car and shut her own door and started her own motor, for she was following them. If Ray had looked back, he'd have recognized the car, of course. He might even have recognized her. But he'd had his arm around the woman and kept ducking his head, presumably to kiss her, and peevishly Cecelia thought they were lucky to know where they were going let alone who was on their tail.

Blood rushing to her head made her ears ring and her brain feel inflated, too big for her skull. Her senses seemed abnormally acute, creating the delusion that she was safe and in control of the situation. She knew it was a delusion, but she'd have sworn she could see the slightest veer of the panel truck on her left, hear the gears of the DeSoto behind her shift as the driver prepared to pass, smell the bittersweet, heady fumes of illicit sex that must be all but propelling the turquoise-and-white Bellaire into orbit. Though she knew perfectly well that these impressions were dangerously off, she was convinced that they made her a far better driver than usual and therefore she could take risks she would not otherwise have even thought of.

The car carrying Ray and his girlfriend—*courtesan*, Cecelia thought wildly, and laughed aloud; *concubine*; *whore*—wasn't going especially fast, but Cecelia didn't resist the urge to speed. She ran yellow lights. Allowing the DeSoto to bully its way in ahead of her, she then shamelessly tailgated in order to keep the turquoise roof of the Bellaire in sight through the DeSoto's big square windows. She gave only lip service to stop signs, made what seemed like clear-headed decisions not to bother with turn signals, and once even took her right front wheel up over a curb.

Cecelia's Aunt Maureen told a story of when she'd been a young woman away from home for the first time, alone one night in the rich people's house where she boarded while she went to the Normal. She'd wakened to find a stranger sitting on the foot of her bed. When she'd sat up and screamed, he'd looked surprised, pulled himself to his feet, and bounded back across the room toward the open window through which he'd obviously entered. Maureen hadn't been about to let him get away with it. Barefoot and in her nightgown, she'd chased him, had hold of his jacket as he got his knees over the sill, before the thought had occurred to her: *What will I do with him if I capture him?*

Cecelia felt like that now. She didn't know what she'd do when she caught up with her quarry. But she wasn't about to let them get away with this.

The three vehicles passed in and out of yellow streetlight glow, like a miniature convoy although they weren't "together" in any meaningful sense of the word, and fiercely Cecelia imagined how that wavy illumination would add to the lovers' romantic atmosphere. Guessing they'd be listening to music, probably classical since that was what Ray liked, she turned on her radio, recklessly steered with one hand while spinning the dial with the other thumb and forefinger.

The DeSoto turned off onto an unpaved side street. But somehow a small white car had appeared in front of her, and the Bellaire was nowhere in sight. She turned off the radio.

A major intersection loomed, the traffic light on the cross street turning yellow right now. She'd have to make a choice in little more than a split second, and she had not the faintest idea what to do.

Evading the threat of hysterical tears, Cecelia gripped the steering wheel and floored the accelerator. As she shot around the white car, two things came into view: the Bellaire, almost a full block west and slightly behind her on a street she hadn't realized was there, and Anna Mary Stevenson on the corner.

Suddenly Cecelia could hardly breathe, and her head was pounding. The crazy thought came to her that there was poison in the air, making all of them act crazy, herself most definitely included. Her tires screeched as she took the corner, searching frantically for a place to turn around so she could follow Ray and his woman before they eluded her entirely. Three men ringed Anna Mary, who, clearly intoxicated, was down on one knee, in a position both suggestive and pitiful, against a bright yellow fire hydrant. Cecelia's arcing headlights caught the bottom half of her face, lips drawn back over glinting teeth, blood drooling from the corner of the mouth.

"Goddammit to hell!" Cecelia shouted. She braked and pounded the steering wheel to make the horn blat. Then she put her full weight behind her fist. The sustained squawk didn't faze any of the four people on the corner. None of them even looked. They all kept on with what they were doing, Anna Mary oozing lasciviously over the hydrant, the three men closing in.

Backing up, gravel spitting from under her tires, Cecelia saw one of the men drop to a half-crouch, heard Anna Mary shriek and curse, and smelled something sharp that for an instant pinched her nostrils shut.

What do you think you're doing? The incredulous, challenging question that flashed into her mind was as distinct as if somebody else were posing it. *This is ridiculous, not to mention dangerous and none of your business.*

She'd meant to turn around and take off as quickly as possible. Now she didn't think she could.

Why in the world not? It won't make any difference. She'll just be back on some other corner some other night, no matter what you do or don't do. You have your own troubles.

From here, over a slight rise and past buildings, Cecelia couldn't see the road the Bellaire had turned onto, and there were no moving lights in that direction. They might already be gone; maybe the woman lived over there and they were on their way to her bed, the car to be hidden in her garage. Surely if Cecelia didn't get there in the next few seconds, she'd lose them.

"Come on, you son-of-a-bitch!" Anna Mary yelled drunkenly, and threw something not very big that clattered into the street. "You think I'm not ready for you?" At least two of the men hooted.

Cecelia stopped at the corner and rolled down her window. This better not take long. She had other things to do. But she had this to do, too. Anna Mary's unwashed, chemical odor—it must be coming from her; she must be tanked up on something other than booze—was sickening, even from this distance. "What's going on? Anna Mary, are you all right?"

That small, really rather silly intervention was enough to break whatever tension had bound these four people together. Casting sidelong, almost flirtatious glances at Cecelia, the men edged and drifted away, leaving Anna Mary draped over her fire hydrant alone.

Squinting at the car, she snarled, "Get the hell away from me!" presumably at Cecelia but the venom could just as well be left over from the departed men.

Hastily Cecelia rolled up her window and started to pull away, thinking she might still be able to catch up with the Bellaire and, one way or another, find out the name of the woman Ray was cheating on her with this time. But now Anna Mary was

115

pounding on the roof of her car, forcing her once more to stop.

"Who the hell do you think you are, you bitch?" was one of the clearer things Anna Mary was screaming.

Cecelia slammed on the brake and flung herself out of the car. It must have been the men—the attackers, if that was what they'd been—who'd smelled so strongly and strangely, for, up close like this, Anna Mary had about her only the eminently recognizable odors of beer and lavender perfume. Fleetingly, though, Cecelia was confused when she remembered that she'd smelled that bittersweet odor off and on during her entire brief pursuit of her husband and his girlfriend. The odor was gone now. The choice had been made; the chase was over. By stopping to help Anna Mary Stevenson, who apparently hadn't wanted any help, she'd lost them.

Are you satisfied now?

Yes, as a matter of fact.

The giddy energy that had propelled her since she'd seen them outside the movie theater now rushed out of her mind and body, replaced by a leaden depression. Through it, she faced Anna Mary. "I'm Cecelia Melchior. Remember me? You screwed my husband."

She couldn't tell whether the other woman knew who she was or not. "Yeah? So? What the hell do you think you're doing here? Sticking your nose in my business? Huh?" But the energy had drained

116

from Anna Mary, too, and she could hardly stand up. Cecelia did not reach to support her, even when she staggered, even when she collapsed—not against Cecelia's car, fortunately, but in the opposite direction against a concrete knee-high wall which shortened her descent.

"I thought you were in trouble. I thought you needed help." To her own ears it sounded laughable, but it also sounded right, the right thing to have done. "My mistake," she snapped, but only for effect; she didn't consider it to have been a mistake.

The whole incident would have been a little clearer, at least later when Cecelia went over the decisions she'd made one after another that night, if Anna Mary had called out a thank you, or had said Cecelia's name, or had waved. But she seemed thoroughly passed out now. Cecelia's bobbing headlights this time caught shoulder and hip, blue dress, shiny stocking with ladders and a crooked seam.

When Cecelia got home, she called the police to report a woman passed out on the corner of 77th and Hancock. Then she paid the babysitter and sent her home. She checked on all five children. She took a bath, washed her hair, and, after some indecision, put on a clean housedress rather than nightclothes. It was scarcely midnight. She had a long, surreal night ahead of her, waiting up for Ray.

Aware that she was trembling, she stood still and thought for a moment. Then, driven by a sense of purpose and anticipated accomplishment that

117

didn't make much sense under the circumstances, she dragged the ironing board out of the closet and set it up in the kitchen, shoving under the wobbly front leg the cardboard folded to just the right thickness and kept in the kitchen drawer for this purpose. She filled the steam iron under the tap, carefully because it leaked, stood it up on the end of the board, and plugged it in by the sink. The clothes she and Karen had sprinkled and rolled that morning lay like kittens in their baskets under damp towels. Cecelia wished she knew when to expect Ray; when he came trailing in, she'd like to be ironing one of his six lightly starched white shirts she did every week.

Her throat tightened. She touched her tongue to her finger and her fingertip to the iron, which sizzled. Thinking she heard a car door slam, she held her breath and listened; it wasn't Ray. She exhaled slowly, so as not to sob, and in further defense against tears began to sing softly, picking up in the middle of some song or other. She unrolled one of her own white blouses, pulled the shoulder snugly over the sleeve board, and set to work. Sweet, sad fragrance drifted up to her from the clothes under her hands.

Chapter Six

Pond-black Nights
(1959)

The car was a pond, black and still, warm. V was
a fish.

The car was a bubble floating through black water, and V was a bug, safely encased.

The car was a pod and V a seed.

Classical music was on the radio. Daddy liked
classical music. V couldn't tell if Mom did or not.
Sometimes, not right now, Mom would sort of sing
along even though you couldn't exactly sing along
with classical music very well because it had all
kinds of stuff going on at the same time.

"Celia, quit it!" he'd tell her, and if he got really

mad he'd yell, "Shut *up!*" which was rude but V didn't blame him. One time Aunt Maureen—she was really V's great-aunt, but V got lost in all those greats and grands so she just thought of her as Aunt Maureen though she knew it wasn't true, which was the way she thought about a lot of things—had been talking about how her father (Mom's grandfather, V's great-grandfather) used to drive Grandma Helen (Mom's mother, Aunt Maureen's sister) nuts by talking when she was listening to the radio. Mom had said she remembered that. Mom had said how hard it was on her mother having Grandpa Harry live with them all those years, because he didn't seem to notice what anybody else was doing. So you'd think Mom would know to be quiet when Daddy's music was on, unless she *wanted* to make him mad.

V didn't know if she herself actually liked classical music—violins sometimes so sweet she thought her heart would shoot right out the top of her head and follow the high gliding notes up and up, sometimes just squeaky so her teeth itched; piano that could make her feel all soft and dreamy or could really get on her nerves. The dark round space of the car traveling through the dark round space of the night was a balloon blown up until one more puff of violins and piano would make it pop.

V *liked* and *didn't like* things. Passionately. She was writing a poem about all the things she liked. It began:

Blue flowers
Tinted clouds
Hula hoops
Noisy crowds

and the poem was one of the things she liked so much it hurt.

V *didn't like* a lot of things, too. Passionately. Her name, for instance. "Virginia Mary Melchior" was one of the things she held against her parents. Especially she detested the Virginia, because it had "virgin" in it, which was embarrassing, and because the "ya" on the end was such an ugly sound. She'd tried all kinds of variations—Ginny, Jenny, Virg; her family mostly called her Ginger—but they were equally loathsome. Lately she'd been trying out just V, signing school papers with V's like flags, meaning to refuse to answer to anything more than the initial although half the time she forgot or, like blinking in a staring contest, succumbed to other people's stronger will.

V hadn't written a poem about things she hated. Maybe she should. A particular slant of light through her Venetian blinds offended her so deeply that she wouldn't go in her room between the hours of noon and 2:00 in winter, 1:00 and 3:00 in summer. The feel of a certain kind of wood, like in tongue depressors and peck baskets, made her teeth and fingernails hurt; just the *thought* of it made her run her tongue furiously over her teeth and curl her fingers in. Walking down her street, she would be overwhelmed to the point of nausea by the *ugliness* of that house on the corner, even though she could tell there was nothing unusual about its shape or color.

Since she'd discovered—what it felt like was that somebody had taught her, but she didn't know who—how easy it was to divide the world into things to adore and things to despise, life wasn't so overwhelming. The world, in fact, divided itself. Each object, event, sensation, person carried as part of its essential nature the quality of thorough goodness on the one hand or utter badness on the other, beauty or ugliness, rightness or wrongness, being *liked* by Virginia Mary Melchior or being *disliked*. Things came that way. She didn't decide; she received, was told how things were, was given to understand. It worked, just as she'd been promised it would.

Her mother's voice came out of the radio music and the roundness of the car in the round darkness, making V squirm. Sometimes her mother whistled, not along with the music but some other tune; that really drove Daddy crazy. This time she just talked, which was bad enough. "They're a little old to be having a baby, if you ask me." Her father didn't say anything, so her mother found a way to make him have to answer. "How old do you think they are, anyway?"

"Henry's older than I am."

V didn't know and didn't care how old Daddy was. Old, though. At least forty.

"Twyla's younger," her mother admitted, "but not that young. I bet she's at least thirty-five. That's old to be having a baby."

V knew her mother had been almost thirty-five when she was born, the youngest of five. Understanding, correctly, that all families have secrets, solipsistic in her conviction that every secret in her family had to do with her, she'd been toying lately with the idea that she'd had an identical twin sister who'd died in the womb. Mom letting it slip that thirty-five was too old to have a baby could be a clue; maybe the secret was about to be told.

V pulled the quilt over her head and tried to fill her ears with violins and piano, but now they made her jangle. The quilt smelled a little bit like dog. That was nice.

"A first baby, I mean."

V heard this amendment, as she was intended to. But because she didn't know what to make of it, what stuck was the conviction—sprung fully formed and stubborn out of a pre-adolescent's craving to take offense—that her mother'd been too old to have her, resented having her because she'd been too old.

V *liked*, passionately:

Round pebbles
Children's noise
Yellow kittens
Certain boys

123

V *didn't like*, passionately: donkeys, the sound of a zipper, the smell of chrysanthemums and marigolds, the shop teacher's sideburns, the color mauve, the word "mauve," the Chinese family who had moved into the house across the alley and went through other people's trash. Her sister Karen said they weren't Chinese, they were Korean, and V knew that wasn't the same thing, but she liked saying it was, and not just to make Karen mad.

Every time V passed the house with the Chinese family, there were more kids. Or maybe she just couldn't tell them apart.

Her first awareness of them had come with the knowledge to put them in her "don't like" category. The very sight of them—shiny black hair, slanted eyes, bright blue and red and yellow shorts and shirts against dusky skin—the very *thought* of them living in her neighborhood and rooting through the stuff she threw away made her stomach turn and her chest tighten. "We do throw away a lot of usable things," Daddy would say. "America is a wasteful country." As if that had anything to do with it. And besides, V noticed balefully, he threw stuff away that in the olden days they'd have used again, just like everybody else did, so he shouldn't talk.

"If it's a girl her name will be Kimberly Ann." V could hear the smile in her mother's voice now. "Twyla says it sounds like running water. Kim-ber-ly Ann." There was a pause. "If it's a boy, they're thinking about Tobias." Now V could hear how her mother's nose was wrinkling in distaste, and instantly "Tobias" got added to the list of things V *liked*. "I guess it's a family name. Tobias Henry Werner."

On the radio some guy had been talking, and V wished he would shut up. Now a lady was talking, too. They must be talking to each other, but something about how their voices came and went made her think they weren't. Through the fogged window above her feet, V saw a little smeary moon.

"It's funny to think of their children and our grandchildren being practically in the same generation."

V scowled and scrunched down in the seat. There weren't any grandchildren. Her oldest brother Phil had just gotten married. Maybe there wouldn't ever be any grandchildren. For her mother to be thinking about grandchildren when she, V, wasn't grown up yet made her mad and scared.

Her mother glanced to the left and prompted, "Ray?"

"What?"

"Did you hear what I said?" This happened all the time. Mom went on and on about boring stuff, and Daddy was rude. V could hardly stand to listen to them.

"I said 'uh-huh.' "

Her mother was skeptical. "I didn't hear you say anything." Now her father really didn't say anything.

125

Her parents had been friends with Twyla and Henry Werner for maybe a year. Before the Werners there'd been other friends, Dolores and Ed. Bud and Trixie. They never saw any of those people at all anymore.

V was bothered and fascinated by how people could just pass through your life and you could pass through theirs and nothing stuck to either one of you. People who used to be your friends and then weren't anymore. People you didn't even notice in the grocery store. People in other cars: If something important happened right *now*, like if the Bomb dropped, maybe years later you'd be talking to a stranger and you'd find out you'd been on the same stretch of road at the same exact time, because the Bomb would make you both remember it, but otherwise you wouldn't have even known. Or your soul mate was in the other car, that big light-colored one there, and he passed you by going the other direction, so your lives had been entwined from this moment and you didn't know it. Wondering what other lives hers was getting tangled up with, V shivered and pulled her jacket more tightly around herself.

When they turned off the paved road onto the Werners' long dirt driveway, V's father snapped off the radio. He always turned off the radio here, maybe to let the quiet of the woods seep in, and any words anybody spoke from here to the Werners' front door were clattery, like stones thrown against something metal. Almost never did anybody speak out loud once they were off the highway or, going home, until they were back out on it again. But sometimes V's thoughts got pretty loud.

She sat up. The woods seeped in, pushed and pulled in, for a minute making her part of them and not of her parents. There was a funny smell, like brown sugar turning bitter when it burned.

Slinking past the car on her side was one of Twyla and Henry's farm ponds. It made an opening in the trees, a black disc like a tiddly-wink on the snow. This was a little one, a puddle, and even though Daddy wasn't driving very fast on the bumpy, slippery road, they were already past it. Its silky surface tension coated V's tongue and the inside of her mind.

One afternoon last summer when she was taking out the trash, all of a sudden the Chinese mother was standing right in front of her. V *didn't like* her. Canary yellow T-shirt, blue short shorts, a baby on her hip. Smiling and nodding, chattering softly, she'd gone through the two sacks of trash right there in V's arms, pressed against V's chest, holding up soup cans and cereal boxes for inspection and comment by her family, a man and three or four older kids who had noiselessly joined her around V in the alley. After they'd all looked and had their say, she'd tuck each item neatly back in, never actually touching V but making the bags twitch.

V's arms had trembled with the strain of holding the bags; her whole body had trembled with indignation and embarrassment. But she wouldn't lower herself to say a thing, or to pull away from the gentle insistent hands. She'd just stood there, with the splitting bags of trash braced against her chest, until the still-smiling woman had stepped back and let her through to the garbage cans beside the garage.

V had tossed the sacks in, ignoring the fact that one or both of them split and garbage scattered. Without looking back, but knowing that the Chinese family had disappeared, she'd run inside the house and up the stairs and into the bathroom, where she'd drawn a steamy bath and soaked for a long time. But for days she'd still smelled garbage on her skin.

The Werners lived in a three-story gray-white farmhouse that looked sort of rundown even though Henry was forever either working on it or talking about working on it. The Melchiors' house was light green, had been light blue when V's brothers were growing up there, which in some way V couldn't explain would have changed how it was to grow up in it. It was longer than it was tall—a ranch, her mother called it, which made V think of horses and rattlesnakes and about the way words, especially names, had littler meanings that spun around their main meaning like moons. If she didn't really concentrate, or if she concentrated too much, it got hard to tell which meaning to pay most attention to.

Sometimes she could *see* the meanings, like the shimmering shadows of all different colors she saw around people. Sometimes she could *feel* the meanings, lurking. Only recently had she begun to suspect that other people didn't see or feel or hear or taste or smell things the way she did, and she didn't yet know what to make of that new bit of self- and other-knowledge, whether to welcome it because it meant she was different from everybody else or fend it off for the same reason.

It was cold when they got out of the car. Snow got her shoes wet; Mom had said to wear boots, but boots were ugly. Snow would be falling on her red knit hat, and briefly she got lost in trying to contrive some way of seeing snowflakes on her hat at the same time she was wearing it.

Henry came to the door before they even knocked, expecting them, glad to see them. V liked it that Henry came to the door before they even knocked. She liked Henry, sort of. She liked Twyla, who talked a lot more than Henry did and laughed. Henry never laughed, although sometimes he smiled, such as now when he came to the door.

She *really* liked:

Copper kettles
Sunsets
Heat lightning
Marionettes

She *really didn't* like the Chinese family. Her sister had actually gone into their house. With reluctant curiosity V had listened to Karen's dinner-table reports.

"Their father is a lawyer or an accountant, maybe, or a banker. He comes home with a brief-case and he wears a suit and a tie and he drives a big white Cadillac."

"Oh, shut up," V had told her. "What do you know about bankers and accountants, anyway?"

Karen had set her fork down and looked at her levelly. "They cook pigeons. They shoot pigeons and cut their heads off and put the head and the guts and the feathers in a big bucket, and then they hold the pigeons over the stove burner and roast 'em."

"Yuck!" V had cried, and Karen had grinned. "Mom, make her stop!"

"We eat chickens and turkeys," Daddy had pointed out. "It's just a different custom."

"Smells bad," Karen had said, eyes still on V. "But it sure tastes good." V had run to the bath-room and tried her best to throw up.

Twyla and Henry had two big black Labs named King and Cole, who licked the plates on the kitchen floor after dinner. V's mother talked about that in horrified tones all the way home, every time. These days she was saying, "When the baby comes things will have to change. They can't have those dogs in the house like that. Licking the plates." V didn't see why not. She *liked* King and Cole. Besides, what about cats? Her mother liked cats. Right now they had two, a calico named Patches and a black and white one named Boots. Stupid, ordinary names. Quilt would be a good name for a calico; thinking of it just this minute, V hugged herself with pleasure that segued seamlessly into apprehension. Had there been cats around when she was a baby? Would she know if they'd stolen her breath?

The last couple of times they'd been with the Werners, she'd secretly stared at Twyla's stomach, but it didn't look as if a baby could be in there. She believed one was, though; lots of things didn't give you any hints on the outside about what was on the inside.

As they went from the cold black-white-gray outside into the warm jumble of the Werners' living room, at least four conversations were swirling around V at once:

"How are you feeling?" her mother was asking Twyla, and Twyla, hands on the baby hidden in her belly, was telling about morning sickness and swollen ankles.

King and Cole were snuffling around on the floor, looking for food, begging for food, asking each other if there was food and warning each other off.

Inside her head was continuous chatter about what she should *like* and what she should *not like*. The snow on the bushes: *like*. The snow on her shoes: *not like*. Her tongue living like a little animal inside the cave of her mouth: *not like*. Her heart caged inside her ribs: *like*. Her brain escaping the cage of her skull: *like*.

Henry was saying to Daddy, "Come out back with me, Ray, I've got something to show you." His voice was thickened with excitement and pride, and something else. This was probably going to be the most interesting of the conversations. It might not be the one she was supposed to pay attention to. She could never tell. Pieces of the others put themselves together in all different ways and made a background that kept spilling into the foreground— her mother telling about when she was pregnant with the twins, Cole crunching something, and a smell as much a taste way in the back of her mouth that seemed to have something to do with good or not-good, ugly or beautiful.

She went out back with Daddy and Henry. She wasn't invited, but nobody said she couldn't. Mom came, too; V had thought Mom would stay in the house and talk to Twyla about baby stuff, and for a minute she was distracted trying to see if she was supposed to like it or not that Mom came, too. *Don't like.*

The Werners didn't have any yard in back, just black woods and a glassy black pond, black woods and water under charcoal sky on top of white snow with black footprints in it, and over her shoulder the tall gray-white house, pale gray smoke coming out of the chimney, black roof peaks. Yellow lights.

Their footsteps hardly made any noise in the wet snow, but V heard ripples, flows. Most of the time, reality flowed along and carried her headlong with it, *liking* and *not liking* getting her across as if she were jumping on stones; but every once in a while reality puddled, and then she knew exactly where she was even if nobody else did. Sometimes passing black ponds did that, and pond-black nights.

Henry said something to Daddy that she didn't catch. Daddy didn't say anything, but she felt something gathering, puddling in him.

Henry stopped. Daddy stopped, and Mom a few steps later. V scooped a gloveful of snow off a waist-high rock, packed it into a snowball, threw it against a tree, and only then stopped. Henry spread his arms. "Right here," he announced. "Right here's the spot." His face must be gray, since for now V was trying to allow herself only black, gray, and white. His hair was black. His eyes and mouth were black in his face; the whites of his eyes and his teeth were white. His gray breath puffed toward her but didn't quite get there.

Her parents were looking around, nodding. "Have you started excavation?" Mom asked politely.

"Not till spring. Hopefully they won't drop the Bomb before then." Henry laughed.

V laughed, too, because it struck her funny that he'd be laughing about the Bomb. The adults all glanced at her, and she hurried a little distance away and plopped onto her back to make a snow angel so they wouldn't tell her to go back to the house. The heavy snow resisted her scissoring arms and legs just enough to let her know she was doing something worthwhile. She hoped Daddy would help her up when the time came, so she wouldn't spoil the angel with fist and heel gouges.

Snow was white and gray on her blue coat—no, it couldn't be blue because she didn't like blue coats. Black coat. A sharp smell in the cold air made her sneeze.

"Bless you."

All she could really move without spoiling the snow angel was her head. That hurt her neck, but she finally made out a girl about her own age on the ground under some bushes on the other side of V from the grown-ups. The girl was on her stomach making a snow angel. V'd never seen anybody do it that way before. A knit hat covered the back of the girl's head and all her hair must be tucked up under it. Her coat was blue—no, black—like V's. She didn't have boots on, either.

Henry said, "Here are the plans. Twyla hasn't seen them yet, but she told me what she wanted before I set to work on them. Look here, Ray," and he crinkled paper in her father's direction. Her father didn't say anything. Maybe he was looking. Maybe he was thinking what to say. Maybe he was just ignoring Henry the way he ignored Mom when she talked about stuff he wasn't interested in, but V didn't think so.

"Bor-*ing*," mumbled the girl with her face in the snow.

"What's boring?" V demanded. "Snow angels?"

She *liked* snow angels. Was there something about them she shouldn't like?

"No, stupid. The Bomb's boring. Fallout shelters are boring."

"Oh, yeah?" V didn't know if the girl's snotty attitude made her mad or not. Waiting to find out, she lay still in the snow, which she had to admit was getting uncomfortable.

The girl had started moving her arms up and down and her legs in and out again, making a deeper angel. V wondered how she was going to get up without leaving knee marks. "Let's talk about what we like and don't like. You know, like blue flowers and donkeys and that wood that peck baskets are made of. That's not boring." Inside her wet gloves and wet shoes, V's finger- and toenails itched at the very mention of that wood.

Warily, V said, "I guess the Bomb's more important."

A snowball hit her in the stomach. She flinched and half-rolled away, spoiling her angel. The girl hadn't come any closer but was up on her haunches, hands already busy between her knees packing another snowball. Her whisper reached V like a yelled curse. "The Bomb's too hard! Don't think about the Bomb! Think about copper kettles and round pebbles and tin foil!"

"But really," V protested, afraid of what she was about to say out loud, "it doesn't matter if I like or don't like that stuff."

A shower of snow fell off a branch over V's head,

cold and wet in her face. The girl hadn't been any-where near that branch, but V knew she'd done it. "That's the whole point, stupid!" the girl hissed, and V was going to go rub her face in the snow but by the time she got herself onto her feet, the girl was gone.

Thinking about tin foil, V furiously brushed snow off her coat and shook out the red hat. Behind her, the angel was ruined; it just looked as if some stupid kid had fallen down in the snow.

One hot afternoon she'd been lying on a blanket in the back yard, eating red strawberries out of a white bowl. *Liking*, passionately, the seed-pricked sweetness of the berries, the smell of her skin under the sun, quilt yellow and brown like sunlight in the bushes, piles of peony petals white and pink on the driveway. *Not liking*, passionately, the hot whine of a baseball game from her father's radio in the house, bugs that kept crawling on her ankles, a bit-tersweet smell from some weed or flower she wished she could find and pull up. All at once there had stood the old Chinese lady.

With a little scream, V had sat up, got up on her knees. Smiling, the old lady had had her hands folded across the front of her long loose gray-brown dress, her feet bare, her face amazingly wrinkled.

They'd stared at each other, and finally V had managed, "What are you doing in my yard? Get out of my yard!"

The old lady had said what sounded like more than one sentence. Insulted to be addressed in a

foreign language, V had tried to think of the comb
under her pillow as a weapon. The old woman had
stepped toward her and said something else, making V scuttle backward against the fence. Then a
small brown hand had reached into the white bowl,
plucked a red strawberry, briefly held it up to the
light, and popped it into one wide sleeve. V had
stared.

The woman then had taken something out of her
other sleeve and held it out. V couldn't back up any
farther. The woman had squatted, fist still extended, and V had found herself holding out her
own hand. Into it the woman had dropped a hard,
glinting bit of tin foil. Still smiling, she'd nodded at
V, said something, straightened creakily, and left
the yard, carefully closing the gate behind her.

Released, V had raced up to her room. The distant, tinny clamor of the baseball game had tried to
follow her, but she'd outrun it. She'd slammed the
door and thrown herself onto her bed, thinking desperately how much she *liked* the chenille ridges of
the bedspread against her chin, *didn't like* the mole
on the side of her forearm, *liked* and *didn't like,*
passionately, the nub of foil tucked into the crease
of her palm.

*You have to decide. It's dangerous not to decide
one way or the other.*

"I figure a year's worth of canned goods and de-
hydrated food and bottled water," Henry was saying. He and Daddy were standing close together,
peering at the paper that crackled in the cold, and

V almost got lost traveling back and forth with the beam of Henry's flashlight. Mom had moved off a little way. "Along the east wall there'll be storage, and the living quarters over here, and here's the door, a high-security hatch facing south away from prevailing winds, for protection against airborne radiation." Henry took a breath and finished proudly, "I think we've thought of everything. Do you see anything we've missed?"

V's father straightened and took a short step backward, changing the perspective between himself and the other man. "What would you do if somebody came to the door?" he wanted to know, and now V did, too.

Mom said quietly, from a little distance away, "Ray," but V couldn't tell what she was warning him against.

Henry said, with a kind of wary stubbornness, "This shelter is for myself and my family."

Daddy said, "If the Bomb fell and you and your family were safe in your fallout shelter and people came and knocked on your hatch and begged you to let them in, what would you do?"

Henry said, "I only have enough provisions for Twyla and me and the baby for a year."

Daddy said, "If they pounded on your door and begged to be let in because they had no other shelter, what would you do?"

Henry said, "They should have built their own goddamn fallout shelter."

Daddy said, "What would you do, Henry?"

Reality puddled, waiting for the answer, and abruptly V understood something new: This was not the same kind of choice she'd learned to make, not about *liking* or *not liking*. *Liking* or *not liking*, she realized, made you think you were making this kind of choice—*right or wrong, good or bad, ugly or beautiful*—but you weren't. Something sweet was burning nearby.

"I'd shoot them," Henry said. Mom sucked in her breath.

Daddy said quietly, grimly, "If we don't take each other in, what's the point? Why survive at all?"

Pride in her father brought reality crystal clear and still, like a true black pond, like the shiny hard bit of foil still in her jewelry box. She put her arms, stiffened by coat sleeves, around his neck and buried her face in his snow-skimmed shoulder.

Hot sweet pride in her father became part of her ongoing poem:

Pond-black nights

Chapter Seven

Love as Something New
(1967)

Sitting in her old place at the table and sort of incredulously watching her mother bustle around the kitchen, Karen thought how some things never fucking changed. Here she was, with all this life-changing shit on her mind—the war, Selma, free love—while her mother, who, naturally, could never possibly understand any of that, filled her own life and tried to fill Karen's with shit she actually thought was important, like washing dishes and putting stuff in scrapbooks and making Christmas cookies from scratch.

That was why you couldn't trust anybody over

thirty. They thought all the irrelevant shit was important, and they didn't even see what was important. On a mescaline trip last summer, when trees had bent to commune with her all up and down the street and she'd felt the rotation of the earth in her own bloodstream, her expanded consciousness had allowed her to see truths, as so often happened when you did drugs, and unlike some of the others this truth had stayed with her after she'd come down: *In order to change the world, individual members of the bourgeoisie will have to be sacrificed. In the larger scheme of things, they don't matter.*

Karen's mother had waited to make the cookies until Karen got home, but Karen had stayed well away from the kitchen while her mother and sister rolled out the sugary dough and cut it with the same star- and reindeer- and Santa-shaped cookie cutters they'd been using as long as she could remember. They'd sung Christmas carols; sometimes her mother had whistled Christmas carols, which had made Ginger giggle and exhort, "Mom!" as she'd always done. Karen's own temptation to join in had warned her how dangerous it was, and her mother's disappointment at her refusal had told her she was right to refuse. Some things never fucking changed, but Karen had, thank God.

Her mother still *ironed,* for Chrissake. One of Karen's clearest and most complicated childhood memories was of her mother spending practically all day every Saturday ironing, thirty minutes for

141

each of her father's six lightly starched white shirts, and then blouses, dresses, slacks, slips, pillow cases, kitchen towels, handkerchiefs. Some weeks Karen had been an accomplice, not totally unwilling, to this degradation, on Friday having sprinkled dry clothes stiff but sweet-smelling off the line with water out of a special bottle, rolling them up into oddly pleasing sausage-shaped bundles and laying them in a special basket tucked in with towels to wait for Saturday.

By lunchtime, her mother's hair would be plastered to her forehead in sweaty sprigs and she'd be complaining that her feet hurt. Hangers holding ironed clothes would block doorways, so you'd have to push through sleeves and skirts and pantlegs; they smelled good, but if you knocked them down they'd get wrinkled and the whole process, from the sprinkling and rolling, would have to start all over.

One Saturday afternoon when Karen's father had come home late from work, he'd blustered that the place looked like a goddamn Shantytown, his voice breathy with moral indignation that Karen had guessed even then was a cover-up for something else. Insulted, her mother had stormed around pulling the loaded hangers down, and she'd yelled back at him, so it had turned into a major fight that had left her tight-lipped and seething and him alternating for days between surliness and an unnatural cheer as if he'd found some sort of moral high ground, precarious and heady.

But she'd kept on ironing his shirts, every Saturday, six of them, thirty minutes a shirt and not a single wrinkle in the collar tips or cuffs or down the front plackets around the buttons and buttonholes. Karen would have told him to iron his own fucking shirts. Karen would have left the motherfucker; five kids or not, why put up with crap all your life? She had sworn every Saturday then and swore again now—although her mother wasn't ironing right this minute, she might as well be—never in her entire fucking lifetime to iron a single fucking thing.

Deliberately, Karen thought of her mother by her name: Cecelia. She'd been practicing: Cecelia and Ray. When she could call them that to their faces, she'd really be fucking liberated.

Ray hadn't spoken to her for the last three months, which was fine with her but fucking weird considering that every Wednesday he picked up her dirty laundry at the dorm and brought her clean. The fact that Cecelia did her laundry was fucking weird in the first place. It was inconvenient, not to mention embarrassing, and Karen would far rather have done it herself in the dorm's basement laundry room that echoed companionably with the sloshing and humming of machines under girls' voices and music from numerous transistor radios, sometimes on the same station and sometimes not, tinny Janis Ian and Bobby Vinton. But because she couldn't grok why doing her laundry was so fucking important to Cecelia and Ray, she didn't have the balls to stand up to them about it.

So on Wednesdays right around five o'clock, the front desk would buzz her, and like a good girl she'd always be in her room, ready. Lugging the week's dirty laundry in two pillowcases down the brown hallway and the brown stairs and through the French doors into the lobby, she'd be trembling with trepidation and resultant fury by the time she saw her father waiting grim-faced with clean and pressed clothes on hangers over his arm. "Hi," she'd try, sometimes even, "Hi, Dad." Nothing. Without a word, he'd hand her the fresh laundry, take the bulging, slightly smelly pillowcases, and leave. He knew something. He was really disappointed in her about something. Shit, it could be anything. If it was sex, she'd laugh in his face, the fucking hypocrite. But it could be drugs, or being part of the anti-war movement, or anything.

"So how are you doing, Sis? Oh, and Merry Christmas. Or Happy Holidays." Ginger looked at Kirk. "Are you Jewish? I'm sorry. I didn't know you were Jewish."

"I'm not Jewish," Kirk assured her in some amazement.

"What are you then?"

Kirk answered readily, "I'm human," and Karen's eyes burned with tears of pride.

Ginger was seventeen, but trying to hold a conversation with her was like talking to somebody a lot younger. She'd make clumsy attempts at being interested in somebody besides herself, but she wasn't really. People thought she was retarded, but what she was was schizophrenic, which meant there was something screwed up about her thought processes but not her intelligence.

It was a trip trying to figure out how Ginger's mind worked. Karen thought Ginger wasn't entirely convinced anybody outside herself was real. Then she thought nobody was sure of that, really. Then she thought maybe Ginger was right; maybe she and Kirk and Ray and Cecelia and LBJ and Judy Collins and Martin Luther King were figments of Ginger's imagination, or her own, or somebody's she'd never think of.

There was something just slightly off about everything Ginger said, so that even a neutral question like "How are you doing?" sounded staged. Maybe it was the "Sis." "I'm fine," Karen answered stiffly. "How are you, Ginger?"

Ginger leaned earnestly across the table, pudgy forearms extended, multiply ringed fingers clasped. "Tell me about your life. I don't know anything about your life."

Karen caught Kirk's eye, but he hastily lowered his gaze to keep, she knew, from laughing out loud. She actually was tempted to share with her little sister some of the important shit in her life, would have enjoyed Ginger's wide-eyed reaction. But their mother, Cecelia, was right there. And, anyway, Karen knew from experience that Ginger's short attention span would have her feeling like a fool for trying to tell her anything that mattered. "Groovy," she said, fervently. "Life's groovy."

Ginger nodded uncertainly. "That's good," she said vaguely. "Your aura looks kind of rusty."

"Rusty?" Karen echoed incredulously, though the word that ought to have inspired incredulity was "aura." Kirk coughed into his hand, but he wasn't laughing. Maybe Kirk believed in auras. Maybe Ginger was on to something.

"How's school?" Cecelia asked.

The question pissed Karen off. "None of your fucking business" sprang to her lips but she was still too chickenshit to say something like that to her mother, even if she thought of her mother as Cecelia.

School was far-out. She could *feel* her life changing right as she lived it, one substance pouring into her and another substance altogether when it gushed out. All kinds of fucking things were happening to her all the fucking time, things that Cecelia would never fucking dream of and that would give her a heart attack if she ever did.

Sex, for instance, and love. Love without boundaries, sex without rules. Karen squirmed in her chair and slipped her hand under the table. Her skirt was short enough that she didn't have to push it up to get to the warm pulsing mound between her thighs. She hadn't worn a bra in a year and never fucking would again, for reasons of both politics and comfort, but she couldn't quite bring herself to go without underpants.

Half-hoping Cecelia would be able to see what she was doing under the uncovered table, Karen enthusiastically masturbated and thought of everybody she could think of who made her feel good: Billy, Ross, Rob, Kirk, especially Kirk, who was grinning knowingly at her now. She loved Kirk and he loved her, and often they made love three or four times a day, which was nowhere fucking near enough.

Karen and Kirk, along with a growing number of other couples they knew, had discovered the secret to making love last forever: space, no obligations, the freedom to be with anybody you wanted in whatever way you wanted, so that every time you came together it was a renewed and passionate choice. Because there were no rules, there were no rules to break, and so there'd never be any reason to break up. Her parents didn't know that. Nobody over thirty did. Sitting in her old place at her parents' kitchen table with her eyes on Kirk and her fingers stroking her labia, Karen thrilled, not for the first time, to the certainty that she was alive in the perfect moment in the history of the universe, and that, besides living her own life in peace and freedom, she was helping to move humanity forward.

"Yeah. How's school? School's great for me." Typically Ginger would mimic the form of social interaction without the content—if there was any real fucking content, which Karen had come to doubt. "Oh, I'm taking drama now, did Mom tell you? I'm in a play. It's called *The Earth, the Sky, and People All Around.* It's all about the war and black people and everything important like that. I almost had the lead, but this other girl got it."

"So how is school, Karen?" Cecelia was nothing if not persistent.

"I got a 4 point," she said grudgingly, and was gratified that, although it was the fucking truth, it sounded and felt like a lie. Her voice quavered guiltily, too, from what her fingers were doing between her legs.

Cecelia half-turned. "Straight A's? Honey, that's wonderful. Daddy will be so proud."

Shit. Like her grades had anything to do with *them.*

"What do you study, Kirk?"

"Life." His answer delighted Karen, who knew both that he meant it and that her mother, Cecelia, wouldn't think he did.

Cecelia glanced suspiciously at him, probably trying to figure out if he was making fun of her, which, though he meant what he said, he was. After a moment, she pressed, with a touch of sternness now, "I meant, what's your major? What are your plans after graduation?"

Karen said, "Shit," out loud. Ginger gasped audibly and put both hands over her mouth in what, from anyone else, would have been mock horror but was the closest she could come to the real thing.

Predictably, Cecelia said, "Karen. Please don't

talk like that in this house." She'd turned her back again.

"Shit!" Karen slammed into the bathroom where she could take off her underwear and put her fingers inside herself as fucking far as she wanted. Exulting in the satiny curves, the rough hair against the inside of her wrist, the contracting and relaxing interior muscles, she wished Kirk had come in here with her. But she didn't need him. She came, a little.

Pulling her underpants back on made her feel fucking morally compromised. At least she didn't wash her hands. Kirk fucking loved the smell of her. She loved the smell of herself on him, in his beard. Ray and Cecelia would be grossed out, if they even knew what the fishy odor was. Fingers to her face, Karen grinned at the mirror. On the back of the toilet, plugged into the outlet above the sink where Ray plugged in his shaver, a truly tacky little ceramic Christmas tree blinked. She hoped it was air freshener, which would have pushed tacky to the limit, but it wasn't.

The smell on her fingers, the taste also reminded her of Rob, who turned her on, too. Actually, Karen couldn't fucking think of a man who didn't turn her on, either actually or in theory, which was cool. Her state of near-constant sexual arousal was also fed by things like the cat that had come out of nowhere to purr on her chest while she was tripping last week, her almost straight hair almost down to the small of her back, the be-ins in the Student

Union with everybody playing guitar and everybody raging about the war, her own honest rage, her 4-point average and all the groovy shit there was to learn about sociology and psychology and genetics, sex and more sex itself.

"Somebody saw you riding down the hill on your boyfriend's motorcycle carrying an overnight bag." The Resident Advisor, only two years ahead of Karen, was from a generation utterly fucking alien, like every previous generation and—though Karen and her friends, misunderstanding the ways in which they were changing the world, did not suspect this—like all those to follow, too. Sitting on the edge of Karen's bed with stockinged ankles neatly crossed, auburn hair curled just to her chin and sprayed there, perfect subtle makeup, the RA had looked genuinely concerned, but about the wrong things.

Karen had swung her hair and asserted, "We fucking spent the night in the Blue Bonnet Motel."

The RA had frowned. "Karen, listen to me. You'll ruin your reputation this way."

Karen had cawed with laughter then, and thinking about it now made her chuckle again. The fucking concept of having something called a reputation was absurd. More absurd was the idea that you had to make fucking moral decisions about sleeping with somebody you loved—or with somebody you didn't love, or with somebody you didn't *know*—when sex was the most natural thing in the world and had nothing to do with right and wrong. There were plenty of things in the world you had to make moral choices about, take moral stands. Sex wasn't one of them. People like the RA didn't give a shit about Vietnam, or they supported what America was doing there. They didn't care about how whites had oppressed blacks for centuries, or they thought the civil rights movement was going too far too fast. Those were moral decisions, worthy of attention. Ruining your reputation was fucking not.

It had taken her and Kirk six months to get his penis to go into her vagina. Now that this was definitely not a problem anymore, the difficulties they'd had at the beginning amused her, in an uncomfortable sort of way. They'd both been virgins, and ignorant, and it had fucking hurt. Finally she'd asked Rob to help out, and he'd showed her how so she could show Kirk.

She loved Rob; he was a good friend. She loved Kirk. The idea of a part of one person's body actually being fucking inside another person's body, that two people could really get that close, got her high just thinking about it, and she fucking thought about it as much as possible. "Look at that! Just fucking look at that!" she and Kirk would moan, touching with their hands the place where their bodies were actually *joined,* twisting to look down in wonder at the juncture. "You're inside me! I'm inside you! We're actually part of each other! Look at that! Look what we're doing! Oh, I love you!" as though love were something new with them, as though nobody else had ever put a penis into a vagina and tightened around it.

The phone rang, and Cecelia answered it in the kitchen. Karen took advantage of the distraction to slide open the bathroom door and stick her head around the corner to beckon to Kirk. Ginger nodded eagerly and started to come, too, and when she didn't respond to frowns and head-shaking and "halt" hand gestures, Karen had to hiss at her, "Not you! You stay there!" Ginger smiled feebly and settled back into her chair then, looking a little hurt but not embarrassed as anybody else would have been.

Giggling and making no effort to keep it quiet, Karen led Kirk down the hall to the room that used to be hers. She barely got the door shut behind them before they were in each other's arms, kissing open-mouthed, clutching each other's genitals, moaning. Karen was transported by psychedelic sexual desire and the absolute trust that it would soon be satisfied, and she and Kirk made quick, hard, joyous love on the fluffy pink rug by her bed without even taking off most of their clothes.

"Jesus fucking Christ," Kirk whispered, and Karen, recognizing it as a declaration of love, tightened her arms around him under his loose embroidered shirt. He smelled good. He always smelled so good.

As she came back down from the high that making love always gave her, Karen noticed that Cecelia had put decorations up in here, too, all shit she remembered from Christmases past that was supposed to make her feel at home and instead made her skin crawl. An angel with a foil-pyramid skirt and yellow yarn hair. A garland she'd made in second or third fucking grade out of interlocking loops of green and red construction paper. None of this had anything to do with her life now, and she itched with fury and pity toward her mother for trying to pretend it did. What was scary was how well-preserved it all was—none of the construction paper loops torn or even flattened, the angel's hair still stuck on.

Except for the Christmas decorations, which she'd flatly refused the last couple of years she'd lived here, this room still looked and felt like her room, which it wasn't anymore. That pissed Karen off. Her Beatles posters were still on the wall over the desk. Her Drucilla doll, as tall as she was when she was six with elastic on its feet she could slip her own feet into for dancing, still sat bandy-legged on the shelf. It was like a goddamn shrine.

Then she started seeing some things that had been changed. The books had been straightened up and put in some kind of order. There were boxes in the closet that she hadn't put there. Some weird thing was on her desk; after a minute she recognized it as a thing sort of like a ViewMaster that made pictures three-dimensional when you looked through it; now *there* was a fucking exciting way to spend your time. It had belonged to some ancestor, her great-grandfather or somebody, and it had always been on the mantel in the living room. It pissed her off to find it in her room.

Retrieving the baggie of weed from inside the wide leg of her purple bells in her overnight bag, she hastily rolled a joint with one hand, lit it, sucked in the smoke with sharp quick inhalations between teeth and stiffened lips, and immediately got a nice little buzz. Holding her breath, she slipped the joint between Kirk's lips and tripped out a little on the way the tip glowed when he inhaled, dimmed when his lungs were full and he quit inhaling, glowed again when he managed one more toke.

"Your sister's a trip," he said in a voice strained from holding the smoke in his lungs.

"No shit."

"Your mother seems kind of groovy."

"She's not."

"I bet she'd understand about the war and shit like that."

Karen grabbed his chin and pulled him down to kiss him again, a gesture as combative as it was affectionate. There was a smell about him she had never noticed before, not the acrid aroma of the grass or his own usual sweaty-sunny body odor. Bitter and sweet at the same time, it was an incredible turn-on, and Karen pressed herself against him. When he opened his mouth on hers, smoke seeped in, making her cough and giving her a sweet little contact high. "Don't you fucking say a fucking word about the war," she warned him, laughing but alarmed, and lightly bit his lower lip to reinforce the order.

"I'll say what I fucking feel." He'd been ready for this. "I won't waste my time talking about fucking trivia. You shouldn't, either." Chastised and challenged, Karen felt her defiance surge to match his, which brought them together again, arms linked, standing up against the establishment in the person of Cecelia Melchior.

There came a knock on the door and her mother's—Cecelia's—call. "Karen?"

Karen resisted the guilty impulse to jump up and extinguish the joint and open her window and adjust her own clothes and Kirk's. They weren't doing anything wrong. She wished, in fact, that her mother would walk right in.

"Your father will be home any minute."

"Yeah? So?" But the blissed-out feeling was spoiled. She took a last quick drag, let Kirk take one, and threw the roach out the window. The cats would get a nice fucking little Christmas trip out of that if it landed in their bowls. The thought of pot smoke curling up with steam from the oatmeal Cecelia always made for them on cold days started Karen laughing extravagantly. She told Kirk about the cats and the oatmeal so he'd laugh, too, and it didn't make much sense so they laughed together for a while, just for the fun of it, putting their hands and ears against each other's wiggling stomachs, the immediate cause of their hilarity long since lost and anyway what they were laughing at was *life*.

Cecelia knocked again. That made them laugh some more.

Karen had forgotten to shut the window. She ought to do that. Though not snowing yet, it was cold out, and the sash stuck, so for a minute she thought she wasn't going to get it shut. She giggled, but her childish relief when it thumped down, and her consternation at the noise, pissed her off; Cecelia wouldn't know why she'd opened the window even if she did hear, and what did Karen fucking care if she did?

"He's here. He just pulled in," Cecelia said, as if her mouth might be pressed against the crack in the door. The door wasn't fucking locked. Why didn't she just open it? This was *her* house, after all. Karen didn't live here anymore.

Karen had already spent more of her fucking life than she wanted to worrying about what her fucking father would do or say or think about her, and trying not to worry, and pretending she wasn't worrying, and practicing what it would be like not to worry. She was finally starting to get herself free of all that, free of him, and the last fucking thing she needed was her mother dragging her back in. When the streets were alive with people marching for peace and justice, and songs about peace and justice were everywhere and constant, and people risked their lives to make the world a better place, what Ray Melchior thought of her couldn't be less important.

Emerging from the bedroom with her head floating, her underwear on crooked, and her lover behind her, she heard her father on the back porch and her heart seized. Then she heard her mother say to him not, "Karen's home," or, "She's in her bedroom with her boyfriend with the door closed," or, "How was your day?" but, "Marie called."

She stepped into the kitchen. "Hi, Dad."

He looked at her and barely nodded.

"Dad, this is my friend Kirk Prinzler. Kirk, Ray Melchior."

Both men hesitated. Then they both stepped forward, right hands extended to show they weren't carrying weapons. The handshake was brief and, both of them having something to prove, firm. Kirk said, "Hi," and Karen was appalled to find herself wishing he'd add, "Sir," or at least, "Pleased to meet you."

Ray lifted his chin and said, "You're the one I saw riding a motorcycle up the Mead Street Hill with my daughter at seven in the morning."

Kirk said, "Far out," and grinned, at the same time that Cecelia, pulling her tacky red Christmas sweater more tightly around her, admonished, "Ray."

Karen said, as if she'd prepared the alibi in advance, "We had a breakfast date." Kirk guffawed, under his breath but plenty loud enough for everybody to hear, and Karen, pleased with herself, imperfectly stifled a laugh, too, as much at the ridiculous term "date" as at the brazen mockery of the half-truth.

Ray's gray gaze riveted on her and she steeled herself to meet it. Making direct eye contact was rare in this family except for Ginger, and you never knew whom Ginger was seeing when she looked directly at you. So meeting and holding her father's stare seemed a fucking crazy thing to do, but Karen did it. As always, his eyes were unreadable. Angrily and with a certain tipsy, gleeful vengefulness, she wondered what he thought he was seeing in hers.

The locked gaze between Karen and her father didn't last long. Neither of them blinked, but Cecelia announced with false brightness that admitted and put to good use its own falseness, "Dinner's almost ready. Go wash your hands, everybody," and everybody did what she said. Karen was tempted not to. Why should she take fucking orders from Cecelia or anybody else? But the best she could manage at the moment was not to use soap.

"Mrs. Kyle died, did you hear?" Obviously having saved up things to report so there'd be something safe to talk about, Cecelia passed this first news item to Karen along with the platter of roast beef.

Karen glanced uncomfortably at Kirk, who wasn't going to know any of the people about to be discussed and who would likely think the whole conversation a waste of time. He seemed to be happily eating, though. "Who's Mrs. Kyle?" she asked, although she didn't really care enough to extend the conversation and although now she thought she vaguely remembered Mrs. Kyle.

Ginger told her, but the associations didn't quite mesh, whether because of Ginger's loosely connected narration or because Mrs. Kyle, and everyone else Cecelia had in mind to mention, were from a different world. Even—especially—if they'd known her all her life, she told herself confidently, they'd never grok who she was now. "Brenda Stevenson married the youngest Colton boy over Thanksgiving."

"Bruce," Karen supplied, surprising herself.

"Oh, he's so nice." Karen raised her eyebrows teasingly, as though her sister's dreamy tone implied what it would from anyone else, a relationship or the wish for one. From Ginger it likely meant nothing other than a scattershot attempt to participate in the conversation. "She's nice, too," Ginger added, in the same tone, proving Karen's point.

Brenda Stevenson was one person Karen had known better than her mother had ever realized, and for longer; after Brenda's alcoholic mother had abandoned the family, Brenda didn't come over to play anymore, and Cecelia had no idea, Karen was sure, that the girls' friendship had continued for years. For a minute Karen thought it might be nice to see her again. Brenda'd been this town's first hippie, or maybe a hippie harbinger, a proto-freak. She'd done drugs before anybody else around here; maybe she was still a source for good weed, or maybe, stuck here, she needed a source.

Brenda used to meet a black guy named Alain at the Allegheny Center Mall on Pittsburgh's north side. Alain would have been conspicuous if he'd come up here, and Brenda had no car, so every Saturday their entire senior year Karen had driven her. They'd always missed the turn and had to go all the way around again, sometimes more than once, on the one-way road that circled the mall and the Buhl Planetarium and the blocky low-income apartments. They'd always cruised the parking garage for a long time, looking for a spot near the elevators so they wouldn't have to risk going across the lot, while Brenda alternately fretted and gloated that Alain didn't like to wait.

The gas-exhaust-urine odor of the garage would, years later when she encountered it again in a Manhattan subway, fling Karen back precisely to 1966 Pittsburgh and that particular adolescent mixture of eroticism and dread. Then she would realize that there was a visceral association, too, between the odor and the poor black people who mostly parked and shopped and lived around the mall, who embodied the bogeymen lurking behind parked cars and of whom Alain was a standout specimen; such racism, virtually instinctive by the time she recognized it, would shame her profoundly, but the association appeared to be ineradicable.

Portly, thirtyish, dapper Alain would meet them in front of Sears. Having eyes and hands only for Brenda, he'd scarcely speak to Karen. Abuzz with lust, they'd hurry off. She'd shop Sears, the National Record Mart, Maryann's, sometimes Spencer's Gifts though it made her feel tacky, and finish with a piece of the best cheesecake in Pennsylvania from Rhea's Bakery, sitting self-consciously on a bench until, finally, Brenda would appear, always without Alain, always hungry, sometimes ebullient and sometimes worrisomely subdued.

These treks to Pittsburgh would acquire various moral implications at various times in Karen's life, their emblematic nature enhanced by the fact that she would never see either of the principles again. For a long time, Brenda would seem tough and self-possessed because she'd refused even to pretend she and Alain were in love, disdaining Karen's persistent efforts to call the trysts romance and the sex passion. Then Karen would come to consider her usurious, white-girl-slumming, and, an overlapping interpretation, Alain as a sexual predator and herself as his accomplice, his pimp. When her own children were teenagers, the thought of them doing something equally risky and sleazy behind her back would cause her to pity her parents, herself as a parent, all parents throughout human history. And there'd come a time when she'd look back on those excursions fondly, as an early example of her willingness to see what would happen in the world. But at Christmas 1967, what she felt was the power of a child successfully keeping a secret from her mother, and she smiled smugly as Cecelia and Ginger's chatter about Brenda and Bruce's wedding segued into discussion of other weddings of 1967 and some planned or predicted for 1968. Kirk, of course, had nothing to say. This must be making

161

her seem awfully fucking bourgeois. Later she'd tell him about her role in the saga of Brenda and Alain.

Ray didn't say much of anything during dinner, either, for his own reasons. The classical music she couldn't believe he really liked, so inconsistent was it with the rest of his redneck attitudes, jangled and screeched from the living room, piano and violins. It wasn't the first fucking meal she'd passed in his brooding silence, but it might well be the last. She didn't have to put up with this shit. She just wouldn't fucking come home anymore, at least not for a long time, like till he was dead. The thought, glanced at and away from many times before in these last few heady months, now embraced her hard, like yet another lover, and Karen shivered with excitement at the attainable prospect of emancipation and estrangement.

When he was done eating, never fucking mind that nobody else was, Ray got up without a word and went into the living room. From her place at the table Karen could see him through the doorway, reading the paper in his La-Z Boy in front of the Christmas tree, feet up, head tipped back, ass sagging, lips pressed grimly together. It wouldn't have seemed so personal a statement, so much like flipping her off, if he hadn't been right in her line of sight. "Maybe we should leave," she said suddenly.

"No!" Stricken, Cecelia quickly patted her arm, quickly took her hand away. "Stay. Please. It'll be okay. It's Christmas. Families belong together at Christmas."

"I notice the boys aren't here." Ginger looked at her in surprise and open admiration, and in fact Karen was rather proud of herself for speaking at least part of the fucking truth hidden like valuable and explosive treasure around here. She knew it was unkind, but it was a lot less so than what had sprung to her lips to say, which was, "This isn't my fucking family anymore. My family is my friends at school, people in the Movement, the family I choose, who love me the way I am now and the way I want to be, who care about the same things I care about. This is just the place I'm from."

Cecelia had an explanation ready. "Philip and Jan can't afford to bring all the kids all this way. Dean has—other plans." And Dennis was in Vietnam, but Cecelia didn't say that.

"Oh, Mom, get real." Ginger scowled theatrically, coyly at Cecelia, all the while keeping the corner of her gaze on Karen and Kirk, gauging their reaction not so much for approval, Karen thought, as for continuous verification of the facts. Ginger's occasional moral confusion arose from her difficulties deciphering what was real. Pitching her voice loud and falsely confidential, she informed her sister, "Dean's in Canada."

Kirk looked up, interested now. Karen said, "You're fucking kidding."

Cecelia said, "Karen, please don't talk like that in this house."

From the La-Z Boy, Ray pronounced, "My son, the draft-dodger. My daughter, the gutter-mouth."

"Well, whaddaya know." Amazement and filial pride were limned with a certain ignoble jealousy that somebody in the family besides her evidently had a conscience. "I didn't know old Dean had it in him." Ginger was looking proud of herself, as if she'd had something to do with it. "Where is he?" Karen asked their mother.

Cecelia's expression had turned sad and almost dreamy, and she shook her head slightly. "I don't know. We haven't heard from him. Dennis told us."

"Dennis is in Vietnam."

Cecelia visibly flinched. "I guess they write."

"Far out," Kirk commented.

"Did Dennis enlist?"

"You bet," answered Ray from the living room.

"He had a low draft number," Ginger said.

"Twelve," Cecelia added, as though against her will. "Dean, too. Of course."

"One twin fighting the war and one twin in Canada." Karen shivered with something like aesthetic pleasure and hugged herself. "It's like two halves of the same person."

Kirk asked for another piece of lemon meringue pie. Karen narrowed her eyes at him; was he fucking trying to divert the conversation into safer territory? Who did he think he was to do that? This was her fucking family.

Cecelia didn't seem as pleased as usual when dinner guests appreciated her cooking. Already primed for combat, Karen took rather deliberate offense at this subtle rudeness. Even as she bridled, though, she was aware of her own disingenuousness, for the last fucking thing she wanted was for her parents to like Kirk.

Anyway, she saw, it was Ray her mother was pissed at. Although Cecelia's back was to the living room and to Ray sitting insolently in his La-Z Boy, she might as well have been glaring straight at him. Her lips were white, her eyes narrowed, her jaw set. Maybe it had something to do with Dean this time, but Karen had seen that look countless times, and nothing ever came of it, nothing ever changed. The familiar futility of her mother's anger horrified her, almost made her laugh out loud. This was yet another thing that was not going to happen to her. She was not going to be fifty years old and have no effect on the world.

Ginger announced, "I made the pie," and folded her arms across her chest as if to protect herself from the torrent of compliments sure to follow. From someone else, this would have been a deliberate diversionary tactic intended to diffuse imminent conflict. Ginger, though, was just saying one of the many things foremost in her mind. Her self-absorption and, more, her social clumsiness enraged Karen, making it a perfect score: Now she was furious with everyone in the house.

Mouth full, Kirk smiled at Ginger with his eyes. " 'S good," he mumbled.

Ginger was off then on one of her monologues,

their connections to anything anybody else was talking or thinking about tenuous at best and utterly irrelevant after the first paper-thin and tortuous transition. This one started out, fleetingly, to be about cooking, but rapidly became a trippy, disjointed discourse on, as far as Karen could tell, only a few of the infinite number of thoughts that populated Ginger's head at any given moment and of which, unlike normal people, she was constantly, intensely, helplessly aware.

Karen didn't know whether her sister actually heard voices, but obviously she didn't live alone in her mind. Nobody did, Karen guessed, but most people, unless they were on something, weren't pressed in on and torn apart by the crowd. Ginger shared her place in the world with an active mob of thoughts and images, minute sensory details like the pattern of the holes in the buttons on a shirt cuff, epic themes about the nature of life and death, memories and stray stimuli and auras and dreams and maybe scenes from the future, scenes from past lives, scenes from other reality streams, all of them simultaneously equally worthy or unworthy of attention and expression, no relative difference between foreground and background.

It was fucking exhausting to try to follow what she said, like being with somebody on acid when you were straight. Kirk said schizophrenia was another label the establishment used to oppress people who didn't accept the party line, and Karen thought that was true, but Ginger was, even so, fucking hard to be around.

School, she talked about now, and how hard it was to keep meringue from drooping, and Joan Baez and Bob Dylan, and how much sugar you put in meringue, and the color of her gerbil's eyes, and how much she loved Christmas, and how close she and her sister were, and how long you beat meringue to make it stiff depending on climatic conditions, and how much she hated Christmas, and *The Earth, the Sky, and People All Around,* which at first Karen didn't remember was the title of a play and thought was some sort of crazy, expansive comment on Ginger's worldview, which maybe it fucking was.

"Far out," Kirk said a few times, more or less randomly.

Every time, that stopped Ginger short. She looked hard at him, then at Karen, to whom she asserted, "Reality just flows, you know? And then every once in a while reality puddles, and there I am."

Understanding, Karen pushed herself away from the table to carry her dishes to the sink. She never could decide the right way to act with her sister. Should you go along with her delusions? Were they delusions? Should you tell her when she was doing something weird? Was it weird? Did she need feedback about consensual reality? Was it real?

It wasn't Ginger's schizophrenia that threatened to drag her into some dank lair, but the fact that they were related by blood, circumstance, and personal history shared imperfectly but significantly. When she wasn't around her sister, it was reassuringly easy to deny connectedness, for they weren't the same kind of people at all anymore. As far as Karen knew, for instance, Ginger was a virgin. As far as Karen knew, she had no opinion one way or another about Vietnam or civil rights, or maybe dozens of opinions, all of them always in the foreground.

"What's wrong?" Ginger demanded behind her, both truculently and pitiably. No one answered. Hanging in the air like a Christmas ornament, the question quickly acquired a universal and symbolic quality, as if it had not been addressed personally to Karen but to the whole household, the whole world.

Knowing Ginger wouldn't let it go, Karen nevertheless said, "Nothing."

A look of terror showed that Ginger knew she was being lied to but not how or why. "Something's wrong," she insisted.

"What's wrong," Karen said with great, careful emphasis, "is that this country is rotten at the core. We're killing babies in a war that's none of our fucking business on the other side of the world, and we're oppressing black people at home, and it's hard to get into the fucking Christmas spirit when shit like that is going on all around." She snorted and added meanly, *"The Earth, the Sky, and People All Around.* Grok?"

Ray's footrest hit the floor with a thump and he was on his feet again, but still he didn't come into the kitchen. Backlit by the lights of the Christmas tree, underscored by the piano and violin music Karen thought she couldn't stand a second longer, he thundered, "You watch your mouth, young lady!

168

You don't like the United States of America, why don't you leave? This is the greatest country in the world, you hear me? Love it or leave it! You hear me?"

"People are dying in your stupid war!" Karen shouted at her father. "Civilians! Babies! Old fucks like you send young men to die!"

"It's *war!*" Ray shouted back. "People sometimes have to be sacrificed in war! That's how it is!"

Kirk began in a quiet singsong, "Hey, Hey, LBJ," and Karen said over him to Ginger, "Fuck off, Sis."

"What do you mean? 'Fuck off' can mean lots of things." There was breathless panic in Ginger's voice but no sarcasm, and her eyes flashed with real anxiety.

"I mean leave me alone."

Cecelia began, "Karen, please don't talk like that—"

"Sure," Ginger said. "No problem. Merry Christmas," and left the room.

Ray had strode into the master bedroom off the opposite end of the living room. The door slammed dully. The absence of his dark bulk made the Christmas tree lights seem garish. The music kept on.

Shaking, Karen admitted to herself that she was frightened, but it was fear in the service of something good and important, almost a holy fear, like standing up to pigs with nightsticks, which she hadn't been in the right place at the right time to do yet. She reached for Kirk. He smiled at her and squeezed her hand, but she could tell he didn't quite grok what was going on here.

169

He was so beautiful, and she loved him so much, and they would always be together because they allowed each other space to grow, and because the love they felt for each other was part of the love they felt for people everywhere. The bittersweet smell of him was almost intolerable. Sexual arousal made her labia feel swollen and her clitoris throb.

To forestall her mother's remonstrance, and to give herself something to do besides tear Kirk's clothes off, Karen offered to do dishes. Kirk said he'd help. They exchanged a long sensuous look, as if doing dishes together were some kind of secret erotic code. Kirk dropped his eyes before she did, which was, briefly, puzzling.

Uncharacteristically, Cecelia hardly protested. She scooped leftovers into Tupperware dishes, burped the lids, stacked them in the refrigerator. She wiped off the table and folded the damp dish-rag before handing it to Karen. Then she went around the corner and through the living room past the Christmas tree to their bedroom at the other end of the little house, and quietly shut the door.

Ray's in there, Karen said to herself. I wonder what they're saying to each other. I wonder what they're doing. She tried and failed to entertain a lascivious image.

So Karen and Kirk performed their first domestic activity together, the first of what would turn out to be not very many. They moved self-consciously, kissing and touching each other's bodies with damp, sudsy hands because kissing and touching

were not as intimate, not nearly as risky as just doing dishes together would have been.

At school they spent hours in a steamy corner of
the lobby of her dorm among dozens of other couples, making out, murmuring proclamations of love
and desire. The pleasure was in the flowing mutu-
ality, not just between the two of them but among
everybody in the big room, an emotion greater than
the sum of its parts, a single organism seething with
the orgasmic life-force. The lobby was largely un-
ventilated, and the smell of sex thickened the air.
Karen would, infrequently, emerge from the super-
heated hormonal brine long enough to speculate on
what it must be like for outsiders—the receptionist
at the switchboard; students who weren't part of
couples; her father, Ray, delivering her clean laundry.

When, on that Christmas Eve in her parents'
kitchen, Karen backed Kirk against the refrigerator
to press her groin against his and kiss him—her
passionate playfulness heightened by the tension of
being in her parents' house, doing dishes in her parents' house, getting high on sex and love and grass
despite her parents' best efforts to bring her
down—he hardly responded. Cold alarm sounded.
She put her hands on the sides of his head, fingers
twined in his slightly greasy blond hair, and kissed
him harder. This time his mouth did open under
hers, but something was wrong. Something was
changing, and Karen knew it as it was happening,
would later look back on that time in Kirk's newly

distracted embrace as a moment when the earth shifted.

Thirteen weeks later, on the evening of March 31, 1968, President Johnson was to make a dual announcement that would bring joy to the streets and to the Student Union where Karen was with Kirk: The bombing of North Vietnam would cease, and he would not seek re-election. In the celebratory pandemonium that swelled like bright balloons, Karen would kiss Kirk like that again, open-mouthed, passionate, giddy with their love that was part of a larger love that had, in fact, changed the world. And he would not respond. And she would plead as she had a dozen times since Christmas, gazing fearfully up into his beautiful face, "What's wrong?"

And this time he would answer—calmly, with no apparent difficulty meeting her gaze—"I just don't love you anymore."

From then on Karen would, in a pale imitation of her sister, always hold two streams of reality in her consciousness: the glories both of triumph and of loss, each informing the other, each at any moment puddling. When her children would scoff at or envy the Sixties—especially when, in jest or in reverence, they'd play a song about gentle people, answers in the wind, society's child—she'd be reminded how, even when you did right things, someone could just stop loving you, and how, even when someone stopped loving you, you still had to do right things.

Before long Cecelia made her way back out of the bedroom, holding her blue chenille robe tightly around her and giving them a faint half-smile as she traversed the kitchen to the bathroom. The soft sliding of the door and softer, tiny clicking of its latch were sad. Sharply not wanting her mother to be sad at Christmas, Karen considered whether this sentiment was worthy of her expanded consciousness, and couldn't decide. She finished scrubbing the last pot, handed it to Kirk to dry, and wiped off the counter.

On her hesitant and hasty way back through the kitchen, Cecelia made a mournful little detour to kiss Karen good-night. "Merry Christmas, honey," she said thinly.

Here, presented full before her, was a moral choice Karen was as sure of as she was of her opposition to the war, her support of racial equality, her embrace of free love. At this moment in history, Cecelia Melchior represented the entire older generation, and Karen's obligation was so clear that she wondered if she could have dropped acid or mescaline somehow without realizing it: *What matters is the cause.* "Mom, wait. I want to talk to you for a minute."

Predictably, Cecelia shook her head, denying or refusing. "I'm awfully tired. I have to get up early to get the turkey in the oven—"

Karen took her mother's hands. Startlement cut through the fatigue and sorrow on the older woman's face, and Karen felt her own pulse quickening. Something was about to change the world. "Mom, listen. We're not trying to hurt you and—and Dad. Neither is Dean. We're trying to make things better for the whole world. It's about love. I want you to understand. It's about love."

Cecelia didn't pull her hands free, but she didn't grasp Karen's, either. She didn't exactly look away, but she didn't meet Karen's gaze.

"Karen." Kirk even tugged on her arm. "It's late. Everybody's tired. Let's just go to bed." She heard the warning in his voice but, knowing he was wrong, ignored it, focusing her energy on this incipient connection with her mother that she willed to break through.

"You're in the boys' room," Cecelia insisted, gasping as if she couldn't get air to make her point strongly enough.

"My stuff's already in there. Karen, come on."

Without taking her eyes off her mother's face—which, in the variegated half-light from the Christmas tree in the next room and the dim fluorescence from the hood-light over the stove, looked drawn and rigid, as if fending off an assault—Karen gestured him away. "You go on. I have to talk to Mom."

After a long moment, Kirk leaned down to kiss her on the mouth—not the peck they'd often mocked as over-thirty kissing but not a real, deep kiss, either. She thought at him, "Stay awake. I'll be in later," but distractedly, so he probably didn't get her mental message. Surely he'd know. He mumbled something in Cecelia's direction, Cecelia nodded tightly, and he shambled off down the short hall, leaving mother and daughter alone together in the circumscribed space they occupied at the moment, never mind that three other people were in the house and billions in the world.

"Let's sit down," Karen said softly, excitedly to her mother. They were at the kitchen table again then, Cecelia stiff on the edge of her chair with her robe pulled so snugly around her that the fabric strained thin across the shoulders. Karen leaned forward, bare elbows on bare knees, hands clasped. "Mom, please, I want you to understand us. I want you to approve of us," was what she yearned to say, but she could only approximate it: "All we want to do is bring peace and love to the world. Make love, not war. That's all we want to do. How can you think that's bad?"

Cecelia nodded raggedly, shook her head raggedly, said, "Uh-huh."

Eagerly, Karen pressed on. "We think it's morally wrong for America to be involved in another country's civil war. Haven't you seen the pictures? Haven't you heard the stories? We don't hate America. We want America to do what's right. We're not against the soldiers, really. It's LBJ and McNamara and the rest of the government, all those old men sending young men to kill and die."

Cecelia had lowered her head and hunched her shoulders, as if waiting for another in a rain of blows. But she didn't argue and she didn't get up and leave. Again she nodded and said, "Uh-huh."

Karen was encouraged. "Doing drugs allows us to experience other realities, instead of being limited to this one. We're opening our consciousness. It's not just for fun. It's *important.*"

Cecelia was breathing hard. So was Karen, and the air was suddenly tinged with that bittersweet odor she'd thought was Kirk, but Kirk was not in the room.

"We believe in free love because sex and love are natural and beautiful things and shouldn't have limits on them. How can that be wrong?" So sure was she of this argument that she laughed a little in delight, saying it to her mother on Christmas Eve. Now there came a long pause that Karen couldn't interpret. Breathlessly she wondered if she should say something more, or if Cecelia was already convinced.

Finally Cecelia pushed herself up out of her chair. It seemed to take her a minute to get her balance. Fingers stiff and fumbling, she untied her belt and opened her robe, revealing white flannel pajamas with little pink and purple flowers, a kid's pjs or an old lady's. The pajamas embarrassed Karen, and this flash of unself-conscious vulnerability, the opposite of Cecelia's habitual wrapping gesture, put her on quivering alert. But then Cecelia did wrap the robe snugly around her, re-tie the belt, cross her arms, and, without looking up, walk out of the room.

Stunned, Karen sat there for a beat or two before she jumped to her feet and followed. "Mom?" The Christmas tree was dark. Something about the thought of her mother, in the midst of what Karen was starting to realize was a headlong rush to escape, pausing to attend to a detail of household safety like unplugging the tree lights—probably checking the water in the base, too; probably turning down the thermostat on the wall as she went past—struck Karen as tragic, a word she'd thought safely reserved for napalmed babies and burned churches. "Mom?"

But the door of her parents' bedroom clicked, rendering it more firmly unassailable than a slam would have done. Karen stood in the dark living room, shut out, horror she did not yet understand beginning to prickle her upper arms and thighs.

Then she heard, from behind the closed door, her mother's sobs. She'd hardly ever known her mother to cry, and this was because of her, a deep, low, terrible sobbing that allowed no space for breath or, certainly, for explanation or apology.

Karen's hands went to her face, but she didn't cover her ears and she didn't move out of earshot. Beginning a process of comprehension that would continue for the rest of her life—that, intending to do something loving, she had done something cruel—she stood there for a long time, absorbing the sounds of her mother's grief. Finally she went to bed before the sobbing had stopped, and Kirk came in, and they made love.

Chapter Eight

The Confession
(1978)

The teepee on the railroad tracks excited Cecelia, the bravery of it, the way it jutted crookedly up out of the prairie. "They're still here," she said, glad. "Let's stop," and slowed the car, inviting if not exactly waiting for her son's assent.

Dennis didn't object. Of all her family and friends, he'd be among the least likely to object to interrupting a Sunday afternoon drive down from Coal Creek Canyon to talk to the little group engaged in civil disobedience at the Rocky Flats nuclear weapons plant.

There were no more than half a dozen demonstrators. One of them carried a sign, unreadable from here. The primitive construction of the teepee imbued it with grim and beautiful symbolism. The medallion she'd worn today, in hopes they'd come back into town this way and stop here, was inscribed: "War Is Not Healthy for Children and Other Living Things"; she could read it like Braille.

Her other children didn't pay much attention to what she believed in. The older she got, the more she felt chronically misunderstood, which wore her down the way a stubborn low-grade fever might have, or persistent mild pain. A commitment to non-violence, for instance, though admittedly never especially focused, had for a long time been fundamental to how she lived in the world, and for the most part her children didn't seem to want to know about that.

Phil, her eldest, lived a thousand miles away and never in a million years would they discuss anything like Rocky Flats, but she had no reason to think his "America-love-it-or-leave-it" stance of ten years ago had altered. She'd long since despaired of Virginia, her youngest, ever grasping an issue for more than a few seconds at a time before she was inundated by all the possibilities of the thing, real or imagined (though how could you tell the difference when it was *possibilities* you were dealing with?).

The consciousness-raising Sixties seemed to have had a more lasting effect on her, though she'd been well past the magic age of thirty, than on the middle three of her children who'd come of age then. As far as she could tell, Dean's life in suburban Vancouver, where he'd fled to avoid the draft, was orderly and conservative and retained no evidence of being any more morally informed than the average.

In college Karen had marched in every protest march and sat down in every sit-down strike she could find. There'd been drugs and sex, probably more than Cecelia'd known about and less than she'd feared; an entire world order had seemed to be in jeopardy, and Karen herself. There'd been one particularly awful Christmas: Dennis in Vietnam, Dean in Canada, Marie—Ray's mistress then—actually calling the house to complain to Cecelia about his shoddy treatment of them both, and Karen home with a long-haired boyfriend, smoking marijuana and having sex right there in the house and Cecelia not knowing what if anything she ought to do about it. For some reason, that boyfriend still sent Cecelia Christmas cards, though Karen said she hadn't heard from him in years and acted embarrassed by the mention of his name. At the time, Cecelia's acute maternal discomfort had obscured everything else, but now she missed her daughter's hippie passions, scattershot and callow as they had been. Strangers to each other back then, they'd each changed position and were still strangers; if Karen had been in the car this afternoon, Cecelia wouldn't have dared stop here.

Dennis, though, gave a nod and a quick smile as she eased the car onto the gravel shoulder. She guessed he'd see this as an enhancement rather than an interruption of their outing, although he probably wouldn't say so; a chatty kid and notably unsurly teen, Dennis had come home from two tours of duty in Vietnam a man of crystalline integrity and unnervingly few words.

While he'd been over there, long months without word from him, Cecelia'd become obsessed with what might be happening to her son. Sometimes she'd tried her best to avoid the terrible news stories and sometimes she couldn't get enough of them: the napalmed little girl running down the jungle road; children shot by soldiers as enemies and often, rigged with explosives or broken bottles, they really were; the bare soles of POWs beaten with bamboo rods.

Dennis didn't cower at Fourth of July fireworks or explode in fury over trifles, but the war had changed him, for the worse and, strangely, for the better. She knew not to ask him direct questions, and did her best to believe what she knew to be true, that this child of hers was not keeping himself from her in particular, was not so much secretive as camouflaged.

Once in a while he'd tell her something, without much detail. He'd been captured. He'd thought he was going to die. He'd escaped. He'd seen on the streets of Saigon children whose legs had been cut off by their parents to make them better beggars. She'd held her breath, hoping he'd say more, hoping he would not.

181

A hot breeze stirred the grass heads, lightening them in both color and density. 80th Avenue had the feel of a barely paved country road, though it led right into the city not ten minutes east. Highway 93 crossed behind them, the scenic back way to Boulder, right up against the foothills as though there were no place farther west to go, although there always was.

Cecelia had nothing particular in mind to say to the demonstrators—three women and two men, she could see now; all of them more than a generation younger than she was, younger even than Dennis. But she wanted to ally herself with them.

Ray would scoff. Just about everything she'd ever considered important, Ray had disdained. Not that he himself hadn't had strong opinions. The Vietnam War, and his sons' various responses to it, had caused him great moral distress. And she still remembered, wifely pride made sad now by a sense of missed potential, how twenty years ago he'd stood up to a friend of theirs who'd insisted he'd shoot anybody seeking shelter in the family fallout shelter. But Cecelia's opinions he'd never taken seriously, whether they matched his own or diverged. This was partly her fault; she'd never expected him to.

Cecelia sighed. Ten years after the divorce, why should Ray's reaction or lack thereof even enter her mind? Let Marie have that along with whatever else she could claim of the rest of him. Ray mocked almost everything about Marie, too, even now that she was so sick, even now that he had, twice, been back in Cecelia's bed.

Cecelia didn't understand why she'd allowed such a thing; it was wrong for all sorts of reasons, and she wouldn't want any of their children, especially Dennis, to know about it. It upset her, even as it gave her a certain satisfaction, to be struggling with questions of sexual morality at her age.

In the back seat Tomt was very quiet, as he usually was. Even his play, though intent, was quiet; he didn't shriek with laughter or cry aloud. This similarity between him and his father, one of many, made Cecelia smile. They even looked alike, though she'd have been hard pressed to say in precisely what ways; it was obvious they were related, this tall broad-shouldered white man with chiseled features and prematurely steel-gray hair, thirty-two years old next month, and this tiny Vietnamese-black six-year-old.

She got out of the car into the wind, wondering uneasily whether the fine dust might be radioactive. Dennis got out his side and wordlessly opened the back door for Tomt, who wordlessly climbed out and reached for his father's hand, then, endearingly, for his grandmother's. He didn't seem to be holding on more or less tightly than would any other child.

"Look, son." Feeling Dennis's gentle tug in the boy's other hand, Cecelia choked up at the sound of the word "son." A flock of brown prairie birds whose name she wished she knew rose out of the grass. Following the ascent, her eyes swept up over several of the five hundred Rocky Flats buildings—all the more ominous because they didn't tick or rumble or emit black smoke—to see a hawk up high, sun on its bright red tail. She caught her breath.

Tomt's hand in hers told her nothing about his response. Looking down for clues in his upturned face, she thrilled again to the dual-sided knowledge that in some ways he was hers forever now, because of a decision her son had made, and in some ways, no matter what anybody did, he would never be hers. This was not totally unlike what she knew about her other grandchildren, but with this one there was a special resonance.

He'd seen the hawk; his brown eyes were following it. Had he ever seen a hawk before? Were there hawks in Vietnam? Did it scare him, remind him of bombs and napalm? Did it please him? He gave no sign.

Dennis had crouched beside the child and dropped his hand to put his arm around him. Tomt leaned into his father's embrace, and Cecelia saw with sharp pleasure how easy affection was for them both. Tomt said in turn, "Daddy, look!" with a slight sweet accent on the diphthong. The hawk had disappeared and they weren't looking upward now anyway but at something in the tall grass around their knees.

Standing a little apart from them, Cecelia was painfully proud of her son for adopting this little boy. But the pride seemed wrong, a denial of what was and what needed to be between father and son, and she could never speak it to either of them without damaging something important. Still, she was proud. Her eyes stung.

Ray had fumed. "Why doesn't he just do the normal thing and marry some girl and have kids of his own?"

Since the divorce, Cecelia had purposely allowed her skill at avoiding arguments with Ray to get rusty, but this time she'd let go two provocations, "normal" and "own."

"He says after what he's seen he'd never bring more children into this world." Dennis had said that to her, the few words like poetry, each meaning much more than you'd suspect. It broke her heart that he thought of this world in such ugly terms. But, confusingly, he didn't seem unhappy.

"Kid'll have all kinds of problems."

"I'm sure."

"Damn fool thing to do."

"I think it's admirable." And she had, though she was worried, too. Her voice had broken with both worry and admiration as she'd tried to say, "I'm proud of him."

Ray had still been scowling when he'd declared, "He's his mother's son, that's for damn sure. They all are." She'd thought it a complaint and been considering whether and what to retort when he'd added, surprising her, "We've got a bunch of terrific kids, thanks to you." Then he'd taken her in his arms and kissed her, which should have been a surprise and was not.

As unwelcome warmth spread up through her at the memory—and, she forced herself to admit, the anticipation—Cecelia knew perfectly well why she was having an affair with her former husband, whom she didn't much like or respect and certainly didn't trust. It was not very complicated or mysterious, she told herself sternly as she started across the grassland: She'd never slept with any other man in her life and had no desire to do so, though she'd dated since the divorce, had once come close to falling in love. The physical attraction between her and Ray Melchior had never diminished, no matter what else had been going on or not going on between them at any given time, no matter how persistent her visualizations of him being equally passionate with other women. Right here, right now, she thought of the way he'd always, from the first night of their marriage, started their lovemaking, resting his fingertips under her ear and then, after a long pause exquisite and excruciating, very gently and slowly drawing them down her neck to the point of her shoulder, down the length of her upper arm to the inside of her elbow, down the inside of her forearm to the pulse point in her wrist, and finally into her palm, where she closed her fingers around them. Her breath caught a little. Just last week, in her bed that used to be their bed, in the middle of a Thursday afternoon, making love with him had been thrilling again. Never mind that it was not love.

"Beautiful," said a hearty male voice off to her left and slightly behind her. "Absolutely beautiful."

He was about her own age, big, thinning gray hair, jeans and a plaid flannel shirt; she'd always liked big men in soft plaid shirts. She'd be willing to apply "beautiful" to any number of things here—the weather, the landscape, the demonstration, her son and grandson—and she smiled at him. "Yes."

He walked over to her. He was much taller than she, and she admired his hands. There was a faint sharp odor about him that she found pleasant, too. "You, I mean."

She felt herself flush. "Pardon?" she asked, shamelessly, so he'd say it again and elaborate.

His eyes were dark, maybe gray, and he had a nice wide mouth. He made an expansive gesture with both big hands. "This is a beautiful thing, all of this, and you're the most beautiful thing about it."

Cecelia was flattered, though she knew better. "What a nice thing to say."

He leaned close and lowered his voice. "Don't let anybody spoil it for you."

She moved back to widen the distance between them again, both touched and put off by what pretended to be but was not entirely admiration.

"I can tell you're a very moral person," the man said seriously.

It was harder to scoff than it should have been,

but she managed, "How in the world would you know that?"

He brushed off her skepticism with hardly a shrug. "It's obvious. You have an aura about you. You're here, which is a moral thing to do. You'll be here again. I admire that."

"You're here, too." She wasn't sure what she meant, but it seemed important to establish his participation in whatever was going on here.

"So give yourself a break. Not *everything* has to be a moral choice."

She didn't know what he meant and, impatient now, didn't care to. "Nice to meet you," she said firmly, and walked away.

"What are you doing?" she asked the first demonstrator she came to, just to start another conversation.

The woman might be in her twenties, hair hidden and face shadowed under a tattered straw hat. A habit Cecelia wished she could break made her wonder automatically if Dennis might be interested in this one. "We're protesting the manufacture of nuclear weapons parts at this plant."

"What's the purpose of the teepee?" Cecelia shielded her eyes to squint at it against the vast bright sky.

"It stops the trains bringing in materials. They have to get out and move it. Then we put it back. Sometimes they call the police and somebody gets arrested for trespassing. Then somebody else takes their place."

Cecelia nodded. "I admire you for taking a stand like this."

The young woman grinned. "Join us."

"It's an uphill fight," Dennis observed, merely a fact unadorned by opinion, interpretation, or nuance.

The woman regarded him and then Tomt. "Rocky Flats is polluting our environment and contributing to the mentality of war. Join us. For your son's sake." Already all but persuaded, Cecelia was won over the last little bit by the woman's ready assumption that Tomt was Dennis's son.

"The government says no plutonium escapes into the environment. The plant is inspected. It's perfectly safe." As Cecelia had suspected, Dennis did know something about the issue. There was no sarcasm in his tone, and no belligerence. He was simply setting out data like young plants.

The protester's attention had shifted to her comrades, who were gathering near the teepee. Cecelia hoped a train was coming. Hoping so, too, the young woman hastened away from them, reacting to Dennis's statements with only a cynical snort.

"Where's Grandpa?" Tomt suddenly wanted to know.

Cecelia found herself blushing, which embarrassed her further. "I don't know," she answered. Fearing that might sound testy, she added, "He's at his house, I guess. With Marie," then thought that might sound snide.

Tomt seemed satisfied, though. He wandered off

in the general direction of the teepee. Across the long rolling sweep of prairie, there was no sign of any approaching train, no sound of it through the low blurred hum of the several encircling highways and the closer, higher-pitched insect-buzz.

Dennis and Cecelia followed the little boy, Cecelia looking around for something commemorative she could put into the scrapbook she was keeping for him in case Dennis didn't think of it; she'd sent bulging scrapbooks with all of her kids when they'd left home, but none of them had seemed much impressed. When Tomt stopped well before he got to the teepee, his interest caught by something closer at hand, so did they. He sat down in the tall golden grass and they stood companionably together. The sun was warm but not too hot, and the breeze was pleasant, if it wasn't carrying pollution onto their skin and into their lungs.

Since there was no way of knowing, Cecelia decided to treat it as an ordinary summer breeze intending no harm, and she lifted her face to it, let it riffle her hair, which hardly had any curl left in it anyway from the perm less than a month ago. The unwillingness of grayed hair to take a perm was, she'd often thought grimly, one of the unsung cruelties of old age.

Tomt's thick, straight black hair glistened in the sun, and above the red-and-white-striped polo shirt the bent back of his neck was golden-brown, darker than the grass and lighter than the dirt. Cecelia's great tenderness toward him seemed somehow distilled from the tenderness she felt for this place, this day. "Don't you wonder," she said quietly to her son, "what secrets are in that little head? We'll probably never know."

Dennis nodded and shrugged, both agreeing and dismissing. He observed, "We all have secrets, don't we, Mom?" and Cecelia flushed again, thinking, *He knows about his father and me.*

She faced him. "What do you mean?"

Uncharacteristically, Dennis dissembled, which she took to be some sort of warning. "We all have things that haunt us," he said, evasively.

She thought, *He must not be talking about Ray and me. You wouldn't use the word "haunt" about that. He wants to tell me something that haunts him about Vietnam, something worse than what he's already told me.* Bravely, steadied by the sense that she was making a sacrifice, actually putting herself in jeopardy, for the sake of her child, she laid her hand on his arm. "What haunts you, son?"

During the ensuing long pause, the voices of the demonstrators twittered like birdsong and Tomt busied himself in the sunny grass. Dennis hadn't stiffened and he didn't pull away, but he didn't respond to her touch, either, and after a while Cecelia removed her hand, wondering unhappily if she'd gone too far. At last he said, "It's hard to talk about," and cleared his throat.

Seriously alarmed now, Cecelia wasn't sure how to convey maternal interest and willingness to hear what he had to say without prying. She settled on,

"If you want to tell me, Dennis, I want to listen," and fervently hoped that was both right and enough.

Dennis didn't take a deep breath to get himself started, as most people would have done. He just plunged in, not looking at her, his voice a bit too loud and harsh. "Something's been keeping me awake nights for years, more so since I've been a parent. Tomt, what is that?"

He left her side to check on his child, and she waited nervously, trying not to anticipate how the revelation on the brink of which they were teetering might alter how she thought about him. In the few minutes before he returned, she considered all sorts of things he might have done in the war and came to terms with them all, some requiring more effort than others. But there could always be things she hadn't thought of, so terrible they'd be beyond her imagination until he forced them in.

The large plaid-shirted man was beside her again, his approach concealed by the grass under his feet and the persistent breeze. There'd have been no way to avoid him on the flat, open prairie even if she had seen him coming. Cecelia pulled her jacket around her. "Don't let him get away without telling you what's on his mind," the man said.

It was an outrageous invasion of privacy, of course, and Cecelia flushed again, in anger and embarrassment this time. "You overheard us talking."

"It wouldn't be right," he pressed, watching her with an odd intensity, "to let this opportunity slip away. It wouldn't be right for either one of you."

"Not *everything* has to be a moral choice, you know." She echoed his tone as well as his words, so the sarcasm couldn't be missed.

His eyes lit up, as though she'd given him exactly the opening he'd been hoping for. "Ah," he said, almost triumphantly, "but some things are."

He grinned and walked off, and Dennis rejoined her, apparently satisfied that Tomt wasn't playing with something imminently dangerous. She steeled herself.

That wasn't enough, though, because when Dennis was beside her again he'd fallen silent. She glanced up at him. He was watching the demonstrators, who were milling and talking among themselves as if something important were about to happen. His profile was skewed by how close she was standing to him, but nonetheless she was struck by how much, superficially, he looked like Dean—the long straight nose, the cowlick—and how little they really resembled each other. Technically identical twins, they'd never been hard to tell apart.

He wasn't saying anything. Cecelia couldn't stand it. "Dennis. What is it?"

"I don't want to tell you," he told her, "but I have to." She couldn't think of another encouraging thing to say to him and felt herself getting annoyed, so it was a relief when at last he went on. "One time when I was in junior high I forgot my lunch and you brought it to me."

"I remember that!" she cut in, realizing the interruption was unwise but so amazed by the clarity of the memory that she couldn't stop herself. It had been a happy, uncomplicated little mother-son interaction, and she didn't want him to use it as a lead-in to the telling of some awful secret. But it was too late now.

"When you came to the school I was on the playground with my buddies. You handed me the lunch sack and I don't think I even said thank you."

"Oh, I think you did," she protested, wonderingly. "At least I don't remember that you didn't. You mean you've been *haunted* all these years because you thought you didn't say thank you? Oh, honey."

"Do you remember the smell?" When, at a complete loss now, she didn't answer, he turned to her, and she was chilled by the anguish in his face. She reached up to grasp his shoulders, but the half-hug seemed to make no difference to him one way or another. "There was this odor on the playground that day. It made my eyes water and the back of my throat burn. Nobody else seemed to notice it. I thought I was coming down with something but I didn't get sick. I remember because there was a Boy Scout camp-out that weekend and I was afraid I was going to miss it, and I was all ready to blame you."

He gave a short chuckle, which Cecelia took as a good sign. She let her hands drop but stayed close by him, and made a point to smile. "I suppose you've you've noticed by now," she said conspiratorially, indicating Tomt, "that parenting can be a pretty thankless undertaking at times. I never realized that until I had children of my own. I don't think a person *can* realize it before they're a parent themselves."

But Dennis wasn't about to be distracted from the past by the present. "It was the same odor I smelled in Nam," he said. "The whole country reeked of it."

Cecelia didn't understand. She waited, aware that she was trembling.

"Then," Dennis said, and she saw how his fists were clenched at his belt, "one of my buddies asked me, 'Who was that old bag?' He knew who you were. He'd been to our house. It was some kind of game, some kind of adolescent-male challenge. And I just said, 'Oh, I dunno.' "

There. It was out. By her son's heavy exhalation and her own silly but considerable hurt, Cecelia knew this was the dreadful secret. What a good man he was, that it had bothered him all these years. How proud she was of him. But thinking of that lanky thoughtful boy he'd been denying to his friends the dowdy, conscientious, probably annoyingly loving mother she'd been brought a lump to her throat that, for a critical moment or two, she couldn't speak around.

Dennis finished, quietly now. "For years I'd think of that at night when I was trying to fall asleep, and I'd have to pull the covers up over my head, I was so ashamed. It got worse in Nam, and now with Tomt it's gotten worse again. I'm sorry, Mom."

What could she say to him that would be both

honest and comforting? "It's all right" would do for any of her other children in similar circumstances, but not for this one because it wouldn't be entirely true. She'd settled on "I'm really glad you told me" and had opened her mouth to say it when Tomt screamed.

They never would know what had frightened him, or whether, in fact, it was fear that propelled the rhythmic shrieks that broke Cecelia's heart and set her teeth on edge. The train was coming; maybe that was it—they could hear it chugging, hear its whistle, and the protesters bunched up determinedly. Maybe a snake had showed itself to him. Maybe he was remembering something, or anticipating something.

By the time his father got to him, and his grandmother right behind, his cries had taken on a momentum of their own divorced from any precipitant, sometimes muffled against his father's chest and sometimes swooping out across the prairie like birds. Dennis held him, crooned to him, stroked his back. At last, as if what was available had only just occurred to him, the child quieted and snuggled into his father's shoulder.

The train full of war supplies approached. The breeze blew, seeming fresh and clean. The demonstrators stood in a short line across the tracks with the teepee between them and the train. Leaving her grandson in her son's protection, knowing she wasn't going very far, Cecelia went to join them.

Chapter Nine

*The Wet Spot
(1986)*

In the midst of foreplay on his office floor—
Gretchen's fingertips fluttering over the head of his
penis, his mouth pursed just far enough around her
nipple that the most sensitive flesh on areola and
lip came into contact—Kirk fell completely out of
love with her. It was a sensation like music ceasing
in the middle of a glorious chord.

He should have stopped the sex then. Physically
he could have, for he was abruptly not attracted to
her, in fact was repulsed, and from one minute to
the next his erection had gone from eager and demanding to purely mechanical and easily denied.

But he thought he should finish, for her sake. He hoped it was a passing mood, though from experience he should have known better, this not being the first time he'd suddenly, inexplicably, and irremediably stopped loving a woman about whom he'd been passionate.

Gretchen was capable of extravagant sexual abandon. Throughout the year or so of their affair, Kirk had found this a wonderful quality in her; now, suddenly, he suspected it of being faked, and, if it wasn't, suddenly he found it a little embarrassing, a little cheap.

He presumed she would write about him and about her own passion, which now suggested contrivance if not outright phoniness; not long ago, knowing that she recorded everything in her notebooks had added to the thrill, but now he was distracted by an irritable curiosity about how she would describe what was happening between them. He'd never read the notebooks, never thought to; now he'd like to pore over every word, and then burn them.

Mostly to stifle her moans and squeals, he kissed her again although he didn't want to. His tongue did its best to curl away from hers. She caught it playfully between her teeth. The times she'd done that before had been among the most erotic they'd had, especially the first time, when the sweet shock of it had made him lose control; once he could talk he'd started to apologize for coming too soon, but then she'd cried out and arched her back and he'd held her, marveling.

Now, he nearly gagged. He pulled his tongue out from between her teeth, scraping it unpleasantly, and wrenched his face away from hers, thinking he really might throw up because she smelled bad, too. Maybe it was perfume; he'd never known her to wear perfume, at one time had loved the sunny, faintly sweaty smell of her. The strong bittersweet odor was alluring in a sick way, rancid, like something sweet that had turned.

He sat up, rubbed his nose. "What's that smell?"

Still in the swoon of her orgasm, if that was what it was, Gretchen didn't even try to answer. Her panting grated on his nerves.

He reached for his clothes and tossed her hers, distressed and taken aback by his aversion to the feel of her bra and panties. Equally strong and equally surprising was his desire—his determination—neither to watch her get dressed nor to let her watch him. He couldn't stop himself from turning his back, standing up, moving away. His lip curled with a contempt he wished he didn't feel. "God, what *is* that smell?"

Naked on her back behind him and at his feet, Gretchen stirred. "I don't smell anything," she murmured. "Except maybe love." Her protest was flirtatious, desultory, but he could tell she'd sensed the change in him, though she didn't comprehend it yet. Kirk didn't comprehend it himself.

It had happened to him a few times before. The

girls he'd fallen in and out of love with in junior high and high school, intense but passing fancies a defining characteristic of adolescence, hardly would have counted in themselves if they hadn't turned out to be the first in a lengthening line. In his hippie college days—almost twenty years ago now, which wasn't as hard to believe as he'd like—there'd been Karen, the first girl he'd slept with, their passion intensified by being part of the larger peace-movement and civil-rights passions; the night LBJ had announced he wouldn't run again, an orgasmic moment if there ever was one, Kirk had been taken aback to discover he didn't love her anymore, just like that. He'd never again been able to work up much interest in her, although for some reason he'd kept in sporadic touch with her mother; the obvious reason would be guilt, but he didn't feel guilty. From her mother he knew Karen had devoted herself to domesticity, was wife, mother, and, incredibly, housewife; hearing this over the years never failed to give him a little self-congratulatory thrill, even though in matters of the heart he prided himself on going with the flow and making no conscious choices at all.

There was no doubt in his mind that he'd once loved Karen, wholeheartedly and sincerely. He wouldn't swear to having loved the girls in high school, but he definitely had loved Gretchen, too. As recently as yesterday, as recently as this morning anticipating their tryst this afternoon, he'd loved her. Exuberantly, as a matter of fact; deliriously.

Obsessively. Recklessly. For months, since the August day she'd given him a ride in her red T-bird with the top down and Joan Baez nostalgically passionate on the tape deck, and they'd ended up spending the afternoon not at the company retreat where they were expected, in fact were on the agenda, but having wild sex on a blanket prickly with pine needles in Rocky Mountain National Park—since then, they'd hardly been able to keep their hands off each other. Co-workers didn't even bother to be furtive about their gossip. More than one client had obviously picked up on the supercharged atmosphere between them when they'd unwisely tried to conduct meetings together.

On their business trip to Honolulu last November, all expenses paid by the company, he'd gone to one or two seminars and she'd made her presentation, but the rest of the week was an erotic blur. Shamelessly groping each other under the thin airline blanket till he wondered giddily why the flight attendants didn't stop them in the name of public decency. Every few minutes rushing off Waikiki back to the pink hotel where they made love on the perpetually disheveled bed or the bathroom floor or the narrow open-air balcony under not much cover of tropical darkness, wet sandy bathing suits peeled off to reveal flesh more sensitive than that which had been exposed, steel drums and orchids riffing air so heavy and sweet it seemed meant for some purpose more exotic than breathing.

Now he wished to hell she'd cover herself. Her

clothes untouched in the pile where he'd dropped them, she sat up, arms around drawn-up knees. Under her pale and slightly flabby thighs, a little beard of pubic hair was plainly visible. Kirk's skin crawled.

Gretchen smiled, stretched with a languor so shameless it must be false, and buried her face in her knees. Unwillingly Kirk imagined what odor she was inhaling. Her hair straggled over her forearms. He'd never noticed before that the flesh under the sides of her breasts sagged a little. Really, she was not an especially attractive woman physically; not having considered her that way before, Kirk felt callow and mean-spirited to be thinking it now, but there it was.

Unhappily he rubbed his face, then immediately regretted the gesture, which had transferred musk—hers, his because of her—from his fingers directly onto his nose. Briefly this overlaid the peculiar bittersweet odor, but soon the sharper fragrance broke through and he heard himself saying, "You've gained a little weight, haven't you?"

Gretchen raised her head, frowning, not so much hurt yet or insulted as puzzled. Under the circumstances it was an appalling thing to say, and Kirk was suitably ashamed of himself. But there was also a nasty little spurt of satisfaction, quite uncharacteristic of him, he hoped, but of which he found himself craving more.

He strode to the other side of the office, as far from Gretchen as he could get without actually leaving the room, and sat behind his desk. His crotch felt sticky and he wanted to go to the restroom to get himself cleaned up. But he found himself reluctant to leave her alone in his office, as if she might soil it. He straightened his tie. "Well," he said, as politely as he could manage, "I need to get to work."

Many an afternoon they'd sexually whiled away in his office or hers, in some motel or other, twice in the corporate boardroom, and never before had work come between them. This time his mind was already mulling the chronic overrun problem at the southeast branch, and suddenly he thought he might have a solution. He itched to plot it out, thumbs and forefingers impatiently riffling the pad of graph paper he'd positioned in front of him. He and Gretchen had reveled in playing up how much they'd distracted each other, how their passion was stronger than they were, how they could not control themselves; there'd been considerable truth to it, and the exaggeration had been an aphrodisiac in itself. The distraction she was creating now was more on the order of a dripping faucet, and all he wanted was for her to go away.

She wiggled her shoulders and sighed, "Oh, baby." The two of them—professionals, solidly in their thirties—calling each other "baby" had been a sweet naughtiness. Now he felt himself flushing at how ridiculous it sounded. She propped her chin on her wrists and gazed soulfully at him; he shifted his position so that the short tower of black plastic in-and out-boxes on the corner of his desk blocked his view of her and, presumably, hers of him. "I told them I'd be in meetings all afternoon, so nobody's expecting me," she said smugly, coyly.

This meant, of course, that her staff knew exactly where she was and what she was doing. Kirk remembered, as though it were a long time ago and he'd been a different person, when he'd enjoyed the gossip about them in the company, the disapproval and open envy. The public character of their relationship, their flaunting and display of it, had been part of the fun. Now, it shamed him.

He had the guilty sensation that somebody was observing them right now, had been watching while they rolled around on the napless gray carpet. Scenes of what they'd have looked like played across his mind like a cheap porno movie: his ass in the air, her legs spread. The slatted shades were closed all the way, though, and the door was still locked.

Gretchen got to her feet, which stirred up and worsened the odor. Kirk was horrified by the expanse of her nakedness—head to toe; mouth to clavicle to breasts to navel to pelvis to pubis to knees to toes—upon which mere hours ago he hadn't been able to gaze enough. God, what if she came over to him, wanting more loving, which she would have every reason to expect? She pulled a face at him, which was obviously supposed to be sexy but which only made her look silly, and made a disgusting kissing noise with her mouth.

To forestall her, Kirk hastily picked up the phone, punched line 1, and dialed the first number that popped into his mind. He had no particular business with that branch office, but he chatted with the receptionist, asked for the manager whom he knew wasn't in, left a message he hoped didn't sound as fabricated as it was. All this time, Gretchen was advancing on him, naked, intending to be alluring and justified in thinking she was. Kirk could hardly stand it when her hands came to rest on his shoulders, then slid inside his collar and down his chest. Once they'd actually had intercourse while he was on the phone with a client, and the effort of keeping his voice steady and his breathing regular had gloriously heightened the excitement and the release. This time he actually felt his scrotum retract in self-protection.

When he hung up, Gretchen swiveled his chair around playfully and started to lower herself onto his lap. Her approaching buttocks loomed huge and comically menacing. He leaped up and pushed her away. "No!" he all but yelled. He cleared his throat, feeling foolish, angry with her for making him feel foolish. "I—I don't want to wrinkle my pants."

Incredulously she demanded. "What?"

"They just came back from the cleaners."

She gaped at him. Then apparently she chose to interpret this as some sort of intimate and affectionate little joke, and she laughed, uncertainly but trusting in his good opinion of and good will toward her, of which she'd had ample and recurring evidence. An hour ago he'd have agreed that he was trustworthy. Now his mind scrambled to defend the blatant untrustworthiness being revealed: Loving somebody didn't imply loving them forever. They'd never made any promises. Gretchen had liked the freedom as much as he had. All of which, though true, he knew to be irrelevant.

"What's wrong, Kirk?"

"Nothing. Nothing." By this time his irritation was beyond endurance. Knowing full well that there was nothing to warrant it, that everything she was doing and saying would have seemed sweetly sexy to him a short time ago, only made it worse. "I have a four o'clock appointment," he lied transparently. "The client's coming here. You better get dressed."

He really could not bear to watch her step into her underwear, pull them up over her hips, struggle to fasten her bra—Lord, what if she asked him to do it? Not a few times that had precipitated another headlong episode of lovemaking when his hands strayed around to her welcoming breasts and her hips pressed back into his pelvis. Now the threat of such a thing revolted him.

"I'm going to the men's room. I'll be back in a few minutes." He restrained himself from adding, "Be gone before I get back," but did actually pledge to himself that one of them would leave; if she wasn't gone he'd have to either evict her by force, verbal or physical, or flee himself, locking her in if possible in order to prevent her from following. He could scarcely believe he was entertaining such extreme notions, especially toward this woman who so recently had given him such ardent pleasure, but he had to admit they were arousing. "I'll call you tomorrow," he flung at her; he wouldn't, but a familiar promise—in the past always happily kept—might induce her to get out of here.

Quickly, before he said or did anything else gratuitously unkind, he left the office, shutting the double-paned door behind him with a quiet click. His heavy breathing and heavy footsteps were stilled in the gray-carpeted, gray-walled corridor, but not the sensation of being in a desperate situation requiring desperate measures.

Another man—white shirt, dark pants, neat haircut; could be anyone—was using the middle of the three urinals along the far wall. For a moment, a bit frantically, Kirk considered taking the elevator up to the next floor on the gamble that the restroom directly above this one would be unoccupied. But his need to clean up had grown urgent.

In here the bittersweet, astringent odor, apparently clinging to his clothes and flesh, was stronger than ever. He was mortified, though he didn't know why he should be, that this guy—probably a CPA or lawyer from one of the other professional offices in the building—would be able to tell from the smell of him what he'd been doing.

Over the continuing loud stream of piss against porcelain, without a glance over his shoulder or any other standard conversational opening, the man boomed, *"Women,* huh?" and roared with laughter.

Kirk felt his face redden and didn't answer. Taking a stance at the sink farthest away from the peeing man, which wasn't very far, he did his best to shield himself as he unzipped his fly, pulled his shirttail out, pushed down the elastic waistband of his shorts to expose his lower belly and pubic hair, stiff with hardened ejaculate and glossy with secretions from Gretchen. The odor was almost overpowering. Kirk moistened a handful of paper towels under hot water, but the liquid soap from the dispenser was cold and so the makeshift sponge was clammy and sent chilly rivulets down the insides of his thighs.

The man appeared behind him in the mirror, leering. Kirk, looking up to meet the reflected gaze, felt himself in mortal danger. He couldn't have said why; the eyes were ordinary brown, no more malevolent than most people's, and the man made no threatening moves. But, holding his limp penis in one hand and the ineffective wad of dripping, soapy paper towels in the other, Kirk was seized by the conviction that something of paramount importance to his life was at stake here, and that in some way he'd already lost.

"Women," the man observed again. "Can't live with 'em, can't live without 'em. Damn crazy system, if you ask me, which nobody did."

Kirk chuckled weakly, hoping the guy would just shut up and leave him alone.

"Can't live with 'em, can't shoot 'em." Boisterous guffaws and a hard slap on Kirk's shoulder.

"Right." Kirk felt compelled to agree, and had the uneasy feeling he was colluding in something other than what he intended.

"What are you gonna do, huh?" The man spread his hands helplessly, reasonably. "Shit, either you love her or you don't. And once you don't, you can't be expected to treat her as if you did. I mean, that would be dishonest." He grinned.

The guy must, of course, be talking about something out of his own life; he could not possibly know anything of Kirk's. In that case, maybe this morally degrading experience was more common than Kirk had realized; maybe he wasn't the only one who fell out of love as thunderously and thoroughly as in, and then was willing to do virtually anything to get free.

He dropped the wet towels into the trash and pulled another handful out of the dispenser to dry himself. The coarse paper stuck to the places still uncleaned, stinging the flesh, painfully pulling out a couple of hairs. When he winced and swore, the man guffawed.

"Asking if she'd put on weight was inspired." He clapped an insinuating comradely hand on Kirk's shoulder. The flesh and bone turned cold rather than warm under his pressure. "I've used that one a few times myself. Gets 'em every time, even if they haven't gained an ounce, and the beauty of it is you haven't actually made a statement you're responsible for—you've just asked a question."

Solace and justification were to be had here, moral absolution that Kirk recognized as slimy and dangerous but that, in a blinding and ephemeral split second, he chose to accept. Almost proudly, he nodded. The odor was causing vertigo, making his eyes water, his ears ring, his hands tremble.

He'd fumbled his clothes back more or less in order, except that his zipper seemed to be stuck. He tugged at it carefully, slid two fingers inside to check for cloth caught in the teeth. The man gave his shoulder a little shake, friendly, man-to-man. Considerably taller than he'd seemed at first, he was looking down over Kirk's head with evident and disconcerting interest. "Something else to try," he advised, the way you might offer a suggestion about a balky car or a complex accounting problem. "Find a way to make her feel just a tad cheap and dirty. Nothing obvious, you understand. Subtlety's the key here. Just enough to make her wonder."

"But she's not cheap and dirty."

The shoulder shake was not quite so benign this time. "So what? We're talking strategy here. You don't love her anymore, right? That's a given. You don't have control over that. But you *can* decide what to do about it. Here, let me do that." By the time Kirk had realized what was meant and had started to protest and pull away, or slug the guy in the teeth, the big hands had pushed around in front of him, freed his fly, zipped it up, patted his crotch the way ballplayers pat each other's asses, and let him go. In the mirror the man met Kirk's startled gaze and gave a jaunty wave. "Trust me," he said, and left the restroom.

When Kirk let himself back into the office suite, Gretchen, still naked, was sitting at his desk. Her breasts and shoulders were striped by sunlight through the horizontal pencil-thin slits in the window shade. She looked up and smiled, but before she could say anything he fairly shouted, "Don't sit there!" With an effort he lowered his voice, but the vehemence was undiminished. "That's a brand-new expensive chair! I don't want a wet spot on the upholstery!"

There was a beat of stunned silence. Then she said, "Jesus." She pushed herself back from the desk and stood up, arms crossed over her chest the way nude women do when they're feeling vulnerable, as though exposed nipples need more protection than any other private place.

Kirk kept his back to her while she put her clothes on, standing in front of the desk and busying himself with the papers in his "To Do" file. Very soon he heard her cross to the door and flip the lock, and then he turned toward her, feeling sadness and imminent relief in almost equal parts. She was carrying her suit jacket and pantyhose over her arm, having put on only what was necessary to cover herself, and her hair was disheveled. She looked, Kirk thought with a certain bittersweet detachment, like a woman coming off a midday rendez-vous, but there was no odor.

"You know," she said to him, "this was a shitty way to do it. You could have just told me it was over."

The instant the door closed behind her, Kirk crouched to inspect his desk chair. Indeed, the dove-gray seat was marred by a dark spot, quarter-sized, drying but not fading. Unwillingly visualizing the orifice out of which this moisture had seeped, he cursed.

He had no idea how to get the spot out. A bit desperately, he thought of calling Cecelia, the mother of his old girlfriend; he hadn't talked to her for a couple of years anyway, and she'd probably have some useful household hint for him. He'd have to come up with a nonincriminating description of the substance that had left the spot.

But he had Cecelia's number at home. Maybe he'd call her tonight. In the meantime, he'd do what he could on his own; if he left the spot untreated it might stain permanently. As he hurried back down the corridor to the restroom for more damp and soapy paper towels, it occurred to him to wonder if the big man would be in there again, and he found himself half-hoping he would.

Chapter Ten

Partial Detachment
(1992)

"It's her own stupid fault." Steadying the VCR while Tobias crawled behind the couch to unplug it, Tommy jerked his chin toward the big picture window that looked out over the backyard and the garden where Grandma Cecelia was working.

Every morning he'd been here, she was out there before he got up and didn't come in till it got too hot. Some mornings he was still asleep when she got done and came back inside, but today when Tobias had roused him it hadn't even been eight o'clock. Tommy yawned. That window didn't open, and the clunky old box fan on the kitchen floor was loud, but he could hear her whistling. He'd known some old ladies sang and some hummed, but he'd never expected one to whistle.

He'd helped her put in that garden, dug up the whole stupid thing for her and carried six or eight flats of little tomato plants out of the garage. That was before he'd even thought about moving into her funky basement apartment, so he hadn't had to help her out. That ought to count for something. She'd paid him, but still.

"I mean," he went on, to Tobias's heels and ass, "the door's not even locked. She's like, 'Come on, just rip me off.' " Grandma wouldn't much miss the VCR. She kept saying she ought to learn how to program it. All she used it for was to watch a movie once in a while, and even then half the time it didn't work right. He'd watched *Gone with the Wind* with her last week. That ought to count for something, too. She told him she'd seen it four times when she was his age. It was a *long* motherfucker. It wasn't all that bad.

Tobias said, his voice muffled, "Shit. That's the turntable. So many cords back here she's lucky the place hasn't burned down."

"So we're, like, doing her a favor getting rid of one, huh?" Tommy laughed, but now that he thought of it that could have some truth to it. When Tobias didn't answer and didn't come out, and there was no tug on the cord of the VCR he was getting tired of holding, Tommy thought he ought to point out, raising his voice, "Turntable's not worth much."

"No shit."

"Anyway, dude, you and me wouldn't even, like, know each other if it wasn't for her. She, like, brought us together, you know?" What he meant was that she was more or less responsible for the fact that they were ripping her off, but he didn't quite get around to saying that.

It hadn't been his idea to move in here. Grandma had suggested it to Dad, and Dad had apparently said no for a while before anybody'd bothered to mention it to Tommy. But then a couple of weeks ago things had gotten so bad between him and Dad and his bratty little schoolboy brother Luke that Grandma'd brought it up again and Dad had said okay and Tommy'd thought why not.

He hadn't known he was going to have a roommate. Tobias was kind of a weird guy, but he was kind of cool, too. Wouldn't be staying long, a night or two was all. There was a warrant out on him. Grandma said she'd known him his whole life and she'd do whatever she could to help him. Tommy shook his head in fresh wonderment. "Just go ahead and rip me off." Jesus.

The cord jerked loose, and the VCR tipped so Tommy about dropped it. Tobias crawled out from behind the couch. "God, smells *bad* back there. Cats must've been pissing on the rug."

"Grandma likes cats," Tommy allowed.

"Sneaky little bastards," Tobias muttered. "I

mean, it's not like they *care* about people."

Tommy caught a sudden whiff and wrinkled his nose fiercely since he couldn't scratch it. "Don't smell like cats to me."

Tobias was resting on his haunches, scanning the cluttered room. "She hasn't got much that's any good."

Tommy looked around, too, ready to defend his Grandma's taste. "TV?"

"Old and small and gets a lousy picture. I tried to watch the game yesterday. Piece of crap. You can tell she doesn't watch much. Ten bucks, tops. Not worth the hassle."

Tommy had noticed that his grandmother only turned on the TV when she had a show in mind to watch, which was hardly ever, and that she turned it off when the show was over. It was so quiet around here it gave him the creeps, like it was haunted or something. There was no TV in the basement apartment, even though she called it furnished, so he'd been spending more time with her than he would have otherwise.

"She got a camcorder or anything?" Tobias asked him.

"Polaroid." Tommy guffawed.

Tobias glanced at him as he got to his feet and straightened his baseball cap. "Every once in a while you say some word makes it obvious you weren't born American. You know that, bro?"

Tommy repeated the word slowly, clowning "Po-la-roid." Even he could hear it, not quite an accent but a kind of turning up at the edges of the syllables. He shrugged.

"That and the slanty eyes," Tobias added as he grabbed the microwave off the kitchen counter and started out the door with it to Cecelia's car in the driveway. She'd given Tommy the keys because he'd said he'd help Tobias get what he needed for his trip, which was the truth but not how she thought.

Tommy pressed his eyes into an exaggerated squint as he followed. Grandma'd told him she'd never used the microwave his Aunt Karen had given her for Christmas except once to dry out a roll of paper towels that had fallen in the sink, and they caught on fire and made a lot of smoke and the fire department came. The cord trailing between his legs made him stumble on the rag rug spread over the threshold, but he didn't drop the VCR.

"Born in Vietnam, huh? What's it like? You remember anything?"

"Nah." He did remember some things, but he didn't much feel like telling them at this particular moment, when he was helping some dude he barely knew rip off his grandmother, whom he loved.

"How old were you?"

"Six."

"I got a son six years old. Maybe he's seven. Lives with his mother back East. Toby. Tobias, Jr., after me, but he goes by Toby."

"Cool."

217

"Kid's been sick. Haven't had a chance to go see him for a while. Gotta go back there this time. Kid needs his real father when he's sick, you know?"

Tommy moved his shoulders in a way that could have been agreement or disagreement, both or neither. He definitely did not have an opinion about whether Tobias ought to go see his kid. "My cousin just had a baby," he offered, as if that had anything to do with anything.

"Your real cousin? In Nam?"

"My real cousin in Seattle. Jenny. My dad's cousin, actually, so what's that make her? Like, my second cousin or something?" Like most aspects of family relations, this was way too tangled for Tommy to think about for very long without getting lost in it.

Tobias was back to talking about his kid, which was pretty complicated, too, but at least didn't have anything to do with Tommy. "Cops'll look for me there, though. Sooner or later they'll make the connection with Cecelia, too, probably. Toby loves Cecelia. She writes to him, sends him stuff."

"They've already been here once."

"What are you talking about?" It was hard to tell his expression through the beard, and his voice was always the same.

"A couple of guys, like, came here asking questions about you. From parole or the FBI or someplace, cops anyway."

"When was this?"

"I don't know, like, last week sometime.

Grandma wasn't home and I told them I never heard of you, which was, like, the truth." He grinned.

"Shit, I gotta get out of here." The words pretended to be worried, but there was a shine in his eyes.

"Like, what'd you do, man?"

Tobias snorted. "Shit, what didn't I do? I don't live by the rules, man, that's what. They don't like it if you don't live by their rules."

Tommy nodded appreciatively. His dad didn't much like it, either. His dad was big on rules. Grandma Cecelia didn't seem to be.

They had tucked the VCR and the microwave into the trunk of the Subaru, and covered them with the blanket Grandma kept in there in case she ever got stranded in a snowstorm, when Tommy noticed some chick in the yard across the street. He didn't think she lived there. Grandma'd taken him over and introduced him to Mrs. Farris, a really old lady, old enough to be Grandma Cecelia's mother, which was almost older than Tommy could think about. Grandma'd said Mrs. Farris better know he belonged to somebody if he was going to be in the neighborhood for a while.

Maybe this chick was Mrs. Farris's granddaughter or something, visiting. Great-granddaughter or something. Or maybe she didn't belong to anybody around here and was just walking by. She didn't exactly seem to be watching them, but Tommy had the feeling she'd noticed them and knew exactly what they were doing, which made him nervous and ready to be either proud or ashamed of himself depending how things went, like having stage fright.

She looked a little older than he was, a little younger than Tobias, twenty-three, maybe, or -four. Lots of hair, long and black and out around her face so her head looked bigger than normal. Even from here, her boobs showed pointy through her white T-shirt, and her tight blue-jean shorts made a V at her crotch that drew Tommy's eyes like a light bulb in a dark room. His sudden hard-on made him hoot and grab himself.

Arranging the stuff in the trunk, Tobias was still going on about Tommy's life story, as if it had something to do with him, as if he had a point to prove. "So she's not your real grandmother, any more than she's my aunt. I just always called her that."

"Yeah, she is."

They'd had this conversation before, ten minutes after Tobias had showed up and Grandma Cecelia had introduced the two of them. "This is Tobias Werner, Twyla and Henry's boy. Your grandpa and I were friends with his parents before he and his sister Kim were born. Kimberly Ann, like flowing water, isn't that a pretty name? And Tobias Henry. I've never known anybody else named Tobias, except your Toby. Tobias has a little boy named Tobias Henry, Jr. Tobias, Sr., needs a place to stay for a night or two and I said he could have the spare bedroom down here. You don't mind, do you, Tomt? This is my grandson Tomt." Grandma always called him Tomt, and he knew that when she said his brother Luke's name she was thinking Luc, not the American Luke.

She'd hardly shut the door behind her when Tobias had said, like a challenge, "Now wait a minute. No offense, but you're black, man. Cecelia can't be your real grandmother."

"Black and, like, Vietnamese, actually. Her son Dennis is my dad." Seeing that Tobias was trying to make sense of it—did he remember Dennis? Had Dennis married some black-Vietnamese chick or something?—Tommy had added, though it seemed stupid to have to, "I'm, like, adopted."

"You're adopted," Tobias insisted now. "Dennis is not your real dad. I'm a dad, I know about this shit. How old are you?"

"Twenty. Why?"

Tobias nodded as if he'd won something. "I'm six years older than you are. I've known her six years longer than you have."

"Go fuck yourself," Tommy suggested, more or less good-naturedly.

"She's not your real grandmother. Any more than she's my Aunt Cecelia. I just call her that."

"She is too real. Hell, she's not, like, fake, you know what I'm saying? She's not plastic." Tommy laughed. He didn't quite have the words to say what he meant, and he didn't quite want to, any-

221

way. He didn't even really know what this contest was about.

Tobias seemed about to argue some more, but a different thought occurred to him instead. "I bet she's got cash in books. Old ladies always hide money in books, don't ask me why. Like you'd never think to look there."

"She's got a lot of books," Tommy nodded. "She always, like, read to us."

Tobias didn't look at him, but Tommy saw him scowl, eyebrows thick as his beard. "Yeah, so? She used to read to us, too. Big deal."

They went back inside. Absently, Tommy massaged his groin. He glanced out the picture window and saw Grandma still on her knees in the garden, her head bent. He didn't hear her whistling now, but she might be. Tobias stood in front of the dusty bookcase, hands behind his back, considering it. "So which one's her favorite?"

Without even thinking about it, Tommy told him, "Poetry."

Tobias said impatiently, "Man, there's a whole shelf of poetry. Which ones? I gotta get on the road."

Tommy took down a skinny blue volume. Emily Dickinson. He remembered the name. He didn't remember any of the poems much—something about being a nobody and proud of it; something about a snake wrinkling. But the feel of the dust jacket, sort of powdery, was a pleasant memory. The book smelled weird now; must be because it was old, or because his grandmother wasn't much for housecleaning. He'd always liked that about her. He riffled the pages twice, from front to back and then the other way, but no bills fell out, making him feel like a loser in front of Tobias.

Tobias was jerking books off the shelves, shaking them by the spines, and dropping them on the floor. For some reason, that bothered Tommy, and he turned his back and moved over to the window so he wouldn't have to watch it. "Hey," Tobias said, "I remember this one," but Tommy didn't care and Tobias didn't tell him what it was or read from it or anything. He wondered what his grandmother was doing out there. From this angle, he could see her twisting her head back and forth, up and down. Her hands in their pink gardening gloves stayed in the dirt around the tomato plants. Maybe she'd got dirt in her eye, or maybe there was a bee flying around her face. The way he used to count telephone poles and lines in the road and steps and drips from a faucet and windows in the school building, especially when he'd first come to this country, now Tommy counted seven ripe tomatoes on plants she could reach from where she knelt, and the basket by her knee was half full. He felt disrespectful, almost, to be thinking of his grandmother having knees and, worse, hips.

"Bingo!" Reluctantly, Tommy looked over his shoulder. Dropping with a nasty thud a leather-bound book lettered in gold, Tobias held up three bills, too crisp to flutter. "Three c-notes. Not bad, huh?"

"Cool," Tommy said.

"Probably forgot which book she put 'em in. Probably forgot she even put 'em in a book. They were in the Shakespeare sonnets." He threw his head back and spread the hand with the money in it over his heart. " 'Thou art more lovely than a summer's day.' " When he dropped the pose, he kept his hand over his heart. "Probably doesn't even remember she had this cash. Won't even miss it."

Tommy couldn't quite get a handle on his feeling that this wasn't right. All he could think to say was a vague "I don't know—"

Tobias shrugged. "Suit yourself. All I can tell you is I had a lady friend once who took money from her grandmother and she says the cops wouldn't even take a report because it was family. So it's not really stealing, right?"

It crossed Tommy's mind again to point out that Tobias wasn't family, but it was too much hassle. He started across the room, vaguely thinking to claim his share of the loot. She was *his* grandmother, after all. When she died, he'd inherit something, so in a way all this stuff was his already.

He thought he heard her calling him. Probably needed him to help her carry a bag of compost or dig in the garden. Tommy was the kind of person who didn't mind helping out when he could.

Tobias stuffed the bills in his shirt pocket and

headed out the door. "Catch you later, bro. Have a nice life."

"Hey," Tommy objected, following.

The chick with the hair had come over and was leaning on Grandma Cecelia's Subaru like one of those old-time TV commercials where sexy women were draped over hoods. His dick was pressing out against his zipper again, a pleasurable discomfort, and Tommy could see why those commercials would sell cars. He heard Tobias say, "Well, hi there."

"Going my way?" he heard the girl say back.

"No doubt," Tobias acknowledged, and they both laughed.

Her hair wasn't black, but brown, and not even especially dark, so Tommy didn't know why he'd thought it was black in the first place. When he came out onto the porch and saw her standing next to Tobias, just down at the end of the driveway so you wouldn't think the perspective would be that different, she looked short, but when he got next to her she was taller than he was. "You know each other?"

Tobias said, "Not yet," at the same time she said something Tommy didn't quite catch that sounded like, "From the inside out."

Now she leaned up against Tommy. Her perfume was so strong he imagined how it would feel in his hands, what shape and bulk it would have, and instead of being flowery or musky it had a sharp smell that Tommy found almost painfully erotic. It reminded him of the smell he'd noticed when Tobias had been unplugging Grandma Cecelia's VCR, and he wondered if this girl had been around somewhere then, maybe standing outside an open window watching them. It did seem to him that she knew more than she ought to, or that she was more involved in this thing with Grandma than she ought to be, or that she had been in his life or Tobias's life or Grandma Cecelia's sometime before. "Well," she murmured to him, in an insinuating way, aren't *you* a cutie. You coming, too, honey?"

He said, "I guess."

From inside the house, Grandma Cecelia called, "Tomt? Where are you?" She must have come in the back door. By now she must have noticed the missing VCR and microwave and the books dumped on the floor. Tommy panicked a little, half-turned away from the girl, not exactly wanting to get away from her but out of a vague impulse not to stay so close to her, either, not to actually touch her yet. It was her odor, her perfume or whatever it was, that confused him. Suddenly he thought that no matter what he did he'd be making a decision, allying himself with her if he let her keep pressing her hip into his groin, ruining any shot he might have with her if he actually pushed her away. So he just sort of inched back, not making a choice one way or another, his head pleasantly full of her aroma and his belly churning with it, as if he'd toked bad weed.

Tobias said, "Let's get out of here."

The girl tugged at Tommy's hand, and he took two steps with her toward the driver's door. "Let's go, Tommy."

"I don't know," he said, shaking his head not so much to clear it as to keep the high going.

"You're part of this, too," she said, and, to seal it, bent her face to kiss him. Her lips tasted the way she smelled; she must have lipstick and perfume to match. The thought struck Tommy funny, and he chuckled while her mouth was still on his, so that he was taking in the taste of her while he laughed and then while he tried to stop laughing.

"Shit, man, drive or give me the damn keys." Tobias stretched his arm across the car roof and commandingly flexed his fingers.

Proud of himself for doing the right thing here, Tommy said, "Like, count me out. She's my grandma," and dropped the car keys into Tobias's hand. Tobias snapped his fingers shut around them and jerked his fist up as if he were tossing them triumphantly in the air, but never actually let go of them. The girl yelped in disappointment and gave Tommy's cheek a little slap, playful but stinging.

Grandma Cecelia came out the screen door onto the porch. She was holding her head funny, tipped to the right as if she couldn't quite see around something, and her hands fumbled with the door frame, the back of a patio chair. "Tommy?" She sounded not quite sure he was there, and sort of scared. "Tobias? I need one of you to take me to the eye doctor right away. I can't see to drive. It's a good thing you boys are here."

Tobias snorted, "What'd you do, forget an appointment?"

"No, something's wrong. The doctor says it sounds like a detached retina and I have to get in right away or I could lose vision in that eye."

Tommy looked at Tobias. It wasn't up to him; Tobias had the keys now. After a minute, Tobias said softly, "Shit."

Tommy asked, "Does it, like, hurt?"

Her head moved from side to side like a bobber on a fishing line. "Just all of a sudden there's a green globe in the right half of the field of vision in my right eye. Like those pictures of the earth taken from space? Bluish-green? Half a sphere?"

She had her arms crossed in front of her and was plucking at the shoulders of her cotton shirt as if she had on a sweater she could pull snug around her. She sounded more surprised and interested than anything else. Grandma Cecelia was interested in *everything*; it could be really irritating. Still, when Tommy went to her and clumsily put his hand under her forearm, he felt how tense she was. "Cool," he muttered, meaning that the green sphere was cool, hoping she didn't think he meant whatever was wrong with her eyes was cool but not searching very hard for the words to make his meaning clear.

She looked right at him and he didn't see anything green in her right eye. "There was a bright flash of light, too."

"Cool. Like that rocket ship that blew up."

"Tomt, there were people on that rocket ship. It wasn't a Fourth of July display, you know." Her eyes had hardened. Still nothing round and green; maybe she was making this up. He had other memories about bright flashes of light, okay? But they were from before he'd had words or a TV to watch it on. What did she want from him?

The chick had fixed Tobias with a hard stare. She didn't say anything out loud, but she was mouthing words and shaking her head vigorously, slicing her hands through the air in "no no" gestures and pointing toward the trunk where Grandma Cecelia's ripped-off stuff was. Why should she care, Tommy wondered. What reason did she have for getting out of here in a hurry?

Cecelia, who obviously could see some, said, "Tommy can take me?"

Tommy said, dropping her arm and sidling back behind her, "He's, like, got the keys."

For some reason, Tobias said to Cecelia, "This is my friend Lila," and the girl grinned, shrugged, nodded. Certain that Tobias didn't know her name and was making this up, Tommy frowned at "Lila" because it didn't fit her. He'd been thinking her name might be Binh, which was also stupid since she was white. Looking at her now, though, over his grandmother's shoulder and more or less out of the corner of his eye so as not to risk meeting her gaze directly, he saw something about her that made him think she could be part Vietnamese, and Binh, a name from his past somewhere, was a good name for her whether it was really her name or not. There was an "h" on the end of it. He remembered that.

"Nice to meet you," she said in Cecelia's general direction. Her fake sincerity, the total lack of sarcasm in her tone, made it obvious to Tommy just how much she was dissing them all, but maybe his grandmother didn't catch it. "The boys and I were just leaving. We're in kind of a hurry. Couldn't you call a cab? We'll give you money." Tobias frowned.

Cecelia protested, sounding more confused than pissed off. "I have money. I always keep a little extra hidden for emergencies. But I can't wait for a taxi. Tobias will take me." She moved away from Tommy, who thought about pointing out that he hadn't *said* he wouldn't take her.

For some dumb reason he found himself thinking about his scrapbooks, two sets of them, one kept for him by his father and one by his grandmother, starting when he was six and, for all he knew, still going on. School report cards, valentines he'd made for other people and gotten himself, ticket stubs from plays and concerts most of which he didn't remember but some he did. There were things in one that weren't in the other, which was kind of weird, but what was weirder was when the same thing was in both—the same trip; the same birthday party—but represented by different stuff, so it seemed like two different events. There was nothing to represent Vietnam. Vietnam just was. Idly, Tommy wondered where the scrapbooks were. Idly, too, he mused about what might go in them to represent and remind him of today.

Trailing her hand along the side of the car until she ran into the door handle, Grandma Cecelia got into the front passenger seat and fastened her seatbelt. When she looked up from the buckle, tilting and bobbing her head, Tommy saw that she was crying. Not sobbing, but her face was scrunched up and wet with tears. "What'll I do if I can't see?"

The girl was between Tommy and Tobias now, one arm around each of them, and Tommy's thoughts were thoroughly muddled by her smell, by the heat and pressure of her body against his, by the tones and rhythms of her voice. This was pretty much his normal state of mind only more so.

She was concentrating on Tobias, massaging Tommy's hip to let him know she hadn't forgotten about him but looking at Tobias and talking about the situation Tobias was in. Tommy guessed she considered him already a lost cause, at least for this time, and he was proud of that even as he couldn't bring himself to break free of her one-armed embrace. "You've got to think about yourself. You've got to think about Toby. He's sick. He needs his dad."

Tommy got distracted trying to remember whether she'd been around when Tobias had mentioned his kid, and then Tobias was saying, "Shit" again, slamming open the driver's door, and practically throwing himself behind the wheel, knocking his baseball cap sideways. Not to be left behind now that the decision had been made, Tommy hastened to get in, too, sitting in the back seat alone. He'd barely shut the door before Tobias gunned it in reverse and they shot backward out of the driveway.

"Slow down, Tobias. You don't want a speeding ticket on top of everything else. It's not *that* much of an emergency."

Grandma tried to laugh, but Tommy could tell she was majorly upset now.

They passed Binh or Lila or whatever her name was walking along the road. The bright sunshine turned her hair almost blond, and Tommy had to turn around in his seat and look twice to be sure it was the same chick. She looked heavier, too, but that could just be because she'd put on a red sweatshirt over the T-shirt; it was definitely her. He waved and Tobias honked, but she didn't do anything to show she recognized them or realized they recognized her. At first Tommy thought neither one of them would probably ever see her again, and he was sort of sorry about that, but mostly he was relieved. Then he had the feeling, more like a seeping odor than an actual thought, that he'd seen her before and he'd see her again, and that also made him both sorry and relieved. He took his first deep breath since she'd showed up, and, though it felt good going into his lungs, it also made him cough.

Grandma asked suddenly, her voice choked and too loud, "Will you come to see me if I move to a nursing home?"

"What are you talking about?" Tobias sounded pissed. "You've got—what? Five kids."

"They have their own lives. I'd never impose like that. I remember when my grandfather lived with us—" She was talking too much and too fast, sort of breathlessly, as if she was either high or panicky. Tommy bet on panicky.

"Oh, for Chrissake." Tobias swerved around the station wagon he'd been tailgating and lay on the horn. "It's just your eye. Chill."

But Grandma wasn't done. "Will you still love me if I'm blind?"

The query and the silence that followed it were shocking. For a minute Tommy had no clue what she meant. Then, when he did understand, he was so profoundly embarrassed by his grandmother's extravagant need that all he could manage to mumble was, "Sure."

Tobias, though, declared out loud, glancing sideways at her for longer than he should have in traffic, "Aunt Cecelia, we love you no matter what happens," and reached across the gear shift for her hand. The rest of the way to the doctor, Tommy gazed at their clasped hands, framed by the bucket seats where the only way not to see them would have been to keep his eyes shut.

233

Chapter Eleven

Magnolias
(1994)

The Mississippi River was brown and wide. The phrase played in her mind to a blues riff; probably you'd have to live here a while before you could think of the Mississippi without wanting to hum or wail. In another life, she'd have an apartment above a sleazy bookstore in the Quarter and be the first white great-grandmother to play jazz sax on Bourbon Street.

"Across the Mississippi," Dottie Frasier mused beside her, all but singing, too.

"What do you suppose it would be like to ride this ferry across the Mississippi to New Orleans every day, like that guy over there with the lunch-box?"

"I guess you'd get used to it," Dottie said, and Cecelia nodded, but neither of them believed it for a minute.

A sudden strong sense of kinship made Cecelia yearn to pat Dottie's hand, beside hers on the rail-ing; she restrained herself only out of hard-earned doubt that such a gesture would be welcomed. She herself would have been more than pleased if Dot-tie'd reached for her in that way, but the fact that people didn't do that was one of the sad mysteries of life.

The guy with the lunchbox had turned his head in their direction as if he'd heard them talking about him. Of average build, probably swarthy-skinned Caucasian though he could be Hispanic or even light-skinned black, he had no distinguishing features, and Cecelia wondered why she'd noticed him in the first place. If later she were called as a witness to something, she wouldn't be able to de-scribe him: Was his shirt blue or gray? Was his billed cap a baseball cap, and for what team? Was that beard stubble on his cheeks and neck or just gritty shadows?

He started toward them with an air of expec-tancy, and she braced herself, eager and wary. Then the look on his face changed to disappointment, maybe, and surprise, as though he'd realized they weren't who he'd thought they were or they weren't about to do what he'd anticipated. As he went on past, just moving to the other side of the deck, he kept his eyes on them, turning his head as far around as it would go like a pirouetting dancer maintaining balance. He, or maybe his lunchbox, had a pungent odor that stung Cecelia's nose; she couldn't identify it—fish? cheese? body odor, his or someone else's?—and she was glad when he elbowed his way through the crowd and was out of range of her sight and smell.

Louisiana in October wasn't hot, but it was muggy, and Cecelia was sweating uncomfortably though she needed her light sweater. Above the water and bleeding into it, the air was wide and brown, too, and wet. They might have been traveling through either element, water or air. Another ferry, soft brown and soundless from here though not very far away, was where the horizon would have been if the air and the water had been more differentiated.

The rest of the handful of people from the Class of '34 who'd come to this reunion clustered on the deck, a couple of them standing awkwardly, most rather precariously on the backless and armless wooden benches. Turning to regard them again, Cecelia thought there was something pleasing about the look of them, herself included, about how they were all old now, really old, soon to be eighty. At the thirtieth reunion, even at the fortieth, they'd all been middle-aged. At the fifth, they'd all been young. For some reason, that progression through time, probably one of the few things most of the classmates had in common by now, struck her as sweet and very nice.

She supposed she oughtn't to be surprised that, after sixty years, attendance was so sparse. There'd been only fifty-two in the graduating class in the first place, and only twelve had come to the fiftieth in 1984 in Carey Jennes's barn.

But, truth to tell, she'd have found the low attendance less depressing if more had been dead. Alice Bennemann, by now a one-woman committee, for the first time this year had separated the "Deceased" page from the rest of the Class Notes, and only fourteen were listed on it.

Orville Herman had been the first, drowned on graduation night, the other three teenagers in the boat with him soaked and sobered but only Orville unable to make it to shore. At the time and for a few years afterward—Cecelia had still been hearing it at the fifth reunion, but she thought not at the tenth—there'd been gossip that the accident had been caused by Marcelline Campinella's forceful objection to Orville's pass. Everybody'd known Marcelline was hopelessly sweet on Fred Buchtel, who was out that night with a girl from another school, but Orville had been just foolish and bull-headed enough for the story to be plausible. Marcelline never came to reunions and never sent information; at one time Fred had been living in Alaska, but he hadn't kept in touch.

Several boys had been killed in the war—only in the context of high school did Cecelia think of

World War II as "the war," as though there'd been no others worth attention before or since. She hadn't known any of the dead soldiers well enough to grieve, which, looking back, seemed slightly preposterous in such a small class. There'd been cancer and heart attacks and car accidents, other than the war no foul play as far as she knew. She didn't know how Lurleen Simpson had died, which did make her mournful; she and Lurleen had been best friends all through school. Regular correspondence had taken years to dwindle to Christmas cards with multi-page newsy letters and then years again to trickle down to mere signatures under "Have a happy new year!"—the exclamation point intended to convey sincere if increasingly ill-informed and impersonal well-wishing.

In these last ten years, two more class members were gone. Sam Dinsmore had "succumbed after a long illness"; Harriet Caldwell Jensen "after a short illness." Re-reading Alice's updates as she'd bitten into a powdered-sugar beignet at the Cafe du Monde earlier today, Cecelia had been unable to repress a moue of frustration. Especially at a reunion, it *mattered* how people had died for the same reasons it mattered how they'd lived. The omitted details bothered her like a button missing from a cuff, something allowed to dangle, something left flapping open that should have been closed.

The absence, then, of the other thirty-two could only be explained as one form or another of rejection. Plain lack of interest, maybe, or interest too pallid to motivate a trip to New Orleans. Misplaced shame, if you thought you hadn't succeeded when you'd been predicted most likely to do so, or had stayed in the less-than-glorious ruts everybody'd expected you to. Nursed grudges, chips still on shoulders after all this time. Some had sent regrets, which Alice had passed along: Several had health problems that Cecelia wished had been specified; a couple had declared, maybe indignantly, that they were just too old to travel so far; this one, maybe huffily, pointed out the limitations of a fixed income; this one had obligations at church every October. Whatever the excuses, they weren't good enough.

A horn cooed like a dove, from this ferry or the other one. There didn't seem to be any reaction to it from anyone on either boat or from shore, and there was no apparent reason to communicate anything, so Cecelia couldn't guess the purpose of the horn, unless it was purely decorative.

Jack Purcell, still burly and sweaty, and tuft-haired (formerly bushy-haired) Maury Cooke were recounting the same stories from high school they'd told at the fiftieth, fortieth, thirtieth, and twenty-fifth, at least, and Francie Steiger Bundtzen's husband Cal, who'd gone to school in Jackson, was once again chiming in. Their voices were somewhat less hearty than they used to be, and Maury wheezed, but they still guffawed, slapped their knees, punched each other's shoulders, interrupted each other. Volume rising with their collective excitement, their memories of recounting these stories before were as much fun, Cecelia suspected, as memories of the events themselves, and as the original events themselves had been.

Every tale had to do with cars and drinking. The steering wheel coming off in Jack's hands, his pantomimed shock and hissed "Ho-ly Shit!" more burlesque with each retelling. The sheriff forcing Maury and "some girl"—every time, Cecelia fleetingly amused herself by wondering who—to lead him to the homemade brew stashed in Maury's father's shed, which the sheriff had confiscated for the purpose, Maury was still convinced, of himself tying one on. Playing chicken on the back roads, boys from their school in one car and boys from Jackson in the other, some in the rumble seats, some on the running boards; Alice reminded them again about the kid whose leg had been crushed and had to be amputated and eventually he'd died, what was his name? Again this sobered them, but not for long. Nobody, including Cecelia, remembered his name; he hadn't been in their class.

Tired of waiting for a break in the talk long enough to cut in, Cecelia observed over them, "Some things never change, do they?" Francie—Fran now, but Cecelia made no real effort to remember that—reacted as if she'd been interrupted and didn't know what Cecelia meant. But Dottie caught her eye and grinned. Just like sixty years ago, the boys performed and the girls, in the same circle, were cheerleaders—listened, laughed, even applauded now and then, exchanged forebearing looks, inserted a civilizing comment now and then. Maybe, Cecelia thought hopefully, this is a characteristic of class reunions and not really an indicator of who we are. Her daughter had described practically the same scene at the first class reunion she'd attended, the main reason it would be the last. What had boys talked about to prove their manhood before there were automobiles? In her parents' generation, not so long ago, had they exchanged reckless boasts about horses?

The brown wide water was thick, muddy, folding rather than rippling. The other ferry inched past them, trailing a sluggish wake. There was no acknowledgment by one boat of the other, no tooting horns now when there'd have been an obvious purpose, no calls or salutes from either deck.

Cecelia was very glad Dottie Frasier was one of the diehard reunion attendees, and regarded this as further evidence, however oblique, of the incipient kinship between them. They'd been together all through school, so it was a good seventy years that she'd been trying and failing to get to know Dottie better, and success always seemed just around the corner of the next discussion topic, just over the next discovered hill of shared values or experience. In the latest Class Notes, Dottie's "Favorite High School Memory," something about winning a regional volleyball championship, had admittedly been discouraging, for Cecelia had been totally oblivious to volleyball. But still she was drawn to the small, wiry, always unescorted woman, and determined to make a real connection with her before the reunions petered out altogether or one of them died.

Cecelia was all but certain Dottie Frasier was lesbian. The idea pleased her inordinately, which, she admitted to herself, would not be the case if she really accepted homosexuality. Over the years she'd twice brought up the possibility, once to Ray, who refused to come to these things with her anyway and so would never meet Dottie, and once, after the twenty-fifth reunion when the world had changed enough that you could put such things into words, to Lurleen.

To Ray she'd announced excitedly, "Guess what? I think one of my classmates is a lesbian!"

He'd rolled his eyes in disgusted, lascivious amusement. "Why? She make a pass at you?" Vastly pleased by his own joke, he'd teased her for days, and nothing from her could get him to stop— not anger, not tears, not calm statement of what she needed, not her retort (which, at least in part, she meant when she said it) that she half-wished Dottie *had* made a pass, not because she had any erotic feelings toward the woman but because it would have been *something*. Only his own boredom finally put an end to it, and that was the dawn of Cecelia's realization that Ray's boredom had become—maybe always had been—the defining force in their marriage. When Ray was bored, things changed. When he wasn't, they didn't.

Of Lurleen, who might know, she'd inquired flat out, "Is Dottie Frasier a lesbian?"

Lurleen wouldn't meet her gaze. "Heavens, I don't think so." It was apparent she'd already thought of it.

"I bet she is."

"Why would you even think of a thing like that?"

From Lurleen's offended tone, Cecelia had known herself to be in trouble, and when she'd put her impressions into a spoken list they'd sounded specious and prejudicial even to her. "Well, she always wore boys' clothes and cut her hair short. Remember how they tried to get her to wear dresses? She's never been married. She's lived with another woman for years—you said they own a house together. They take vacations together. She used to play a lot of sports. She's always had a certain walk, a certain way of talking."

She'd expected scoffing or chiding. Instead, after a rather long pause punctuated by the clipped sounds of whatever household chore she'd been occupying herself with, Lurleen had sighed unhappily. "Well, I surely do hope you're wrong. Because I really like and admire Dottie, and if you were right I wouldn't be able to anymore."

"But—but, Lurleen." Cecelia had been shocked. In light of this terrible responsibility, she'd been uncertain whether she ought to argue or to let it go. "But, Lurleen, why couldn't it work the other way? If somebody you like and admire turned out to be homosexual, maybe it could make you think differently about homosexuality instead of differently about the person." But Lurleen had been shaking her head in fierce warning, and the subject had been thunderously dropped.

"I guess we're docked," Dottie said now, peering toward what apparently was, for crossings in this direction, the front of the ferry—the bow, maybe, or the prow.

Cecelia'd felt no jolt, and the motion of the ferry had been so lugubrious that she hadn't noticed it stopping. "How can you tell?"

"Everybody's getting off," Dottie pointed out reasonably, and they both giggled—like, Cecelia thought happily, schoolgirls. She'd have loved to link arms, but didn't dare; she did, though, stay close behind Dottie so they'd be walking together when they stepped onto land. The man with the lunchbox was standing off to the side and Cecelia found herself thinking, oddly, that he was waiting for them, or waiting for something to happen that had to do with them. His odor was thick as fog; not altogether unpleasant, though she thought it should be, it had a definite if invisible shape to it as they passed through.

A gravel road curved away from the river around an official-looking building that made Cecelia wonder if this little place might be the parish seat. Knowing the term was "parish" rather than "county" made her feel positively cosmopolitan. The road became a street, paved but barely, with the haphazard sidewalks and random plantings of a pleasantly rundown small town.

The three men and Francie had bunched up just ahead, and Alice was hastening toward them while glancing worriedly back at Cecelia and Dottie. Cecelia liked it that they'd look as if they were walking together, which was true only technically and by happenstance, and deliberately ambling in order to talk, although the fact was that she, at least, could hardly go any faster anymore.

Maury boomed, as if Alice were much farther away or as if he wanted to make his disdain known to the world, "Hey, Miss Alice, you're the tour guide. Where do we go from here?"

Even from behind, it was obvious that Alice was wringing her hands, a gesture familiar from high school although otherwise she didn't look like the same person at all, was even, Cecelia would have sworn, a good six inches shorter. She thought about saying something to Dottie about Alice, but they heard her exclaim, mouselike, "Oh, my, I don't know! I just thought the ferry ride would be fun."

Maury chuckled and the other three in his group joined in, Francie simultaneously frowning to show she wasn't to be lumped in with this silly female. "It *was* fun," Cecelia declared as they caught up.

"Let's just walk around," Dottie agreed. "See what's here." Cecelia tried to catch her eye and exchange a comradely smile, but Dottie had already started off, striding, swinging her arms as if on a playing field. Cecelia noted fondly, as she had at every reunion, that Dottie still had the square, confident stance of a lifelong athlete; it wasn't difficult to imagine her in aerobics and yoga classes, probably not even for senior citizens. Cecelia would have given a good deal to know what, if anything, Dottie was noting about her—the occasional arthritic stiffness in her hip and knee? the way she tilted her head to see things outside her peripheral vision? the pound a year she'd gained since high school?

Reunions weren't by any means the only situations in which Cecelia found herself caring more about relationships than anybody else gave evidence of doing. In fact, during most periods of her life—this one prominent among them—she'd be hard-pressed to think of a relationship that was truly mutual. Her nearby children couldn't be said to neglect her, would be there in a heartbeat if she needed anything, and hardly ever turned her invitations down, but none of them shared her craving for closeness. Virginia was the exception; she couldn't be counted on in an emergency, and she longed for intimacy, too.

Once in a while, somebody made an effort to get or stay in touch with her, but this was rare and usually baffling. One of her daughters' old boyfriends, for instance, over the years since he and Karen had broken up had sent her occasional postcards and now occasional e-mail messages; Cecelia had no idea what he wanted from her, but it certainly wasn't anything she would call friendship.

When, meeting someone new, she felt the little spurt of hope—*"Yes! This could be a friend"*—she nearly always made the first move, the first several moves. Her granddaughter Jenny, Phil's girl whom Cecelia hadn't seen since she was a child and then no more than once a year, had recently moved with her husband and two-year-old into Cecelia's basement apartment. Something was wrong there. Jenny wasn't stern and sharp-tongued like her father, and she seemed to have everything gonig for her—good job, good marriage to a good man, beautiful child. But not far underneath her bright surface were Phil's bitterness and contemptuous boredom, and she hardly seemed to notice little Dylan, who, Cecelia thought, had a funny look in his eye. He was in day care ten hours a day. He hardly got home before it was bedtime. Cecelia was worried, and intrigued. They were family. They lived in her house. She wanted to get to know them better. She'd been considering taking down some of this year's peaches, but that might be too forward.

People she'd known forever, such as Twyla Werner, almost never called but acted glad to hear from her when she did.

Seldom were her e-mail messages not replies or dinner invitations not reciprocations; when even those didn't come, she *really* didn't know what to think, because the few times she'd had the courage to point out that lack of response could be read as lack of interest, the offenders had pleaded I've-been-so-busy, I-think-about-you-a-lot, don't-take-it-personally. It was, of course, precisely the *im*personality that bothered her.

Though Dottie's small pointed face wasn't animated, she was looking around at the pastel houses and pale autumn gardens. Cecelia chafed. What did she have to put forth that might get Dottie's attention? Her vision problems? But they were minimal, and wouldn't bear much scrutiny. Her failed marriage? Tawdry; boring even to her, unless she included sleeping with Ray after the divorce, which she didn't think she would. Her involvement in the peace movement, the encirclement of Rocky Flats, the march on the State Capitol to protest the death penalty? She was proud of that, but as a conversational gambit it was risky: Dottie might disapprove of her politics, she might disapprove of Dottie's, and then where would they be?

She could talk about her children. You were expected to talk about your children at reunions. She could come up with succinct, high-concept, reductionist descriptions to make them interesting to Dottie, like pitching a movie idea. The erstwhile hippie daughter turned housewife *in extremis*. The twins, one a Vietnam veteran and one an expatriate in Vancouver. The eldest, whom she knew so little she'd have to make up a thumbnail sketch whole cloth, unless what she talked about was knowing him so little. The youngest, Ginger, a schizophrenic poet who sometimes demanded more intimacy than Cecelia could supply or tolerate and sometimes scarcely could make out what a mother was among all the other objects, animate and inanimate, that constantly vied for her attention.

She considered. The temptation was strong to tell Dottie about Ginger, as a kind of offering. But that would be disrespectful, and cheating.

From the Class Notes she knew Dottie had nieces, nephews, grand-nieces and -nephews important enough for her to have listed under "Family." If they'd been children and grandchildren, asking after them would have seemed natural and normal. "I see you have nieces and nephews and their children living nearby," was the best she could do, chagrined by her own clumsiness.

Dottie smiled and nodded. "They're great," she said, warmly but not very forthcomingly.

After a moment, Cecelia pressed. "Did I count five grands?"

"Six. Four grand-nephews and two grand-nieces. And one on the way."

"That's wonderful. Congratulations." *Tell me more*, she was silently urging. *Tell me what it's like to be a beloved aunt and great-aunt instead of a mother, grandmother, great-grandmother. Tell me about your life.*

Dottie said, "Thanks," and nothing more. They continued along this pale Louisiana street in a silence that might or might not be companionable.

Schizophrenia allowed Cecelia a measure of ease with Virginia that she could achieve fleetingly at best with anyone else. She'd accepted—albeit long after her daughter's peculiarities had become undeniable, notwithstanding occasional relapses into hope and despair—that Virginia was quite impervious and, for all her ritualized behavior, quite unpredictable, so she didn't try anymore to figure this daughter out. Whatever Virginia was, she was; whatever Cecelia touched in her, she touched.

But over everyone else important or potentially important in her life, Cecelia stewed. Did Twyla's silences mean she'd just as soon not hear from her? Since nobody in the family appeared even aware of traditions precious to Cecelia—baking complicated fruit-filled Christmas cookies, planting tulips in fall and pansies in very early spring, dancing in the kitchen to Mozart on NPR among dancing rainbows from the prism in the window—was she to infer that such things mattered only to her and quit imposing? Should she keep reaching out to Jenny, or, much as it pained her, risk letting that potential go unrealized? Was there a subject she should broach with Dottie—families, flowers, homosexuality—that would break through and make them friends at last?

Looking for guidance from Dear Abby, Ann Landers, Miss Manners, she'd come to the conclusion that no one else had precisely her dilemma, and she'd never had the nerve to write in herself. A few times during their marriage she'd consulted Ray about it; impatient that she even concerned herself with such silliness, he had, though, said once, like a ruby he hadn't quite meant to give her but hadn't taken back, "You're the heart of this family, Celia. You're the soul."

She could see that unrequitedness was a theme of her life, and had not much hope of putting it to rest. Besides, she got intermittent reinforcement, the kind behavioral psychologists considered most effective: Ray's long-ago soul-of-the-family comment, or a long missive in January from someone to whom she'd been sending Christmas cards as if into a void, or the letters and peculiar little gifts that intermittently arrived from Twyla's sick little grandson, a relationship she cherished even more since his father, whom she'd known all his life, had also written to her from jail—once; no response after that to any of her letters.

Again after this reunion, she could foresee already, she'd restrain herself until Christmas, when she'd draft and re-draft notes chatty but short that to her seemed restricted nearly to the point of secrecy yet risked being too confessional. Some classmates wouldn't respond at all, and unhappily she'd visualize their distaste. From others she'd get cards back, maybe with a confusing "keep in touch" or "so glad to hear from you." Not once had anybody showed the slightest inclination to correspond otherwise. Not once had anybody ever called her until it was time to start working on the next reunion.

This always hurt her feelings and made her mad; it would this time, too. She knew perfectly well her own craving for real contact, which sometimes seemed to her an indication of neurosis and sometimes of a generous spirit she rather admired. But there was a moral imperative about it, too: In this difficult and wondrous world, people *ought* to be in touch.

A house on the other side of the street, pale green with a double porch, was festooned with cats. Cats on the porch roofs, railings, steps; vivid furry feline mounds among the less colorful plants along the sidewalk; a tabby tail twitching out from under low-hanging branches of the front-yard tree. Dottie and Cecelia halted together and exclaimed together, then both burst out laughing. A commonalty seemed about to be discovered, a likeness to be revealed. "Are you a cat-lover?" Cecelia asked confidently.

Dottie shrugged mildly. "Not especially. I'm not a cat-hater. I don't have much feeling one way or the other, I guess," and Cecelia was rendered speechless on this subject not so much closed as never opened.

The others were almost a block ahead of them by now, hurrying, it seemed to Cecelia, and for no good reason. There was a ferry every half hour. The reunion event scheduled for the evening was dinner at 6:00 at a restaurant, with what she supposed was a Cajun or Creole name, right there in the French Quarter.

She couldn't make out words, but the timbre of the voices that reached back to her was distinctly male. It pleased her to be walking just with Dottie Frasier in this funny little town—not the least bit quaint or exotic or racy; bearing no relation that she could see, although there must be some, to gaudy New Orleans just across the wide brown Mississippi.

"Do you live alone?" she found herself asking, as a way of asking about the other teacher, the woman, she'd once known Dottie was living with.

Dottie had stopped to regard the elaborate stained-glass window in the attic peak of an otherwise unremarkable gray house. Cecelia, craning her neck, had seen it, too, bright blues and reds, and was gratified that the others had obliviously passed it by, even though it was probably not true that only she and Dottie paid attention to details or appreciated beauty. "Yes, I do," Dottie replied, head tilted back and hands folded in front of her as she gazed up at the window. Her manner betrayed nothing—no uneasiness or caution, no regret or relief, and no particular interest in either continuing with or abandoning this topic of conversation.

Now Cecelia was left with no way she could think of to fill in the gap between two of the very few things she knew about this woman's life: that Dottie had lived with another woman for a long time, and that she didn't anymore. What happened? she longed to ask. Did you break up? Did she die? Did you love each other? What was it like? "I do, too." She didn't really want to talk about her own single life; what she wanted was to talk about Dottie's. But maybe sharing something of herself here would make her questioning seem less like interrogation and encourage a give and take. "Living alone has its advantages and disadvantages, like anything else, don't you think?"

Dottie smiled. Waiting, Cecelia saw that there were flecks of yellow in the window, too, but couldn't discern an actual design.

When Dottie said nothing else, Cecelia finally offered, hesitantly, "I'm divorced," as if confiding. Immediately she felt dishonest; this was a commonplace disclosure, not in the least daring, costing her little.

"I'm sorry," Dottie said automatically.

"It was a long time ago." After a moment, she risked inquiring, "Have you ever been married?"

"No." Another pause, during which Dottie finished contemplating the stained glass window and resumed walking. Afraid she'd gone too far, Cecelia didn't say anything else for a while, and caught her breath when Dottie went on, "There've been times when I've thought it would have been nice to have had a husband, maybe children. But I don't see very many happy marriages."

"In another life." Cecelia nodded. Dottie glanced at her in a way she took to be inquiring, and she was happy to elaborate, "There are a lot of things I'd like to do and never will, other forks in the road. Not that I regret the ones I have taken, just that I'm aware there are other ways of life I probably would find just as rewarding as the one I have. Like playing jazz sax on Bourbon Street." She grinned and so did Dottie, nodding. "So, 'in another life,' maybe you'll have a husband and children."

"Maybe." Dottie was absolutely noncommittal, and she did not, as Cecelia hoped, add any other "maybes" that might have been clues to the choices or the serendipity of her life.

"Not," Cecelia added hastily, awkwardly, "that there's anything wrong with the path you have taken. As far as I know, I mean. I mean—" She stopped, for fear of saying too much or too little, and Dottie said nothing to help her out, though she gave no indication, either, of discomfort.

"Good day, ladies."

The source of the creaky voice was a man in boots and overalls, about their own age, sitting in shade on tall porch steps. "Good day." Dottie stopped, turning full toward him, and Cecelia liked her for it. "Care to view my magnolias?"

Tempted by the unexpectedness and unadornment of the invitation, but thinking of the others headed, no doubt, toward the ferry back to New Orleans, Cecelia glanced at Dottie, who apparently had no such qualms. "Sure," she said readily, and started along the skinny sidewalk abutting the house to a head-high wooden gate.

"Meet me back there," the man instructed, as if he'd known they'd be unable to resist. With a stout cane he pushed himself to his feet, then retreated into the shadows of the porch, and a screen door swung open and closed.

Dottie had carefully shut the tall gate, as if Cecelia might not be following her, or as if she would take care of her own responsibilities and let others tend to theirs. Cecelia made her way to it, tugged it open, shut it when she was through. Drawing a little savoring breath of anticipation, she turned into the stranger's back yard.

It was quite an ordinary yard, though, and disappointment started right away to seep in. No flowers were in bloom. The grass was greener than at home, but not much. Plain gray flagstones led from where she stood at the gate to a corner of the wire fence where Dottie and the stout overalled man were looking at a bush, about which Cecelia saw nothing in the least remarkable, either.

Reading up on New Orleans before the reunion, she'd learned a little about evergreen magnolias. The state flower of both Louisiana and Mississippi, the trees could grow over a hundred feet tall. This one barely reached the top of the fence. Their flowers were large, fragrant, white or pink; even with diminished vision, she doubted she could miss them. This one was not in bloom. The encyclopedia had unhelpfully described the foliage as "laurel-like," which Cecelia took to mean glossy and dark green. The leaves on this bush were unremarkable, dull, as close to gray as to green; to be sure, she went closer, laid a twig across her palm.

Dottie wasn't looking at the man, nor was she saying any more to him than she did to anyone else—than, say, she had ever said to Cecelia. He wasn't talking much, either; Cecelia'd assumed that, hailing strangers off the street like that, he must be a lonely old man desperate for human contact, but that wasn't proving to be so. The two of them stood more or less together, not talking, certainly not touching, and the delicate quality of attentive engagement between them took Cecelia's breath away.

The visit didn't last long. Nobody asked anybody else's name; no personal details were offered or asked for. After fifteen minutes or so, they all just took their leave, and Cecelia and Dottie carefully shut the gate and wended their way along the narrow walk back to the public sidewalk. The man was already sitting on his top step again, his boots and the bottom six inches of his cane in hazy sunlight and shadows over the rest of him. "Good day, ladies," he observed, as if closing parentheses, and they both waved.

It seemed to Cecelia that something ought to be said. "What a nice man," she ventured. Dottie just smiled. An image occurred to Cecelia and she voiced it without much thought: "Do you remember my grandfather's tulips?"

"Pink and purple ones," Dottie acknowledged. This shared memory, and the fact that back then Dottie had noticed something about her, pleased Cecelia enormously, but she didn't know what to do with it and the moment passed.

It wasn't far to the ferry stop at the edge of town bounded by the Mississippi; they had only to close the rough rectangle whose other three sides they'd already walked. Cecelia was getting weary and her hip complained. She couldn't tell whether Dottie was tired or not, because she didn't know her well enough to have a baseline for comparison. As they neared the river, the air took on a certain crisp, crinkled fragrance, which after a moment she recognized as the odor she'd associated with the man on the ferry carrying the lunchbox. He was nowhere nearby now, though, and Cecelia wondered if she was smelling magnolias after all or if this was the smell of the Mississippi. It wasn't unpleasant, but it made her nostrils constrict, and she was feeling a little light-headed.

The ferry was approaching. There was no sign of the rest of the reunion group. Only a few people were waiting this time, and all of them were strangers, floating around like bobbins in that heady odor.

An impulse overtook Cecelia. She turned to face Dottie and blurted, "There's something I've been wanting to apologize to you about since seventh grade."

Watching the ferry, or maybe gazing at the city dimly visible across the brown water, Dottie merely raised her eyebrows.

Cecelia pushed on, ignoring her own bubbling giddiness although she knew very well it was a danger sign. "Do you remember in Mrs. Sattler's room we were talking one day about exchanging names at Christmas? It was seventh grade, the year somebody cut off all the tulips in town and the Tulip Festival was ruined, remember? It was also the year my dad lost what little money he had in the stock market crash, but that was a lot less important to me at the time than the Tulip Festival."

Dottie chuckled but said nothing to indicate whether she remembered any of this. Cecelia, abruptly self-conscious and awkward, briefly lost her train of thought and then stammered a little as she went on.

"The boys were—I don't know, making a big deal, as only seventh-grade boys can do, about not knowing what girls would like. I wanted to play along. I said something about you that I didn't mean as an insult, if anything I'd have meant it as a compliment, but to tell the truth I didn't have any intention at all, I was just talking, and that's what's bothered me all these years, that carelessness."

"That was a long time ago," Dottie said mildly.

But Cecelia was determined to say her piece. "Do you remember this?"

She was pleading for something here, some kind of help. She didn't know whether she hoped Dottie remembered the incident or not. But she wasn't to find out yet, for Dottie only shrugged.

"I raised my hand, ever the good little student, proud as punch to know the right answer."

Suddenly she stopped. Though she'd gone over this scene numerous times in the intervening decades, she was recalling a detail now that had hitherto escaped her: the person across the aisle from her, nodding and grinning, raising an encouraging thumb. Who had that been? No specifics came back to her, not even the gender of this classmate let alone a name or face, but the image of having been urged on was vivid and disconcerting.

"When Mrs. Sattler called on me I stood up and looked right at you and said—" Here Cecelia gave her best simulation of a self-conscious, showing-off adolescent. She threw her weight—a hundred pounds more than then—onto one hip, flung her hands in extravagant gestures considerably less lithe these days, her smile almost a leer, her tone heavily sarcastic. " 'Well, *most* of us would like perfume or hair ribbons. *Most* of us, but not *all* of us. Not all of us, right, Dottie?' "

At first, repeated it out loud like that for the first time, it didn't sound so bad. Maybe that long-ago carelessness didn't matter after all. But Cecelia knew it had mattered, to her if not to Dottie, and she held her breath.

In the ensuing pause, she began to wonder if she'd been careless again, made a wrong choice again, again put her own needs before Dottie's though she'd thought she was doing just the opposite. What did she want here? Forgiveness? Acknowledgment of long-ago good intentions gone awry? Really, she saw too late, this had not been an overdue apology. It had been a ploy, dishonest and usurious; it had been bait. All she wanted was *contact* with this apparently kind, apparently loving, apparently interesting woman who'd never had a thing to offer her, and for that she'd been willing to risk hurting and embarrassing Dottie again.

Dottie smiled, nodded, but maybe not even at Cecelia, maybe not in response to Cecelia's confession. The ferry came. The crowd oozed aboard. The man Cecelia had noticed on the way over, whom she still doubted she'd be able to describe to anyone else but whom she recognized instantly and would recognize anywhere she saw him, was among the passengers. He raised his lunchbox at her in a jaunty salute, and the sharp odor struck her again, made her turn her head away, but not before she saw him raise his circled thumb and forefinger and wink. "Nice job," he seemed to be telling her.

This odd sensation of being wordlessly praised by a stranger passed out of Cecelia's mind as quickly as it had come in, leaving an unsettling impression of the similarity between sweetness and decay which would linger as her predominant impression of New Orleans. Cecelia glanced at Dottie, who was not looking at her, but whose not-looking carried with it no significance, only a lack of intent, indifferent to her as nature. On the trip across the wide, sluggish, brown Mississippi, they didn't talk, and they went to their different hotels in the Quarter to rest until dinner.

For the rest of the reunion, they were not again alone together, and they exchanged scarcely half a dozen words. Dottie's pleasant, remote manner hadn't altered. Cecelia, feeling sullied by a secret whose shame would be incomprehensible to anybody else, found herself with not much to say until abruptly, toward the early end of the evening, the name of the boy who'd died after his leg had been crushed in that game of chicken more than sixty years ago popped into her mind.

She dearly wanted to tell it to Dottie, but Dottie was at the other end of the table looking at the pictures of Francie Steiger's dog that were being passed around, and Cecelia couldn't reach her. So, leaning across Cal, she said it to Alice, who didn't know what she was talking about. "Garrett Roop. Remember him? Garry?"

Though she was exhausted when she got back to the hotel, Cecelia wasn't ready for bed just yet. The reunion had left her restless and vaguely troubled. And, since she doubted she'd ever have reason to come back to this town, she wanted to take in every drop of it she could, never mind that she was already uncomfortably over-stimulated.

She didn't quite know what to do, though. For a while she sat on the settee in the tiny lobby, marveling at the thick swampy air and the fact—she swore she'd have sensed it even if she hadn't already known—that this whole city was below sea level. She fancied she felt a little like one of those dead bodies you heard about now and then floating up out of the New Orleans cemeteries. No one came in or went out.

Back outside, Royal Street, like everything else here, was super-saturated, colors and shapes and sounds and odors and tastes and surfaces, textures, consistencies bubbling in charged, volatile suspension. She couldn't imagine how there'd be room for her. But instead of resistance, there was a welcoming sensation with a definite sinister edge to it, a sort of sucking, and she slid right in.

Music from everywhere made the night lose its shape like unset Jello. The air smelled swampy and sweet. Two small black girls in bouffant dresses tap danced loudly amid the throngs; Cecelia dropped a dollar into their basket and was ashamed of herself for noticing that they didn't thank her. In front of a store-front beer-and-hurricane bar, a silvery-faced mime twisted wiener-shaped balloons into animals; Cecelia was shocked by the price but paid it anyway, then didn't know what to do with the thing but couldn't bring herself to discard it. There was probably not a person in this city who didn't already have more than enough balloon animals. Could she take it home to her great-grandson? It was a problem, the sort she knew she'd fret over, but when as she approached Bourbon Street she was pressed between knots of partiers and the balloon horse soundlessly burst, she felt a pang of regret.

Atop a teetering stool next to a rusted trash can, a person of indeterminate gender, age, race, and intention was playing a sax. The sorrowful excitement saxophones always aroused in her, as well as the difficulty of pushing her way through the suddenly thickened crowd, brought Cecelia to a halt nearby. The face of the musician was layered with paint and sequins; the hands were sheathed in shimmering, variegated gloves, and the thin body, bent like a paper clip, in sheeny patchwork. A row of hoops sparkled red along the arch of one eyebrow; Cecelia's revulsion was very nearly erotic, and it embarrassed her that she could hardly look away.

The placard taped to the trash can read GARRY ROOP, PLEASE GIVE in a shaky, elaborate scrawl. Cecelia shivered, tried to figure out what was meant. Was it that this person's name was Garry Roop, like that boy dead long ago, and he was asking passersby, including her, to give? To give what? Or maybe there was someone named Garry Roop whom the musician was specifically entreating, or hoping to entreat.

Cecelia held her position for quite some time. The sax went mellow and screechy and whispery by turns, and the few tunes she might have known were so wildly interpreted—or inexpertly played—they seemed something else entirely. As far as she could tell, the musician never noticed she was there.

In the end, weary and full to the point of nausea, she dropped all the money left in her purse—which really wasn't much, wasn't enough—into the trash can. The thin multicolored heap already in there looked like trash. Not knowing anything else to do and on the verge of tears, she made her way back to the little hotel on Royal Street to pack for tomorrow's flight home.

Chapter Twelve

Orphan
(1995)

Toby couldn't back up fast enough. He was suspended, stuck in water. His feet didn't touch the floor of the lagoon, and he wasn't a very good swimmer anymore. He was paddling furiously with his hands and scissoring his feet as hard as he could, but not going anywhere. The thing was coming closer, and he couldn't get away. He kicked at it, but he was too weak and small to do any damage and the water slowed him down. He splashed. The thing kept right on coming, huge in the water where it belonged and he didn't.

Toby was dying. When you were dying, you

didn't belong anywhere. They said the fish thing was sick and scared, too. It didn't act like it. And anyway, what did he care?

"Toby, it's okay. She won't hurt you, buddy." That was his dad, beside him in the water. But what did his dad know? He hadn't kept Toby from getting cancer, had he? Just because Toby was named after him didn't mean they had any special magic between them or anything, no matter what Toby used to think when he was little, before he'd spent any time with his father, before he got cancer, before he even heard of cancer. Toby would never trust his father or anybody else as long as he lived.

That struck him as hilarious, but when he tried to laugh his stomach hurt more and he got water in his mouth, which made him sputter and scared him more. He did manage to let out a sort of laugh, as loud and mean as he could make it.

He didn't know why Mom had let him come all the way down here to Florida with his dad, this guy he barely knew and she obviously didn't know as well as she thought she did, just to swim with some stupid fish. Maybe she didn't know about the swimming. Maybe she'd thought it was like the one other time when his dad and his grandma and her friend Cecelia had taken him to New Mexico. Maybe Mom had just gotten tired of taking care of a kid who was dying. You couldn't blame her. Toby was tired of *being* a kid who was dying.

Something had almost happened on the way down here. Unless he'd been dreaming. He did have weird dreams because of the medicine and the chemo, but usually he knew they were dreams even when he was having them. This one he didn't think was a dream.

They'd been sleeping in the truck. Naturally, his dad couldn't afford a motel. Toby couldn't believe anybody would let a dying kid sleep three nights not in a bed, but it was kind of cool so he didn't say anything. He'd been sound asleep, in a sleeping bag in the bed of the truck with his dad right beside him, and then this weird smell had woken him up and at first he thought he was going to throw up— so what else was new?—but he didn't.

His dad wasn't beside him. Toby heard him talking to some lady. It figured that his father would leave him because of a female. That's what had happened in the first place, according to Mom. When Toby raised up on his elbow he could just barely see their outlines, but he could hear everything they said.

They were sitting on top of one of the picnic tables with their feet on the bench. They were smoking dope, but he was pretty sure that wasn't the smell that had woken him up, so maybe they were doing some other drug, too. When they sucked on the joint and passed it to each other, a little red dot blinked on and off.

"Fuck, Lila, I hate this." That was Dad, and Toby knew he was talking about him.

"It must be really hard." She sounded super nice and understanding.

"He pukes all the time and he shits himself and he's in a pissy mood all the time."

"You didn't sign on for this. It's not fair."

It seemed to Toby that his dad and this Lila person must have known each other before. Just listening to them, he'd think they were old friends. But he didn't see how that could be, and trying to figure it out made him too tired.

"I just thought we could spend some—you know, quality time together. Father-son shit, you know."

"I think that's sweet." There was a pause, like maybe they were kissing. Maybe Toby would barf.

"This dolphin thing wasn't my idea. There's this old busybody, a friend of the family, and she thought it'd be good for him—good for both of us, is what she said—and she paid for it and I sort of got roped into bringing him."

"That's asking a lot."

Toby's dad laughed, but Toby knew nothing was funny. "Shit, Cecelia always asks a lot."

"I know." That made Toby think Lila might be a friend of Cecelia's or something, but that would be *really* weird.

His dad didn't pick up on that. His dad was pretty oblivious. Now he was sounding mad at Cecelia, but it wasn't her he was mad at. "Nosy old broad. Fucks around in other people's lives. I rented her basement for a while. Couldn't stand it."

Left without paying rent, Toby knew. Left the place a mess. He'd heard his grandma and Cecelia talking. His grandma was more upset than Cecelia.

"Now her granddaughter's in there, and she's got her panties in a knot over the kid. My mom says Cecelia says there's something wrong with him. Well, so what if there is? He's not her kid. It's like part of the rent is you have to let her into your life. She's doesn't tell you what to do or criticize, but it's like you can't measure up, you know?"

"People like that think it matters what they do," Lila said, like it was the dumbest thing she'd ever heard of.

"And Cecelia always gets what she wants. That's what pisses me off the most. Everything always turns out right."

Toby defended Cecelia in his mind. She was divorced. That wasn't what she wanted. He'd overheard her crying to his grandma about her kids. That wasn't what she wanted. He bet she had other bad things. Everybody had bad things. But he found himself mad at her, too, because she didn't have cancer and die when she was ten years old.

"Don't you hate people like that?" Lila said with a nasty laugh, and ferociously Toby thought, *yeah.* There was a pause. Toby wondered what they were doing. Then she said, "You deserve some good times. You owe it to yourself. We could have some good times together, you know? I mean, it's not like you can really do anything for him." Her voice sounded funny now because she was holding the smoke in while she talked. "He's gonna die no matter what. Why put yourself through this?"

His dad took a hit. His voice had that tight, cartoony sound, too. Toby didn't know why people who smoked weed did that. "Yeah, but he's my kid."

"It's not like you raised him or anything."

"He's my kid, though."

"Suit yourself." She got down off the picnic table and walked out onto the highway.

"Shit. Hold on." Toby's father followed her. Toby's heart raced. If they left him here, what would he do? She stopped and waited, and his dad caught up with her, and they were swapping spit and groping each other, and Toby thought he really would throw up now but he couldn't quit watching them because he was dying to know what was going to happen.

Dying to know. He snorted. Cracking sick jokes made him feel better in a weird way, even though they also made him and everybody else feel worse. If he said stuff like that out loud, the doctors might nod sadly or pat his head, but what they were really interested in was his cancer, which was fine with him. His cancer was all *he* was really interested in, too. His mother would just look away, or she'd get tears in her eyes, and he guessed she'd like to leave the room but she didn't dare because he might die while she was gone. His friends laughed once in a while, but he could tell they didn't get it. Anyway, he didn't have friends anymore. It was hard to be friends with a dead kid.

His dad would say, "Shit," or "Shut up, Toby." Or he'd pretend he didn't hear him. Toby could tell all this really got to him, the cancer and the jokes and having a son in the first place. Served him right.

The lady had left, and his dad hadn't. Toby didn't know why. He'd been curled up on the sleeping bag, sick and scared and shaking, when his dad climbed back into the truck. "Shit," his dad had said softly, and he'd held Toby until the sun came up and it was time to hit the road again.

He hadn't wanted to come to Florida. It was hot in Florida. He didn't want to go in the water. He didn't want a stupid fish coming anywhere near him. He didn't want to die.

The pain in his stomach got worse all of a sudden. It did that, got worse or better for no reason. The medicine helped when it felt like it, and Toby hadn't figured out any other way to control things. But he still tried. Tried to fight the pain and the hurling and the stupid disease. Tried to fight stupid dying, or to run away from it, or something. He didn't want to die. It wasn't fair. He was ten years old and he was going to die and it wasn't fair.

When he was three or four years old, he'd climbed up on the porch wall and dropped a frog onto the sidewalk just to see what would happen. Just before he'd opened his fingers, there'd been a strong smell, which he'd thought came from the frog, and he could swear he heard the frog's har-rumphy voice telling him, "Go ahead, drop me. Who cares?" When it hit the cement porch, the frog had exploded. Its guts were green like the outside of it, and brownish-red. Now Toby felt like that frog, wriggling in some kid's hands just before it dropped and died, some kid who didn't mean to be mean but just wanted to see what would happen.

Floating in the water and knowing that fish-thing was going to *do* something to him, Toby tried to bring his knee up to his chest to ward it off and to ease the pain. But all that did was make him tip over onto his side. Losing your balance in water was different from losing your balance on dry land. Surprised, he bobbed.

The dolphin or whale or whatever it was was right in his face now. Toby could see its eyes, one at a time when it turned its big head back and forth. Its eyes were on the *sides* of its head instead of in front where eyes were supposed to be. They gave him the creeps, made him think of some sort of demon. One at a time, they looked right at him. Its nose was long like a baseball bat, an alien nose, a devil's nose.

"Her name is Orphan," the trainer beside him said quietly.

"Stupid name," Toby said right away.

The trainer didn't get mad or anything. When you were a dying kid, people didn't get mad at you no matter what you said or did. "She really is an orphan, though," the trainer explained. "The adults in her pod were killed by whalers. Orphan's just a baby."

Just a baby. Right. She was *enormous*. Determined not to show any interest, Toby found himself asking, "How big *is* she?"

"Eleven feet long, maybe a thousand pounds."

Toby snorted. Just because he had cancer didn't mean he was a total idiot. "Doesn't sound like a baby to me."

"She's only three or four months old. We've had to feed her by hand. Somebody stays with her round the clock. We think she's going to make it now, but it's still touch and go."

That made Toby furious. This thing that wasn't even *human* was going to make it, and he wasn't. All these people were taking care of this thing that wasn't even a person, saving it, and none of them bothered to save him.

He was sorry he'd dropped that frog. It had taken him this long to get sorry; one day not very long ago, the memory of standing up on that wall in the sunshine, holding against his chest the squirming frog that was about to die because of him, had all of a sudden made him sick with shame. He'd been sorry ever since. He was sorry now, for all the good it did him or the frog. His stomach hurt. Sometimes, when he was bored, he imagined how the cancer was spreading through his gut.

The trainer kept on talking, as if Toby cared, which he didn't. Why should he care about anything, when he probably wouldn't live to be a teenager? Would never drive. Would never have a girlfriend, Heather Campos or anybody else. Would never even *go* to high school let alone graduate. "Now we have to teach her to be a dolphin."

"What's to teach? She's a dolphin and you're not." Toby guffawed.

"How to keep her blowhole out of the water. How to propel herself with her tail."

"You mean she doesn't know all that stuff? Instinct or something?" Toby wished he would quit acting interested.

"Dolphins learn how to live from other dolphins."

Now Orphan was just a few inches away from him, making loud clicking noises and a kind of soft squeal. He could actually smell her, not fishy the way he'd expected, a smell sort of nice and sort of nasty at the same time.

"Get that thing away from me!" He tried to yell, but his voice wasn't very strong anymore and nobody paid any attention. Instead, the trainer hoisted himself out of the water and left Toby alone with the dolphin still coming. He had cancer, he was dying, so what did he care if he got drowned by a dolphin first? But he was *scared*.

Other times in his life he'd been scared of things that turned out not to be worth being scared of; then he hadn't known to be afraid of cancer till he got it, and cancer was what was going to kill him. Thinking how he'd been tricked enraged him.

He'd been scared of the black ponds on his grandparents' farm, but nothing had ever come up out of them to get him. He'd been scared of his grandfather's bomb shelter—a big thick gray metal door out there in the woods, a dug-out room that might make the whole ground collapse; by the time he'd understood what it had been built for, nobody, including his grandfather, had been afraid of the Bomb anymore.

He'd been scared of the tarantula he'd come across when he was nine, on vacation in New Mexico with Dad and Grandma and Cecelia. The spider was as big as his fist, brown and hairy, right there where Toby'd just about put his hand. It smelled bad. It was just too hideous to live; knowing that tarantulas were poisonous was extra, an excuse. Something told him to kill it, so he did. Without hesitation and expecting no second thoughts, he'd squashed it with a rock. Then, transfixed, he'd squatted there in the hot sun and watched it tremble as it died. "It's just a *spider*," the little voice in his head had insisted. "What's the big deal?"

Now, dying of cancer, struggling in the water in the path of the huge oncoming dolphin, he quit thinking about the tarantula when he heard his father say something and the trainer say something back. His father came up behind him, leaned down to grab him under the arms, and pulled him out of the water. On the shore, both of them still in life jackets and dripping wet, he rocked Toby in his arms. Toby didn't think his dad had ever held him before he got sick; probably he ought to be mad about that, but he was too tired. Dad whispered, "It's all right, guy. It's okay. You're safe," which was a dumb thing to say but did make Toby feel better.

He was sorry about the frog. He was sorry about

the tarantula. Brand-new perceptions fountained up in him, briefly and painfully dazzling him: It *had* mattered. And: Maybe that smell he'd noticed both times had been the smell of his victims' fear. Or of death. Or of his own young soul, choosing; choosing wrong. And: The frog and the spider had been alive, and then they had been dead. And: They'd had a place, and he'd intruded. He hadn't had to kill them. And, in a profoundly new way: He was so sorry.

Crying into his father's shoulder, he saw the dolphin out of the corner of his eye, practically motionless in the water. Then the trainer called its name a couple of times, and it turned slowly and went away. Desperately, Toby wanted to know how its skin felt.

"Dolphins aren't fish."

Toby scowled. He'd never said they were.

"They're mammals, like us. In fact, some scientists believe dolphins and humans share a common ancestor."

This was so ridiculous that Toby made a big show of laughing—whooping, even though it was thin and hurt his throat; slapping his knee, even though both his knee and the heel of his hand ached. A common ancestor with a *fish?* What, like his great-great-something-grandfather the whaler was also the great-great-grandfather of Orphan? Or maybe that dude had killed Orphan's great-great-great-grandfather, or Orphan's great-great-great-grandfather had killed him?

When Toby was a little kid he'd played whaler, with sticks for harpoons and the backyard for the ocean and rocks or just his own imagination making whales. He'd gotten bored with the game and quit playing it a long time before it had dawned on him that if you were a whaler you'd actually *kill* whales.

"Dolphins have a sophisticated language. They talk with each other—maybe better than humans—and we believe they try to communicate with us just as we try to communicate with them."

The guy had to be lying. People lied to you a lot when you were ten years old and dying. Did he really think Toby was dumb enough to believe that you could, like, just swim out there and maybe ask Orphan what time it was? Or was she scared to be a dolphin in a world full of human beings, and they were taking care of you but you wanted your mother and your father and your friends? Or what death was? Or why bad stuff had to happen anyway?

"Dolphins are conscious breathers," said the trainer. "That means they have to *think* about every breath they take. It isn't automatic the way it is with us."

So what, Toby thought furiously. His own breathing didn't work right anymore. So what.

"We have a lot to learn from dolphins," the trainer went on. "About life and about death."

Toby hated Orphan. He wanted to blow her up. He wanted her blood to turn the water red or whatever color dolphins' blood was. He wanted, himself, to be strong enough and mean enough to throw a harpoon straight into the dolphin's heart. She smelled funny. He could taste her smell, and it gagged him.

Then he thought, as clearly as if somebody were whispering it inside his head: That's why I got cancer. Because I killed the frog and the tarantula and I'd kill the dolphin if I could. That's why I'm going to die. Oddly satisfied, because any explanation was better than none, he let himself relax in his father's arms.

The next day Toby went into the water again. Not because he wanted to but because he didn't have the energy to argue. He'd been really sick again, throwing up, and his head was killing him and his stomach hurt *a lot* and he didn't much care if he lived or died.

His father wanted him to go in. Said it would be good for him. What did he know about what would be good for Toby? Toby hated his father. He got to grow up and have girlfriends and have adventures and get put in jail and have kids and one of them was going to die but the others would all grow up because they wouldn't get cancer. It wasn't fair.

When his father picked him up to help him into the lagoon, he held him for a while. Toby tried to stay stiff and distant, but he was too tired. "I know it's hard, son," his father said softly. "If I could do this for you, I would. I wish it was me instead of you, buddy, I really do." Startled, Toby tried to see his father's face, but couldn't get a clear view past the beard and the baseball cap. "I love you, Toby."

He was lowered into the warm water. There was no use fighting. His head hurt. The pain in his stomach was exactly as if something was eating a hole in him, which something was. Dad kissed the top of his head where there was hardly any hair and set him down in the water.

The trainer told him a few things he'd probably told him before. A lot of the time now, Toby didn't pay attention to anything outside his own body. "Remember, keep your hands away from the top of her head. That's called the melon, and it's where the blowhole is."

"Hey, don't worry," Toby wanted to say but didn't bother. "I won't be touching any *fish.*"

"And avoid the genital slits on the dolphin's underside. On the male, there's one slit, where the penis is carried inside the body. On the female, like Orphan, there are two, one for the mammary gland and one for the vaginal opening. Don't touch."

Gross. Toby tried to think of something just as gross to say back.

"And don't grab the dolphin's fins. There's actually a law now that humans can't ask for rides. If she invites you, though, you can accept."

Then Toby was alone in the water with Orphan right beside him. He couldn't believe they'd done this to him. This must be "free swim," which he'd heard them talk about, but until this second it hadn't registered that he'd be left alone with the dolphin.

She was coming at him. He thought about backing up, but floating in the water made backward and forward and sideways and even up and down all run together. She was making that weird clicking noise that the trainer said was sonar, hunting for him.

The way he'd gone hunting for frogs—not exactly *planning* to squash one, but squashing one was as good as anything else to do. Waiting for the dolphin's sonar to lock onto him, wondering if he'd feel anything when it did, Toby found himself remembering his mother's smile when she'd told somebody he'd gone frog-catching, a happy and innocent way for a little boy to pass a summer morning, and when you grew up yourself you'd say in the dreamy way adults sometimes talked about when they were kids, "Summers we used to go frog-catching down at the swimming hole," like that was your right. Toby wouldn't say that because Toby was never going to grow up.

Orphan swam slowly around him a couple of times. He felt her bulk and her warmth on all sides. Then she came around front and pressed the square end of her nose—*rostrum*, he remembered unwillingly—right on his forehead in the exact spot where it hurt worst. The shifting of their bodies made waves; Toby had to remind himself to tilt his head back so his nose was out of water. His head ached less.

Opening his eyes, he saw the dolphin's blueblack skin glinting in the sun. It looked like a wet tire. He touched it with his fingertips, then his palm. It felt like a wet hard-boiled egg.

The pain in his head was gone.

Orphan repositioned herself so that her rostrum rested against his belly right over the pain. She was *doing* something to him. He felt something come from her into him, kind of a vibrating like a long, gentle electric shock. Toby had learned to be on guard for anything that would cause him more pain. But he didn't think this hurt.

Three or four or five times she did it, whatever it was. Then she backed away so she wasn't touching him anymore. Before he knew what he was doing, Toby had pushed himself through the water as if he could follow her, as if he could press himself against her instead of the other way around, but she was out of reach. Squealing softly through her blowhole, she swam easily around him one more time, and left the lagoon out the other end through the holding pools into the wider bay. Toby's stomach didn't hurt anymore.

By the time he went to bed that night, the pain was back, but a lot less. He must have fallen asleep, because he woke up. His first thought wasn't the usual "It hurts" or "I've got cancer" or "I'm going to die." His first thought wasn't a thought at all, really, but a feeling. *Sad.* He was so sad.

In the bed on the other side of the tiny room, his father was snoring. For a minute it made Toby mad that somebody could sleep while his son was dying of cancer. But the anger was way far back in his mind. What he felt mostly was sadness. He thought of the word *sorrow;* this must be sorrow, but it didn't seem to be for himself, exactly. He was sorry about the frog and the tarantula, not so much because he'd killed them but because he hadn't even thought about it before he killed them, hadn't thought it mattered. That was part of it. More, he had the sensation of this *sorrow* coming into him from somebody else.

His whole body was tingling. Even his belly, where it hurt, was tingling. There was a weird feeling in his chest, around his heart. Not pain, exactly—Toby was an expert on pain—but a pressure that came and went, came and went, like another heartbeat.

It was hard to breathe. Not hard, exactly, but he had to *notice* his breathing in order to do it. He paid attention to his breath in and his breath out.

Then he was thinking: *Orphan.* Wanting to be in the water with Orphan. Wanting to be with her, to pet her incredibly soft skin and listen up close to her clicks and squeals. The pain was getting worse again, but the sorrow was stronger than the pain. The desire to go to Orphan was strongest of all.

Early in the morning he got himself up and dressed, which was hard, and went out and found the trainer before his dad was even up. The trainer was squatted down talking to some other kid, some geeky bald girl in a wheelchair, and he didn't like it when Toby interrupted to tell him he had to free-swim with Orphan right away. "You're on the schedule for Thursday, right?"

"It's got to be now," Toby insisted. "Now."

"Why?"

None of your business, was what Toby wanted

to say. He managed to get out instead, "She needs me."

The trainer looked at him for a minute, then said, "Okay."

It was afternoon, though, by the time they could arrange it, and Toby could hardly stand waiting. What if he died between that morning and that afternoon? Things were alive one minute and the next minute they were dead. What if Orphan swam away and never came back? What if *he* did?

When finally he got into the lagoon, the warm water on his legs, stomach, chest, shoulders, neck, face eased the tingling a little. Orphan was already there, huddled up against the shore, and *sorrow* was coming from her toward him like light out of a flashlight.

Following its beam, Toby swam and floated over to her. By the time he got there he was exhausted, but it was so nice to lean against her, to run his hands along the silky body that stretched farther than he could ever reach, to look up close into the wide eye.

He laid his arms on the huge curve of her body. She was too big for him to really hug, but he held her, pressed his cheek against her smooth side. He was sure she moved against him, snuggled into his arms, which was a funny thing to be thinking about something that was eleven feet long and weighed a thousand pounds. But she was just a baby, and she was scared and sick.

After a while his arms cramped and his lower body got chilled from being in the water. He moved away a little. The dolphin stirred, and Toby's body tingled again. Around his heart was a sudden, strange pounding that felt like fear, although he didn't think *he* was afraid. Maybe the frog had been, dangling in the air just before he'd dropped it. Maybe the tarantula had been, right when the rock was coming down. But for the first time in a long time, Toby wasn't afraid.

He paddled through the blue water till he was touching Orphan again. He stroked her. He stretched himself out so as much of him as possible was in contact with as much of her as possible. The tingling and pounding in his body had stopped. "I won't leave, Orphan," he said out loud. "I'm here. You're not alone."

He stayed there a long time. Other kids—all of them sick; all of them dying—came into the lagoon and swam with the other dolphins, but they left Toby and Orphan alone. His dad came and sat on the shore, but he didn't say anything and after a while Toby noticed that he'd gone away.

Toby kept talking. "I know you're sad. I know you're sick and you might die. But you're not alone, you know. We're in this together." He had no idea what you were supposed to say, but he paid close attention to whatever came out of his mouth.

Late in the day, when Toby was exhausted and his stomach was hurting a lot and he was starting to panic about having to leave Orphan at all, the dolphin started moving. Sweeping her powerful tail back and forth, back and forth through the water, she went away from Toby and then came back. She was clicking. With her rostrum she gently nudged him away from the shore so she could go all the way around him a couple of times. Then she swam up right beside him and stopped. She waited. She wanted him to do something.

"What?" Toby demanded.

Then, realizing that her dorsal fin was practically in his grip, he grabbed onto it with both hands. A child herself, Orphan didn't give him time to get ready. She was off, speeding around the lagoon before Toby had a good hold on her fin, and he whooped in surprise and delight.

Air and water rushed over him. The dolphin took him fast around the lagoon three, four, five times, never slowing down. People on shore were applauding. The water rippled wildly.

Orphan was just a baby, and she was sick and not very strong for a dolphin. So the ride didn't last long. But it was a gift. When it was over, Toby was laughing, and Orphan lay tipped on her side, one eye looking up at the sky and the other, Toby guessed, down through the water maybe to the bottom of the lagoon. She was trembling. Drops of water flicked off her to glisten for a minute while they floated up into the clouds and down into the water. Coming up from the water and down from the sky were shadows that kind of looked like animals—frogs, spiders, dolphins, humans—and kind of not. Toby got dizzy and lost track of where Orphan was.

He missed the next whole day at the lagoon because he was too busy being sick, throwing up and lying on the floor wiped out from the pain. His father held his head when he vomited and washed his face in between heaves, gave him the medicine that was supposed to help the pain and maybe it would have been worse without it, sat on the floor beside him.

Finally his dad pushed him in a wheelchair down to the shore. He was cold, even in the noontime heat and under the blanket his dad had tucked around him. The misty sun stung his eyes.

The first thing Toby saw when they got to the lagoon was the little crowd on the shore, kids and parents and all three trainers. Some people were crying. Some were just standing there looking out over the water. Some were talking way too loud.

Toby's father pushed him right to the edge of the water, the wheels of the wheelchair making thin tracks that filled up right away. Not far from shore, three grown dolphins had made a circle around Orphan, their rostrums butting into her like the petals of a dark daisy. Toby could see right away that she was dead. The other dolphins were keeping her body afloat, but she'd rolled sideways and it didn't matter now that her blowhole was underwater.

A thin, high, sweet whistling drifted through the air. You could hear it better in the water. "Put me in," he whispered.

Dad didn't hesitate and didn't ask anybody's permission. He gathered Toby up out of the wheelchair, held him for a minute and kissed the side of his head, then lowered him into the water right by the dolphins.

Toby was so weak it was hard for him to keep his nose and mouth above water, and impossible to kick or paddle with his hands. He flailed, came into contact with the dorsal fin of one of the dolphins, and grabbed on. You weren't supposed to ask, but Toby didn't dare wait to be invited. *It doesn't matter. It's only a dolphin,* came into his mind, but he knew it did matter; he was making a choice. Pressing himself against the dolphin's smooth side, which was a browner gray than Orphan's, he managed to drag himself slowly through the water.

Orphan seemed small now next to the adult dolphins. Toby seemed smaller. She wasn't moving. She wasn't making any noise. When Toby laid his face against her, there wasn't any warmth.

The whistling from the others was no louder here, but it was clearer, purer. The water hummed with the dolphins' song. Toby's body hummed.

Then, one by one, the big dolphins went away. Slowly, they swam out of the sheltered lagoon into the open water beyond. Toby didn't watch them leave.

He lay against Orphan's drifting, slowly sinking body and let his eyes close. He thought about his breathing, breath in and breath out, long space in between.

287

Chapter Thirteen

Dylan Finds a Fly
(1998)

The fly landed on Dylan's arm. Dylan hadn't seen it coming, and because he didn't know where flies came from, or even really what they were, it was wonderful and magical and a little scary and a secret.

Nobody knew where he was. Daddy was at school. At Dylan's school they had snacks and played with trucks and had naptime and watched videos. Maybe Daddy was napping right now. Mommy was somewhere. He heard her singing, but not to him. Dylan hadn't seen Grandma Cecelia today, but he guessed she was upstairs in her part of the house. Nobody knew he was out here in the playhouse. Nobody knew a fly had come to visit him.

He lay very still. The fly walked down his arm. It had tiny legs and feet so little he didn't even see them and it had wings. Dylan tried to count the legs but they kept moving and he wasn't sure of the numbers. "One . . . two . . . four . . ." Dylan was four. The fly tickled. It buzzed. Dylan loved the fly. Grandma Cecelia always said be gentle, be nice, and he was. He was careful not to squish it. He held his breath so he wouldn't blow on it. Very slowly and carefully he turned his arm so by the time it got down to his hand he could hold it. He was going to let it go. He just wanted to hold it for a minute. It was his.

He'd show it to Grandma Cecelia. "Grandma C!" he called softly.

"Hi, Dylan."

At first he didn't know who it was. It wasn't Grandma Cecelia. It wasn't Mommy; Mommy was busy, and anyway she wouldn't be looking at him like this, paying attention just to him.

It was Mommy's friend Rose. Dylan knew her by her smell. He liked the way she smelled, even though it made him kind of sick. "Hi," he said back to her, but he didn't know if she'd want to see his fly so he closed his fist.

Right now she was his same size. Mommy and Daddy were always lots taller than he was. Rose was, too, when Mommy was around, but right now she was his size but still a grown-up lady. This was no more or less remarkable to Dylan than many other things in the world. Than flies, for instance, this fly wiggling and buzzing in the creases of his palm. She was looking right at him. She smelled funny, good and bad both. Dylan rubbed his nose with the hand that didn't have the fly in it and put the hand with the fly in it behind his back. Rose said, "Dylan, your fly is beautiful."

Dylan was four. Magic was real, and reality magical. It surprised him that the lady Rose knew he had a fly and it was beautiful, but not any more or less than a million other things every day surprised him. He took his hand from behind his back and opened it. She put her big hand under his hand and poked the fly. It was crawling. "Ooh." She looked up at him and he thought she was going to kiss him and he didn't like it when people kissed him. She didn't kiss him but she held on to his hand so he couldn't get away and her face came real close to his and he felt really special and really mad. The smell of her made his head feel funny. "I know some fun things to do with flies. Want me to tell you?"

He didn't know if he wanted her to tell him or not. He nodded.

"Pull off his wings."

He gasped. "It'll hurt him!"

"Flies don't feel pain."

He stared at her. The fly tickled his palm.

"It's just a fly. It doesn't matter. Go ahead. Pull off one of his wings."

"I don't want to."

"Really, Dylan, it's okay. You know me. I'm Mommy's friend. You trust me, don't you?"

Dylan had no idea what she was asking him, but he understood what she wanted him to say. He whimpered, "Yes," felt like a bad boy, ducked his head.

"What? I didn't hear you. Say it louder. Do you trust me?"

"Yes!" He was afraid of her. He was afraid of the fly.

"All right then. That's what I like to hear." He'd done something right. He'd pleased her. He peeked through his fingers and she was smiling at him. "You're a person, Dylan. This is just a fly. You're a lot more important than it is. You can do anything you want to it. Pull off its wings. It's fun. Everybody does it."

The fly flew away. Dylan burst into tears. "I don't want to!" he wailed. "I don't want him to go away!"

Rose was big now, bigger than Mommy and Daddy, bigger than anybody. Dylan couldn't see her face, just her legs. He wasn't even sure it was Rose now, because that smell was gone. "Oh, well," she said from way up there, and she sounded just like Mommy did when he'd disappointed her. "There will be other chances. There are lots of flies in the world." Then she went away, too.

Dylan waited for his fly to come back. It didn't.

He waited for that lady Rose to come back. She didn't. He waited for Mommy or Daddy to call him or come looking for him. They didn't. He curled up on the floor. Maybe there'd be a spider. There were spiderwebs but no spiders. Dylan wasn't entirely convinced that spiderwebs and spiders had anything to do with each other except what you called then. He fell asleep. Grandma Cecelia came and got him and carried him into the house. He could tell Grandma was mad at Mommy. Dylan didn't know why, but it had something to do with him. Mommy didn't get mad back. He didn't think Mommy even knew Grandma C was mad. Mommy didn't say anything about his fly. Dylan didn't either.

When he woke up from his nap Rose was there. First he could smell her, and he was a little scared to open his eyes. Rose had never been in his room before. He guessed it was okay; Mommy must have said it was okay. Maybe Rose was babysitting him. Sometimes Mommy forgot to tell him she was going away. He pulled his blanket over his head and called, "Mommy?"

Rose was right beside him. She was really big, bigger than anybody, and that scared Dylan and made him feel safe, both. She could take care of him. She could swallow him up, or fall on him and squish him. He could feel how big she was. He hadn't looked at her yet.

"Hush, sweetheart," she whispered. She was going to tell him a secret. He could feel her breath. That smell of hers filled his nose and his mouth and his whole head and his whole body like air. "Mommy and Daddy had to go do something. It's just you and me, kid. Look. Look, Dylan. Look at me."

Dylan opened his eyes and screamed and tried to burrow into the bedclothes. Rose was a giant fly. She filled up his whole room. Her head was as big as he was. She was all black and shiny. Her eyes were like beach balls and they were looking everywhere at once, seeing everything at once, and Dylan saw pieces of himself in them again and again and again. She had a long pointy sword thing for a mouth and it was going to stab him. He screamed. She had wings like blankets to wrap him all up. Her big feet were all sticky and there were lots of them. If she touched him with her feet he'd stick to her and he'd never get loose and the monster fly Rose would carry him away and eat him. "Daddy!" he sobbed. The monster buzzed like a lawn mower. Dylan was terrified of lawn mowers.

"Dylan sweetie," the fly buzzed softly. "Pull off my wings."

Tears and the odor that exuded from her huge body made him cough. "No! I don't want to!"

"I'm just a fly. It's okay. It'll be fun. Go ahead."

Her wing brushed over his hands and over his body and settled over his face. It was like the whole world landing on top of him, softly, lovingly, lightly, holding him down, squishing him, making it so he couldn't breathe. He grabbed on to the wing and yanked. It tore. The fly screamed. He pulled harder and the whole wing came off in his hands. The fly screamed. The wing settled onto him like a tent, like a Halloween ghost costume, like somebody else's skin.

Dylan screamed, "I'm sorry! I'm sorry! It was on accident! I'm sorry!"

The fly wasn't mad at him. Rose wasn't mad at him. Daddy got mad at him when he was trying to study and Dylan bothered him. Mommy never got mad at him because nothing Dylan did bothered her because he couldn't get her attention enough to bother her. Rose was really paying attention. Even with his eyes squinched shut he could see that he was the only thing in all her eyes.

"It's okay, Dylan. It doesn't matter what you do to me. You're more important than anything else in the world. You want to pull off my other wing, don't you?"

He didn't say anything.

"Don't you, Dylan?"

"Yes."

"So do it. It's okay. It's no big deal. Go ahead."

And he did. It was easier this time. Now he knew how hard to pull and how far to twist. Now he knew that hurting flies didn't matter, and that flies couldn't really scream.

Chapter Fourteen

In Another Life
(1999)

Jenny and Charlie McInnis had been happily married for nine years, long enough to know what to expect from the life they'd set up together. Their son Dylan and their daughter Elizabeth were healthy and adorable and no more difficult than any other preschooler and infant, certainly no more difficult than had been expected. Charlie was in law school, doing well, liking it, as he'd known he would. Jenny was Manager of Guest Relations for a midsized hotel, exactly the work she'd gone to school for; she'd gone back to work six weeks after the birth of each of her children, just as she'd planned.

In the life they were constructing together, there'd been no surprises, and none was likely. Even their arguments were predictable.

"Don't tell me how I feel."

"Then *you* tell me how you feel, because I don't have a clue."

The exchange scarcely made sense anymore, although they both delivered their lines with practiced pacing and creditable emotion. This was not a serious argument. Jenny and Charlie didn't have serious arguments. But they said the same things to each other, every time, and nothing changed. Jenny was getting worn down.

What was getting worn down, specifically, was her concentration. She was finding it harder and harder to concentrate on being Elizabeth and Dylan's mother, Charlie's wife, Manager of Guest Relations at the hotel, Jennifer Janet Melchior McInnis altogether. A strong impulse had come upon her to play with the facts of her life.

Lately, for instance, she'd found herself beguiled by the notion of living alone, which she'd never in her life done and which was not likely to happen in the foreseeable future. Completely alone, with responsibility for no other person and with no one whatsoever to take notice, in a town full of strangers who stayed that way, with no human interactions but the most functional and no expectations beyond basic civility. Not for long but vividly, she

imagined herself walking along a crowded, anony-
mous, treeless street, pleased to be greeted by no
passerby; buying a quart of milk in a friendly,
impersonal store where she was not spoken to by
name; letting herself into the close, dim rooms
where she lived by herself; eating supper standing
up; wailing along with loud blues on the stereo in
the middle of the night.

"Mommy? Mom? The baby's crying."

Or, she'd like to be a contemplative mystic in an
abbey in the mountains, speaking rarely or not at
all, consciousness given over to music and prayer
and—rarely, rapturously—the presence of God.
Plain cotton would soothe her skin, abrade gently.
Light would break through the tiny stained-glass
disc at the apex of the narrow window, no more
than a hand wide but ten feet tall, in the end wall
of the dark nave. Music, clearly heard, swelled her
heart. Something began in her that she guessed was
a prayer.

She could do that. She wouldn't, but she could.
From an article in the paper last summer, she knew
the location of such an abbey; a scrap of newsprint
with the address and phone number, unlabeled,
was tucked behind the credit cards in her wallet,
the clipping itself discarded long ago. Tonight she
could go out for milk—it was true that they were
almost out of milk—and call the abbey from a pay
phone to make a reservation. After Charlie and the
kids left in the morning for day care and school,
she could take a taxi to the airport, use an alias to

buy a ticket, and by this time tomorrow be in her new life, hidden and revealed. She wouldn't, but she could.

"Mom, Mom, Lizbet's crying. She's screaming."

Somewhat dreamily, Jenny let Dylan pull her into the baby's room. The baby wasn't crying. Jenny put her hand on her daughter's back, very lightly so as not to wake her; the warmth, the rise and fall of the baby's breath, should have moved her. Sometimes Charlie would stroke Elizabeth's pale hair or rub Dylan's broad little back until they woke up; he claimed he didn't mean to, he just wanted to touch them, but Jenny knew he could never get enough of his kids. She, on the other hand, was just as happy to let them sleep. Quickly she withdrew from both the sleeping Elizabeth and the wakeful, watchful Dylan. Dylan didn't follow her out of the room.

Overhead, Grandma Cecelia's footsteps had stopped, as well as the tune she'd been whistling. Jenny listened upward, wondering how long the silence had been going on. Should she be alarmed? She never could decide. Grandma's health was good. There might be some forgetfulness, a lapse in judgment now and then, but it was unclear to Jenny whether these were age-related changes or basic personality traits. There'd been some sort of eye surgery years ago—Jenny had a vague memory of her father spending a week or two out here helping Grandma and, as if in payment, bringing home new targets for his mockery: Aunt Ginger, who wasn't right in the head; Uncle Dennis's adopted Vietnamese sons; Aunt Karen's slavish devotion to her husband and kids; Grandma's housekeeping; Grandma's social activism. But lopsided reading glasses were the only residual effect of whatever the problem had been; Grandma still sewed, read regular print, drove. She was in her eighties, though. Thinking about all that was wearing, too, and often boring, so Jenny didn't think about it any more than she had to.

From the start she'd understood they weren't to be mere tenants. Grandma looked out for them, too; her attentiveness was sometimes excessive and often a bit off-target—she'd fuss about things that weren't problems and miss things that were—but the mutual regard was, for the most part, both convenient and congenial. Increasingly, though, Jenny chafed at the entanglement.

Charlie came and stood at a little distance from her, as if wary of approaching her, as if the argument had meant something. Vastly annoyed, she snapped, "What?"

"I'm sorry, Jen."

"I'm sorry, too." Neither of them was apologizing for anything particular, only for the unpleasant disruption. The exchange was part of the routine, and it should have been enough to move them on to the next phase.

This time Charlie wasn't satisfied. "I love you."

He wanted something from her. The best she could do was, "You, too," and even that was too much for her. Though not nearly enough for him.

Dylan had popped up between then, babbling, telling one of his endless stories. "Mommy!" he'd insist if he could sense her attention wandering. "Mommy!" She had done all this before, ad infinitum, ad nauseam.

A whiff of an unclean odor made her sinuses ache. With a sigh she added to her mental weekend chore list "clean under the sink." Making lists made her feel she'd accomplished something. Later, if she had to, she'd go so far as to make a written list.

Grandma walked across the kitchen above this kitchen. She must be wearing slippers; her footsteps swished. The phone rang. Jenny and Charlie both glanced at it. Grandma would answer; it was probably for her anyway. Sometimes Jenny could hardly stand sharing a phone with Grandma. Sometimes she could hardly tolerate the intrusiveness of the thing ringing at all. Its second ring was interrupted by Grandma's two-tone interrogatory murmur.

Suddenly distraught, as though from a profound need long unmet, Dylan cried, "I'm *hungry!*"

"Dinner will be ready soon," Jenny told him perversely, knowing full well that if he had any concept of "soon," it would likely add to his distress when it wasn't soon enough.

"No!" Already he had progressed to desperate shrieking. "I'm hungry *now!*"

Jenny's step backward brought her into collision with her small, distraught son, who'd flung himself supine onto the rug in front of the sink. She did not kick him. "Well, Dylan, I can't make the biscuits get done any faster."

He howled. Jenny gritted her teeth. The telephone rang again and Grandma answered it again. How many times was this pattern destined to repeat itself? The fact that it was comforting contributed to her feeling of suffocation.

Two years ago she had barely known her grandmother, contact with her father's side of the family having been minimal since her parents' divorce when she was nine. The vacancy of the basement apartment in her father's mother's house, in a suburb of the very city where Charlie'd been accepted to law school, had been serendipitous; moving in had been a temporary practicality. The fact that they were still here and making no plans to move was testimony to the overall agreeability of the arrangement, she supposed, as well as to inertia. Things just sort of went along.

Jenny told herself, as she frequently did: *This is a good life,* which it was. Yet the wish not to be here had strong, sustained, shameful and exhilarating, almost erotic appeal.

Here, in this white kitchen cooking, listening for Grandma and not knowing what she was listening for, vaguely hassled by work problems she found it hard to care about, vaguely besieged by the impossible and unfair demands of her children, arguing with her husband over things that didn't matter and could never be resolved; here, in an upwardly mo-

301

bile career different in no significant detail from the one she'd prepared herself for; here, in this bright blue and brown-gold part of the country whose once breathtaking beauty was beginning to seem barren; here, in this life. Here, instead of anywhere else.

Charlie repeated helplessly, "I love you, Jenny."

"I love you, too," she answered at once, meaning it, if in a skeletal sort of way. The other was just play; it didn't hurt anybody.

Overhead Grandma Cecelia stomped three times, the signal that the phone was for them. Still locked in their nebulously hurtful conflict, Charlie and Jenny didn't immediately respond. When the three thumps came again, Jenny thought she would scream. She snatched up the phone.

"Hi there, girlfriend."

"Rose," Jenny breathed. The gritty, gray tension began at once to seep out of her, replaced by another kind of tension—warmer, more brightly colored.

"Did I catch you at a bad time?"

Jenny smiled at the coyness. "Yes, and I'm glad you did."

Rose laughed her wide-open laugh. "So I'm psychic, right?"

"I *guess.*"

"We're psychically linked."

"Apparently."

"Want to get together later?"

Jenny ran through in her mind the requirements

of the evening ahead, which were somewhat fuzzy. "I should stay home tonight," she told Rose. "I have things to do around the house and for work."

"Oh, come on. A break'll do you good. They won't even miss you."

"Give me an hour," she agreed, a little giddily. "I'll meet you at Sherman's."

Charlie was frowning and shaking his head as she hung up. "I've got an exam tomorrow. I need every waking minute to study." Then he added, "I told you. We had a deal, remember?"

This was quite true. They were meticulous about division of labor; she'd agreed to let him study tonight. Nonetheless, something like a sonic boom went off in her head, and there was a quick shift in the way the world presented itself to her. "Rose needs me," she insisted, and knew that was true although she couldn't have sworn that "need" was the right word. "I won't be out long. Get Grandma to watch Dylan until bedtime if you don't have time for him." That was unfair and mean-spirited, of course, and Charlie's face hardened.

"I love you," Dylan announced, whether because he'd perceived a crevasse opening in his life or out of an impulse not to be outdone, or just because he'd lately mastered the phrase.

Scooping him up, Charlie put his free arm around Jenny, pulling the three of them into a single embrace. Tingling with dangerous pleasure and affection, Jenny leaned her head into the warm seam at the juncture of her husband's and son's bodies.

This was a good life. She could call Rose back and make plans for some other time.

But she couldn't stay like that for long; she could hardly breathe. Extricating herself, she pretended not to see the dismay flicker across Charlie's face. By the smell, she knew the biscuits were on the verge of burning. Her shirt was streaked with flour; she'd have to change before she left the house.

Although she'd known Rose Quinlivan ever since she'd lived here, she couldn't quite remember how they'd met. That their paths had crossed that first time, whenever and wherever it had been, never ceased to amaze her, for their lives were very different; Rose was unmarried and childless by choice, also by choice vastly underemployed, and really they shared no interests other than each other. It wasn't easy to say what drew them together. But something did, more and more. Whenever Jenny tried to discover what it was, she found she couldn't keep her mind on the question for long. Once or twice she'd asked Rose, who'd laughed and patted her arm and told her not to bother with things that didn't matter.

Often Jenny marveled that she hadn't known Rose all her life. At the same time, she couldn't quite call her to mind—her appearance, her voice, her manner. Nothing caught her essence. Nothing explained how well they fit together.

She brought herself back. "Let me get dinner on the table."

Charlie loped off to check on the baby, with Dy-

Ian now crowing in his arms and clutching his black wiry hair. From a filmy distance, Jenny understood that, here and now, she was happy.

But instantly came the caveat: She could also be happy somewhere else, with someone else or no one, living a wholly different sort of life with its own features that would be dear to her. This life, then, would be one of the possibilities she'd missed; would she yearn for it? Would she tease and torment herself by imagining a life like this? Would one life still bleed into another? Would she still find it impossible to live in only one? Would she still know Rose?

The biscuits were perfect. She arranged them on a flowered plate, taking some time with the presentation as if anybody else would notice. She ladled the stew into blue bowls, put an ice cube in Dylan's to cool it, then felt bad because she'd done it too soon, the cube would be mostly melted by the time he got to the table and he'd miss the crackling.

When she called, "Dinner!" they didn't come. The meal was perfect. The table was perfect. She'd done her job and done it well, and it wasn't good enough. "Charlie! Dinner!" He didn't answer. Jenny stood in the middle of the room, not touching anything, eyes closed, imagining herself leaving the blue bowls and the flowered plate on the table and just walking out. She'd go to Sherman's. She'd wait for Rose. Rose would listen carefully, would hear implications and nuances Jenny would not have been aware of until Rose heard them, would give her to understand that Charlie and the kids would get along fine without her, that she deserved better, that she owed it to herself to be happy. Rose was a good friend.

Dylan was crying. Jenny was instantly alert, moving toward him, listening for Charlie's intervention. Then she smelled that sharp odor again, and the noise retreated until it was like static from headphones somewhere, leeched of meaning, unattached to her or any other person, requiring nothing of her. An unmoored feeling swept her. Everything around her receded and flattened into only memory, only imagination, no more real than any other life she might have lived. Dylan was crying. When she returned to this time and place, it was to mourn a subtle, complicated, profoundly compromising loss, and Charlie was saying, "He put a pillow over her head."

"What?" Jenny covered her face, uncovered it. Suddenly everything was unnaturally vivid. "What?"

Charlie was carrying the baby. "Dylan put a pillow over Elizabeth's head."

Jenny rushed to him and reached for her daughter, but he would not give her up. In order to put her arms around the baby she had to embrace Charlie, too. Dylan was crying. "Is she okay? Oh, God, is she okay?"

"I think so. I don't know how long the pillow was there, but she's breathing and I think she's okay."

"Why did he do that?" She turned on her son,

grabbed him by the shoulders, screamed into his crumpled face. "Why did you do that? Why did you hurt your sister?"

Dylan and Charlie answered together. "She was crying."

Charlie said, "I don't think he meant to hurt her."

Jenny held Dylan at arm's length and stared at him. There was something here she didn't understand. There was something she'd missed.

Blinded, deafened, numbed by insensate rage, she shook the child. Shook him again. Shook him again, savagely. Shook him again. "Jenny! Stop it!" The baby was crying now. Dylan was screaming. She shook him again. Charlie grabbed her arm, shoved her, yelled at her again. "Stop it! Stop it, Jenny!"

She stopped. She could be somewhere else, anywhere else. She let go of her son, got to her feet. Her ears were ringing, her vision blurred, her head swimming, her hands and feet tingling. As she stumbled out of the house, Charlie called after her, but her clearest thought was, "Rose."

Sherman's was just barely within walking distance of Grandma Cecelia's house. Every night the coffee house had live music of some sort, but on weeknights hardly any customers; tonight's lone acoustic guitarist was playing mostly for himself, and seemed perfectly, solipsistically content. Rose had been at the counter chatting with the proprietor, but turned toward the door with two huge mugs as

Jenny came in. They hailed each other and smiled.

"Hey," Rose said. They sat at a table by the window, not hiding, not pretending.

Jenny had anticipated telling Rose about the incident at home—how Dylan could have killed Elizabeth, how she could have hurt Dylan, how Charlie had been protecting everybody from everybody, how she'd walked out. On the way over she'd run through the story again and again, experimenting with which details to emphasize, interpretations to suggest, predictions to hazard, beginnings and endings to offer. She told the tale like Scheherezade, fighting for her life, even saying some of it aloud when no one would hear, and the rhythms of it came to match the rhythms of her heartbeat and footsteps and breath. By the time she'd reached Sherman's she'd known what she was going to say.

Instead, she found herself—quite as if coming upon herself after having been estranged for a while; as if rounding a bend in a dim forest path and there she was—found herself telling Rose how she could have studied abroad her junior year in college. She'd gone so far as to fill out the first series of applications before losing nerve or simply interest. It wasn't exactly that she regretted not having gone, or that in hindsight she thought she'd made the wrong choice. But she had made a choice, and she could have made another, and if she had she would be somewhere else now, living a different life. There was a keen pleasure in imagining who she'd have been then, a swirling temptation to imagine as far as she could go.

"Ah, London." Rose sighed and nodded. "London's a wonderful place." Later, Jenny would muse only fleetingly, and with more delight than unease, that she was almost sure she hadn't specified a destination. "We should go there sometime," Rose declared, and Jenny was nonplussed by her own eager assent. Why should she believe that someday she'd go to London with Rose Quinlivan? And why should believing it give her what could only be called a thrill?

"I don't know—" she demurred.

Rose patted her hand. "It's just a dream. Where's the harm in dreaming?"

She needed to think about her son. She could not. She could not keep her mind on him; what he'd done and could have done seemed far less real than going to London. Her passport was still good. With or without Rose, she could go. She wouldn't, but she could. When she made love with Charlie that night—fierce, even painful sex, as if he knew he wasn't getting through to her—she was also making love with Nigel, the Englishman she had never met but could have met and fallen in love with, still could. Stroking Charlie's dear, familiar, portly body, she exulted in Nigel's thinness, his skin very nearly the same hue as his ash-brown hair. She knew from Rose there was no harm in this; Charlie had no access to her fantasies, and so they wouldn't hurt him. "I love you," she breathed to Charlie, and truly she did, but she could as easily have loved Nigel, and then where would she be? The possibilities were delicious.

They'd been lying together quietly for a while when Charlie stirred and said, "Jen, we need to talk."

Jenny pretended to be asleep.

"What happened between you and Grandpa?" It had taken her this long to ask, out of shyness and deference but mostly because it kept slipping her mind.

She could place Grandma and Grandpa Melchior's divorce in her personal time line because it had happened at about the same time as her parents'. Her father and his younger siblings had all long since left home; Jenny and her brother had still been in grade school. Scott had wanted to talk about it all the time. Tiresomely, he'd never stopped wanting to talk about it, how it had made him commitment-phobic, workaholic, irresponsible about child support, addicted to nicotine.

Jenny remembered obsessively reading books she could scarcely tell apart but that allowed her to feel less present, watching every day for weeks and months hours of undifferentiated TV that took her not to anyplace else in particular but *away,* immersing herself in school despite her profound boredom with everything about it, spending a lot of time at friends' houses absorbing the ambience of their family lives.

She didn't think she'd really blamed herself or anybody else. She didn't think she'd ever even tried to guess why it had happened, any more than you'd try to come up with a reason for the storm that ruined your picnic or the sore throat that kept you home from your friend's birthday party; there *were* reasons, of course, clouds and germs, but they didn't explain why this had happened to *you, today*, and in any case you still missed the picnic and the party.

And if you'd gone to the picnic, you might have drowned in the lake, or gotten salmonella from the potato salad. If you'd gone to the party, who knows whom you'd have met?

Loss and bafflement, she remembered, and also an epiphany of sorts: For the first time, she'd seen that there were many lives a person could live, by choice or by happenstance, and that the life you thought you were in at any given moment wasn't necessarily the one you'd live out.

Sudden images of Rose Quinlivan, vivid though inchoate, made Jenny too restless to sit still. She went into the kitchen for a glass of water. When she turned on the tap, she was acutely aware that water could be running like this somewhere else at this very moment; the play of this light on the back of her hand as she reached for a glass in Grandma's cupboard reminded her of another light in another place and someone else—Rose, say—perceiving her hand and its motion; then her point of view shifted so that she was the watcher and the sunny living room and the objects in it—the quilt on the floor, the piano at the far end, the old woman and little boy looking out the window together at the squirrel in the birdfeeder—altered in some slight but crucial way from what she had left minutes before.

A not entirely unpleasant disorientation flooded her. For just a moment she didn't quite know where she was. She paused at the threshold, savoring the possibility, however slight, that the couch she had been sitting on would be covered in a different fabric now or in a different place in the room, that the people she was about to rejoin would be different people from the ones she had left. But everything was the same, and Jenny struggled to breathe.

Grandma and Dylan were admiring a quilt spread in the pale gold parallelogram cast through the big west window onto the carpet. "My mother made this quilt," Grandma Cecelia was saying, and as Jenny came in she glanced up to include her. "Your mommy's great-grandma. Your great-*great*-grandmother."

Genealogy was lost on Dylan, of course, and Jenny knew nothing of her great-grandmother except her name: Elizabeth, unfortunately called Libby. Elizabeth was a family name in Charlie's family, too, although those Elizabeths had been called Liz and Betty; she hadn't shared Charlie's filial satisfaction at naming their daughter Elizabeth, but she could live with the name. She could have lived with just about any name, except Jennifer; there was a certain wry, vaguely pleasing irony in the fact that she had a better fix on "Libby" than on "Jenny."

The quilt wasn't especially beautiful; Jenny didn't sew, but it didn't look very complicated, either. Its most impressive feature was the fact that it hadn't fallen apart. "Just imagine the hours of work." She shook her head. "I don't have the patience."

"It's what they call a crazy quilt. No plan to it, just pieces stitched together any which way and you see how the design turned out when you're done." She reached to pat the ancient calico cat asleep on the window sill. "That's why this one's name is Quilt. Your Aunt Ginger came up with that."

"Stream of consciousness," Jenny said with a laugh.

Grandma nodded, pleased. "James Joyce with a needle."

Jenny sank onto the dusty couch and made to pull her son onto her lap. Giggling and screeching, he crawled away from her to sit cross legged on the far edge of the quilt, making faces at her. "Dylan," she told him, uncertainly, "don't mess up Grandma Celia's nice quilt." How tired she was of the stream of decisions, simultaneously minuscule and monumental, that a parent was called upon to make.

"It's okay," Grandma assured her. "It's been around a long time. He won't hurt it."

Dylan beamed at Grandma and cast his mother a triumphant sidelong look. Undone by the illogic— if the quilt hadn't been damaged in fifty years it couldn't be damaged in the next five minutes—Jenny just gave an all-purpose frown and shake of the head.

He was into something else by now, anyway. That was another wearing aspect of parenthood: By the time you'd figured out how to respond to one issue, the kid had moved on to another. He'd crawled up onto the desk chair and grabbed something, off the top of the desk or maybe even out of a drawer. A child's picture, in green; for an instant Jenny thought he'd drawn it, but it was far more sophisticated than that. "Dylan," she said again, with real anger now, and started to get to her feet.

Grandma reached him first, and instead of pulling the picture out of his grasp, as Jenny would have done and likely both ripped it and broken his heart, she picked him up, settled him onto her lap, and looked at it with him. "A friend of mine drew that for me," she told him. "It's a frog. My friend's name is Toby. He's been really sick. I haven't heard from him for a while." Dylan was squalling and squirming to get down now as if Grandma Cecelia had held him for a very long time against his will. She let him go and smoothed the frog picture. "I ought to get this framed," she said, and Jenny made a mental note that matting and framing the drawing might be a good birthday present; concern that she might forget brought instant anxiety. Grandma slid Toby's picture back into the drawer and turned back to Jenny. "How was work?"

Jenny sighed. She rather liked her job, but a lot

of the time it didn't seem to *matter* very much. "Oh, I don't know. Sometimes I think I should have been—I don't know, a concert pianist." She flexed her fingers. "Not that I have any talent to speak of."

Where had that come from? She'd never even taken piano lessons as a kid. Hadn't Rose mentioned playing the piano?

Dylan had flattened himself and squirmed partway under the couch. Jenny said automatically, "Dylan, leave the kitty alone," then saw Quilt on her way into the kitchen and mused that cats fleeing from small children were probably the source of the phrase "high-tailing it." She kept a weary, wary eye on her son's protruding legs and feet, resenting that generalized parental hypervigilance.

Dylan was dead. It was only fantasy, with no power actually to make things happen, but the audacity of it took her breath away. The scene played out rapidly in her mind, as fully realized as if it had gone through numerous careful revisions: One early evening when she'd worked late and Charlie was at the library, Jenny came to pick her son up from Grandma Cecelia's and both the child and the old woman were dead of carbon monoxide poisoning from the faulty furnace. A peaceful death. A harrowing grief. A direction her life might take, terrible, of course, but strangely exhilarating.

"I know just what you mean," Grandma said wryly. "In another life, I'm going to play jazz sax in some little dive on Bourbon Street."

For a guilty split second, Jenny thought Grandma

somehow knew about her awful, seductive death fantasy, then realized it was the concert-pianist fantasy she was responding to. "Jazz sax? Really? Do you play?"

"Not a note."

They both laughed. " 'In another life.' That's an interesting way to put it."

"Well, it certainly isn't going to be in this one."

"Do you believe in reincarnation?"

"I don't think so. And if there is such a thing, I doubt that whoever I am next time will like jazz just because I do."

"Does that bother you?" Jenny asked, keenly aware of the need for caution. "The things you'll never do? The places you'll never go and people you'll never meet? Everything you've given up in order to have the life you have?" When she'd asked the same question of Rose, Rose had insisted there was no need to give anything up, that you could have it all.

Grandma was quiet for a few moments. "When I was sixteen, I was engaged to a boy named Johnny."

"Sixteen! So young!" Grandma only smiled. "Why didn't you marry him?"

After a pause that hinted at much unsaid, the older woman answered, "It turned out he was in love with somebody else."

Emerging from under the couch, exclaiming to himself, tawny hair tousled and striped shirt hiked up to expose tender skin, Dylan brought with him a glossy red card in a torn envelope. Solemnly, proud of himself, he scooted over to his great-grandma and presented it to her, saying something emphatic that might have been, "Here."

"Thanks, sweetie." Grandma seized any chance to kiss Dylan, and she kissed him now. "Guess I haven't cleaned way back under the couch for a while. Since Christmas, anyway, huh? I hope this is from *last* Christmas!"

Dylan had his eyes on the card and was waving his fingers at it, making the "uh uh uh" sound that meant, "I want that!"

"Dylan," Jenny admonished distractedly.

"You may have the card. I'll keep the envelope. It's from a high school friend. I only hear from her at Christmas and I'm not sure I have her right address." Handing him the card, which had a shiny Santa Claus swooping across the top, she fingered the envelope's ragged edge and gave a small ironic laugh. "In another life, I swear I'm going to know that woman better," and, once again, Jenny had the feeling that more was unsaid than said. Dylan plopped down happily on the quilt, singing a recognizable version of "Santa Claus Is Coming to Town."

"Did your mother make the quilt for you for a special occasion?"

Grandma Cecelia ran her hand thoughtfully over a section of the quilt done mostly in pinks. "She didn't make it for me personally. During one period of her life they said she made a lot of quilts. She didn't even give it to me." Grandma hesitated. "Truthfully, I don't even know which mother made it."

Jenny searched her memory for any clue to this "which mother" business. But if she'd ever known the story, she'd completely forgotten it.

Grandma supplied, "My natural mother's sister adopted me. So one way to look at it is my aunt was my mother and my mother was my aunt. Or I had two mothers, if you use different definitions of the word, but then you really need different words, don't you? Funny how all that really threw me for a loop at one time, and now it just seems like one more thing, you know? Anyway, nobody knows which sister pieced the quilt."

With a wistful smile, she leaned absently to trace a nubby blue fabric that showed up here and there in the quilt; following her grandmother's fingertips, from the near corner to a spot somewhere in the center third to the far edge where the blue scrap blended with the dark gray backing and would have been hard to spot on her own, Jenny glimpsed a pattern, but it vanished when Grandma brought her hands back to her lap and again took up the story which might or might not turn out to have a plot.

"My Aunt Maureen, the youngest of the three sisters, sent it as a wedding gift when Ray and I got married." She looked pensive suddenly, and Jenny expected a segue into reminiscence about the wedding, marriage, divorce. Instead, Grandma said,

"Now *there's* an interesting life in terms of—what? Serendipity? Maureen's, I mean. The family story is that their mother—my grandmother, your great-great-grandmother, Dylan's great-great-*great*-grandmother"—she shook her head in amazement—"died giving birth to her."

Grandma didn't reminisce very often, certainly couldn't be accused of living in the past or wishing to. She was unabashedly interested in the past, her own and everyone else's, but she was unabashedly interested in her own and everyone else's present and future as well. "Aren't we human beings *fascinating?*" was a favorite phrase, sometimes a rhetorical question, sometimes a true interrogatory requiring a reply, sometimes an exclamation delivered with a chuckle of appreciation or an ironic, discouraged sigh. More than once Grandma had declared Rose fascinating; something about the way she said it hinted that she didn't like her much.

"I've always thought," Grandma was saying, "there was more to it than that."

Out of politeness and because she'd utterly lost her place in the conversation, Jenny felt compelled to inquire, "What do you mean?"

"Oh, I don't know, really. More than anything else, it's a feeling that things are not what they appear to be. I've come up with theories, but I'll never be able to confirm any of them because anybody who knew the whole truth is long gone. Maybe Aunt Maureen wasn't Grandfather Harry's child. Secrets like that seem to run in the family, and my life, at least, has definitely been affected, not so much by the secrets themselves as by the sense of things being hidden, which gives them more power than they'd have had otherwise."

This inspired Jenny to pose the question. "What happened between you and Grandpa?"

Again Grandma hesitated, and Jenny was sorry she'd asked. "Do you mean what caused the divorce? Because a lot of things *happened* between us, you know. We were married twenty-six years."

Wishing fervently she'd not started this, Jenny stammered, "The—the divorce, I guess. If you don't mind. I—I didn't mean—"

Grandma patted her knee. "I don't mind, honey. It's part of your story, too, and it's been a long time. A lot of things have happened since then, too. Ray and I got to be—well, I wouldn't say friends. But we came to peace with each other."

Dylan was shredding the Christmas card. Bits of red and white paper sprinkled the quilt like tiny new scraps to be worked in. Grandma's expression as she watched him was indulgent, so Jenny decided she wasn't expected to stop him or interact with him in any other way.

"The simple answer is that there was another woman."

"Marie."

Grandma nodded. "Actually, there'd been quite a few other women before Marie, and there were other women while he was married to her." She grinned, looked down, looked away. "Including me."

Jenny managed not to gasp.

"But Ray wasn't just unfaithful to his wives. He was unfaithful to his own life. Still is. He told me the other day the only thing he feels when he looks back is regret." This time the shake of her head was emphatic. "That's no way to live."

Jenny shivered. "God, when I'm eighty I don't want to feel like I've missed something."

"But you will, honey." Grandma gave her the same indulgent smile she'd bestowed on Dylan. "Everybody misses things. I wish I'd learned to play the saxophone. I wish my marriage had been different. I wish I'd seen Australia."

"No." Jenny was suddenly so resentful she was afraid to say more. She swallowed. "I won't settle."

Grandma regarded her seriously. "You'll miss the life you didn't live. Can't avoid that. But you don't want to also miss the one you do live, which can happen if you don't pay attention to it."

There must be some way, Jenny thought stubbornly, perhaps as an eightieth birthday gift, to take Grandma on a trip to Australia, find her a saxophone teacher, get her back together with Grandpa Ray, investigate the true story of Great-aunt Maureen. Maybe Rose would know how.

The phone rang. While Grandma went to answer it, Dylan approached his mother with a small bulging handful of colored paper scraps, one palm tenderly tented over the other as if cupping a fragile live creature whose existence depended on a choice he needed help to make. Her skin crawled. She got up and strode away from him before he could pull her in.

"Jenny?" The strain in Grandma's voice sent alarm coursing through Jenny: *Fight or flight! Run! Strike back! Defend yourself Save yourself! Absent yourself!* "Jenny? That was the day care. They're waiting for you to pick up the baby."

"Oh my God, the baby." She had forgotten about the baby. Incredibly, she'd forgotten she even *had* a baby; realization of Elizabeth's existence and relationship to her washed over her now in frigid waves. "What time is it?" Checking for her watch, she grasped her left wrist with her right hand, found it bare, held on tight. Wildly she looked around for a clock.

"Six forty-two," Grandma supplied.

"Shit." At a fine of a dollar a minute after six o'clock, this lapse was going to be expensive. Still, utter astonishment rooted her to the spot for another long moment. "I *forgot!*"

"It happens," the older woman tried to assure her, though she couldn't help looking at her askance. "You have an awful lot on your mind."

"It slipped my mind." The turn of phrase was deliciously apt. Wonderingly, horrified, she repeated it. "It completely slipped my mind."

"Go ahead, go get her. Dylan can stay here with me." She didn't move. "Jenny? Are you okay?"

Grandma made shooing motions. "Go!"

It took an actual nudge to rouse Jenny into motion. Rushing out of the house for her daughter, she felt Grandma Cecelia's disapproval and alarm behind her like a siren, and wanted nothing so much as to put herself out of its reach.

She would tell Rose about this. Rose would help her understand.

"It happens." Grandma Cecelia had said the same thing, but it meant more coming from Rose, accompanied by a languid shrug.

"I felt terrible. I still feel terrible." That had been true when she'd sped to pick up Elizabeth, when she'd faced the day-care provider, when she'd confessed her lapse to Charlie, and still while she'd been waiting at Sherman's tonight for what had become her regular tryst with Rose. Now, in Rose's company, self-castigation no longer seemed called for. Rose's bittersweet scent might have been aromatherapy; exquisitely, Jenny relaxed.

Rose snorted, and a dramatic, dismissive flick of her magenta-tipped hand swept a wave of fragrance full into Jenny's face. There was a blip in Jenny's consciousness, like a split-second cocaine rush. "Jenny, Jenny, Jenny," Rose was clucking. "Trust me, it's no big deal. Happens all the time. There's no harm done. Your daughter's fine. Don't beat yourself up over it."

The shift in perspective was palpable, a turn of a few degrees that made everything look new. Jenny felt silly that she'd ever thought forgetting the baby at day care was serious.

"Charlie has left me," she confided. This wasn't true, but it could be. Contemplating how, if this were true, her life would assume a variant form set her heart pounding.

The bassist was plucking the strings on his instrument's lowest belly, *chung chung chu-chu-chung*, tones so deep they were as much tactile as auditory by the time they traveled through the air to her. "Oh, girlfriend," Rose murmured with appreciative sympathy.

Jenny's throat hurt a little. "He just doesn't love me anymore."

"And what happens next?" Encouragement: Not *you'll be all right* but *It's a game. Let yourself go.*

"Raise the kids by myself, I guess."

As though this other life had been dropped whole into her experience, she knew exactly how it would feel to be a single parent. The fatigue. The loneliness. The power. The freedom of not being required to consult another parent about Dylan, the anxiety of not having another parent to consult.

Watching her intently, Rose nodded. "What else, girlfriend? Keep going."

Reality swirled and then abruptly puddled. "Charlie took the kids and left me," Jenny managed to say though thick hot grief. "He says I don't care about any of them." This was not true, but it could be.

"Oh, honey." Rose's voice broke, too, but her eyes blazed.

This was still too easy, did not demand enough of her. Watching Rose's features change in the diffuse, shifting light, she tried, "I've just met this guy named Charlie. He's nice enough, but there are no bells and whistles, you know? I can't imagine it turning into anything serious." Saying that, to such a good listener, she knew what it would mean never to have married Charlie, never to have had Dylan and Elizabeth, and liked it. Recognition of this disloyalty to her husband and children didn't keep her from eagerly awaiting Rose's response.

Rose was intensely attentive, like a member of an improv troupe taking split-second cues, anticipating by the slightest purse of lips or twitch of eyelids what the partner was about to say and saying it with her in apparent unison. This gave the stories a disorienting and seductive three-dimensionality, like full-sensory multi-dimensional dioramas opening up and closing in.

Daringly, Jenny pushed it a step farther. "The baby's dead." She wept. The sorrow was real even if the referent was not. "Elizabeth's dead." She was wailing now. "My daughter's dead! My son killed her!"

The bassist finished his solo. There was scattered applause. Then came a single sustained trumpet note, impossibly high and pure. Jenny thought she would not be able to bear it. Rose took her hand. "Oh, girlfriend, I'm so sorry." Her husky voice played counterpoint to the sweet wail of the trumpet. "And I'm so proud of you."

Now the drummer began a tight solo that would turn wild before it was done. Rose took Jenny's face in her hands. Jenny felt a savage little vibration in her sinuses, letting her know that, with just a tiny shift of the thumbs, Rose could crush her skull. "The whole world of possibilities is ours, if we just don't get too attached to any one of them." Pitched loudly enough to be heard over the rising drums and cymbals, her voice boomed in the sudden silence when the percussionist paused.

"I'm scared!" Jenny whispered.

Rose's fingers tightened on the bones of Jenny's skull. "Don't be afraid, girlfriend. You've got me. You'll always have me."

The percussionist finished her solo to thunderous percussive applause, which was an extension and elaboration, a carrying-on, of what she'd set in motion.

Rose leaned even closer, forehead and then chin and then the front of her lacy white shirt flickering as they passed over the red-globed candle, and kissed Jenny full on the mouth. Jenny felt her lips move as she promised, *"Anything.* With me, you can have anything."

"But none of it matters," Jenny managed to whisper into Rose's mouth.

Rose's long, deep breath of satisfaction tugged at Jenny's lips, throat, lungs. *"Yes."*

* * *

As it turned out, Dylan was the one who died.

It was a summer Saturday. Charlie was at the library studying. Grandma Cecelia was off somewhere, doing something. In her room at the back of the house, Elizabeth had been wailing virtually all afternoon, making it harder for Jenny to concentrate on the quarterly reports she'd brought home to finish. Natter from the TV in the living room told her Dylan was occupied; every now and then she listened in that direction and then let him slide out of her mind.

Birdsong drifted in, presumably from the branches of the tree whose trunk passed by the window above the sink. She'd been drinking coffee all day and by now it was leeched of any flavor but the suggestion—perhaps the memory, perhaps only the idea—of bitterness. Dylan was prattling. The statistics she entered in columns and rows on the report forms, together with the narratives she wrote to support them, repeatedly wandered out of context, so that she had to keep checking her notes to remind herself what all the data referred to. Elizabeth was crying. Dylan was at her elbow chattering. It didn't matter whether she paid attention to them or not; their needs were endless, undifferentiated, insatiable, and it was impossible to discern that anything she did or didn't do made any difference.

"Mommy, look. Mommy, look. Mommy."

"Dylan, *what?*"

"Look." He mimicked her exasperation.

She didn't look. "Mmm hmm. That's nice."

"Mommy, this is for you, Mommy."

He laid the green paper with the crayoned scrawl on her keyboard where she couldn't help glancing at it. Impatiently she flapped it at him when he didn't take it back. "It's *nice,* honey." What more do you want from me? "Now go find something to do. Mommy's busy."

She was practicing for an important recital, and this little boy she scarcely knew would not stop bothering her. Where was his mother? The keys vibrated under the pads of her fingers.

She was on a plane bound for Australia, where she would embark on a walkabout to meet her spirit guide and be told the meaning of life. This little boy kept kicking the seat behind her and demanding that she admire his scribbles. She'd never seen him before, and after this eighteen-hour flight she would certainly never see him again. Where was his mother? The plane jounced over bumpy air.

Dylan wasn't satisfied. No matter what she did, he was never satisfied, so what was the point? "It's a tree. It's got birds in it. They're singing. See?"

"Put it up on the refrigerator so Daddy can see it."

"Mommy, play with me."

"I can't, Dylan. I'm working."

"He could play in the bathtub."

Jenny started, although she knew it was Rose. She always knew it was Rose. Rose was never a surprise at any time or in any place. Still, blood rushed to her cheeks and her head swam.

With the screen in front of her and bright sun behind, Rose was a fuzzy silhouette, but her voice was clear. "He likes to play in the tub, don't you, Dylan? That'll keep him out of your hair for a while."

Face alight, Dylan had run to greet her. The screen door wasn't latched and she knew she was always welcome, but Rose liked to be let in.

Rose picked Dylan up and exclaimed over his drawing. She knew it was a tree with birds in it without being told, and she took it further, pointing out details Jenny was sure he hadn't meant to be there, praising his color choices as if they'd been anything more than random, telling him the birds looked so real they could fly right off the page. Dylan was thrilled. Jenny felt a little guilty, vaguely repulsed, distantly uneasy, but mostly she was just glad to be spared.

From the voluminous pocket every piece of her clothing seemed to have, Rose produced a bright plastic toy. "I brought you a present," she told Dylan coyly.

He squealed, and not for the first time his mother noticed how a child's delight and distress could mimic each other. "A boat! Look, Mommy, Aunty Rose bringed me a boat!"

"Brought."

"You can play with it in the bathtub." Something about Rose's insistence on the bathtub struck Jenny as peculiar, even slightly sinister, but she couldn't get a handle on it before it slipped out of her mind.

329

"Mommy? Can I?"

"What, Dylan? Can you what?" One of the more numbing aspects of motherhood was the obligation to make countless spur-of-the-moment decisions, choices, inferences, interpretations, judgment calls—any one of which might have salubrious or disastrous effects, or no effect at all.

Dylan and Rose repeated together, "Play in the bathtub." In another life it could be musicians waiting for her to bring down the baton, that electric moment before the first note, under her command.

"Sure. Why not?" She waved them away.

After a pause, Dylan pointed out, "I need you to put water in the tub."

"Aunty Rose can do it."

"No," Rose said, with an odd emphasis. "That's your job."

"It was your idea."

Rose just stood there holding Dylan, both of them implacable. It wasn't worth the energy to argue. Jenny saved the data on the screen, turned off the computer so Dylan wouldn't play with it, and stalked past them to the bathroom. In the room across the hall, Elizabeth, miraculously, was quiet, finally asleep or at least for once not crying. Thank God for small favors.

Getting the bath water the right temperature was a long, vexatious process; several times she thought she had it right, stood up, dried off her hand, then forced herself to check again and found it too hot or too cold. Only after she'd added bubbles did she remember that sometimes Dylan didn't like bubbles; only after she'd dumped in the bucket of bath toys did she realize she should have let him choose. The sound of the running water muted by the bubble bath suggested waves on sand. Without even closing her eyes she was on a beach in a storm, a northern beach, Alaska, sky and water and sand variegated gray, bitterly lonely, about to walk out into the water until it closed cold and gray over her head.

"Not yet," Rose said behind her. "You have things to do."

Deliciously alarmed, Jenny turned. "Not yet what? What do I have to do that matters?" The array of possible replies to both questions was infinite. She held her breath to hear what Rose would say.

Rose said, "Sure, go ahead. I'll help Dylan into the tub."

Jenny thought she must have missed a line or two of dialogue. Not infrequently she resurfaced from somewhere else into an ongoing conversation. This time, though, she picked up right away what was intended. She was to check on the baby, who was not crying. She was to go into the room across the hall and see which of the myriad possibilities she would find.

She paused in the doorway to savor the sensation that her next step, her next action or inaction, would transport her into another life. She'd longed for something like this, a discreet moment that would change her life forever; not for her Grandma's patient and incremental "*everything changes your life.*"

The baby was not in her crib.

The baby had been kidnapped. The terror that filled her throat was laced with and diluted by giddy images of detectives, reporters, ransom notes, milk cartons. It was several seconds before she turned on the light.

Elizabeth lay on the floor against the far wall, completely wrapped in blankets and towels but still instantly recognizable as her child. Jenny cried out, sank to her knees, crawled to the inert little bundle, put her hand on it.

The baby was dead. Terrible sorrow swept toward her like a tidal wave, from another life, from someone else's life, from this life.

The little body moved. In another life she was kneeling in the filth of a Calcutta street ministering to someone else's baby. She tore into the suffocating layers of cloth over her daughter's face. A bath towel. A spit-up cloth. Dylan's baby blanket, soft blue with a tight, non-porous weave; he still slept with that blanket.

Dylan's blanket.

Elizabeth was breathing. Her skin was warm and pink. Her long-lashed eyes, still murky blue, seemed almost to focus on her mother's face before they flickered away, and her rosebud mouth curved into what might have been her first true smile.

Jenny bellowed, "Dylan!" The baby started,

arched her back, and shrieked. Splashing and gales of laughter came from the bathroom, but no answer. "God damn it, Dylan!"

She gathered up Elizabeth, who, terrified by now, shrank from her. It was not lost on Jenny that she, not Dylan, had caused the baby's hysteria; *the law of unintended consequences,* she thought in a kind of calm, wry hysteria of her own. She cuddled the child, cooed to her, all in all did her best to soothe her. In another life she could be a pediatrician examining an infant for signs of abuse. In another life she might walk like this into a room like this, with summer sunshine dimmed by sea-green blinds, and ache for the child she had never had, the nursery that would always be empty. In another life maybe the light would have a Mediterranean cast—more liquid, somehow; more golden—and waiting in the lovely room would be her much younger Greek lover, maybe a woman with honey-colored hair long and sweet enough to cover them both. In another life she might put the baby—with whom she now felt only the most minimal connection—back where she'd found her and tiptoe out of the room and nobody would know the choice she'd made.

Rose called her name, and two thoughts leaped clear and hot as fire in her mind: *Rose would know* and *This isn't it. There's something else. Pay attention. There's another choice to be made.* Rose called her name again, and Jenny noted how much she liked the sound of it. Kindly, distantly, hastily she laid the baby, who was still sobbing, back into the crib and left the room to find out what Rose wanted.

Rose said, "Come sit with Dylan. I have to go."

Jenny said, "He doesn't need anybody with him. He's a big boy." She thought to say, *He tried to hurt his baby sister,* but now that seemed not quite true, not quite real, an image breaking through from another life. "You're leaving?" *Don't leave me alone with these children who came from another life into this one through me but surely not out of me in any intimate sense, surely not.* "Where are you going?"

Rose said, "Oh, here and there. To and fro. 'Round the earth, roaming about." She laughed. "I'll be back, though. I'll always be back. You'll be in my thoughts. And I in yours, no doubt." With a jaunty hug and kiss, she was gone.

"Mommy, look. Mommy, Mommy, Mommy, look."

Dylan was dunking his head underwater, ostentatiously holding his nose and blowing loud bubbles. Rose must have put some of her own perfume in with the Winnie-the-Pooh bubble bath, because the bathroom suddenly reeked, psychedelically bittersweet.

Dylan popped to the surface, very pleased with himself. "See? See, Mommy? I can put my head underwater. See? Mommy, see?"

Jenny knelt on the wet floor beside the tub and

rolled up her sleeve. "Do it again," she told her son tenderly.

Delighted by her attention, he made a great show of holding his nose and squinching his eyes shut, then plunged. Jenny put her hand on the back of his head and held him down. He struggled, but not much, as if accepting her attention, as if it didn't matter much one way or another.

Jenny felt a dreamy sort of panic. She leaned her forehead against the warm porcelain and breathed deeply. In another life, this was not happening. In another life, before and after this one, the living and dying of one little boy wouldn't matter at all. In another life, she and Rose were traveling together around the world.

Chapter Fifteen

The Viewing
(2000)

Sepia-colored light gave no hint as to the time of year or time of day. Sound was sepia-colored and imprecise, too, as was pain.

Cecelia heard someone say, "Well, look who's here. I haven't seen you for a while." Jovial, friendly, hail-fellow-well-met.

Was this somebody she should know? Male or female, old or young? From the recent past (a singer from a dream, someone reading aloud, her granddaughter who lived alone in the basement apartment and often could be heard talking to herself, what Cecelia took to be her own moans, someone crooning to still her moans) or the distant past (the car radio in the dark, the chortle of a small boy bringing a rock down on a big ugly spider)? Nearly everything now reached her from some part of the past; the present was no longer present by the time she was aware of it.

"So where've you been?"

Was the query addressed to her? She'd been here, right here, in this bed or, at most, up in the chair by the window. Where was the window? In an attempt to gather information, though the motion could have been interpreted as greeting or even as plea, Cecelia meant to reach out her hand, wasn't sure whether she actually did.

"Oh, you know." Someone else was answering, pretending to be casual and modest, but with a dismissive shrug, twist of the mouth, toss of the head that belied a chilling self-satisfaction. This voice was even more familiar than the first, though Cecelia couldn't place it, either. "Here and there. To and fro. 'Round the earth, roaming about."

"Making trouble, no doubt."

"I don't *make* anything. I just point out possibilities." Cecelia felt movement, herself included in an expansive gesture.

A sharp odor had worked its way into her consciousness, or out of her consciousness, and now gave the impression of having always been there. Bittersweet, pungent, suggestive. Cecelia was alternately sickened and intoxicated by the odor. Nausea washed over her more or less randomly these days anyway, and exhilaration similarly intense and transient. The exhilaration had come as a surprise to her.

"Hi, Grandma. It's Luc. How're you doing?" Her grandson Luc, grown up.

His presence in her life had from the beginning been a miracle. He'd changed her life forever. When you came right down to it, everything changed your life. Her death would change his. *I'm dying*, she wanted him to acknowledge, but she didn't want to have to say so herself.

"Grandma, look. What is this thing? Dad let me have it. He said it was yours."

The name for the object surfaced immediately in her mind but was too hard to utter. *Stereopticon.* It wasn't hers.

"These cards are weird. The exact same picture on both halves."

Not exactly the same. The details are important. God is in the details, and so is the Devil. It's the little differences that matter.

Luc was shuffling the thick cards. "The Chicago Fire. The Alaska Gold Rush. The San Francisco Earthquake. Here's one of a little kid sitting on a potty."

He laughed too heartily. He was watching her. She smiled, but it might not have been apparent to him.

"Here's one of flowering bushes in the moonlight. There's no title. What are these, rhododendrons?"

338

The shaft of the stereopticon drifted into her field of vision like a spaceship in an old science-fiction movie. Cecelia reached up, partly to defend herself, partly to grasp it, and must have pulled the viewer over her eyes, for suddenly she was in a scene three-dimensional with color and texture. She heard crickets, a rushing stream, someone weeping and singing, and the aroma of the rhododendrons was the medium in which she and the rest of it floated. Apples grew on trees; she could smell them, and a snake in the grass.

She was moving. There was no sensation of walking or crawling or flight, but there were paths every which way and she was moving, stopping, moving again. This way or that way? Let this pebble lie or pick it up, set it down here or here or here, throw it into the water at the bottom of the ravine? Pluck this cluster of buds or leave it to spend itself still attached to its stem? Walk across this bridge, pause at the thirteenth or twenty-seventh or any other plank, turn around and go back?

"It doesn't matter what you do."

But every choice, one thing or another, this or not, *did* alter the scene in which she moved, transformed if only minutely the way it was constructed and the way it would from then on be viewed.

Another scene engulfed her. Again, her means of passage through it was unclear, though this time it had an exoskeletal feel, something having hardened around her that was now carrying her rapidly along. Dimly, at the edge of her peripheral vision: on a corner sliding past, someone in distress, someone who had harmed her and who, now, she had no reason even to notice. She *had* noticed, though, and so: To stop or not? She could go on by, and no one would ever know, including the woman on the corner.

"Why bother? Would she do the same for you? Would she even think about it?"

Here was a scene aflutter with hair ribbons, pink and green and white. The optical illusion collaged a young girl's face with the same face sixty years later, sharp-featured as a fox. What to say? What to say about what she had said?

"Oh, lighten up, Cecelia. No one else even remembers what you said back then."

She was on the phone with her husband, who claimed to be working late again tonight. She was listening to her daughter talk about peace and love, and her heart was breaking. Over the playground fence she was handing her son his lunch—

"Grandma, talk to me." The viewer was removed from against her eyes and Luc's face replaced it, not resting on the bridge of her nose and her eye sockets but nonetheless filling her entire field of vision, too close, so close it was hard to distinguish features, though she guessed it was Luc. She did see tears. "Grandma, please. I'm scared. I'm always scared."

These days her gaze wandered and lost focus of its own accord. She brought it back to Luc, but it slid away again. He lowered his head to her shoulder, as if she could put her arms around him.

She would try.

A sardonic chuckle, gently but pointedly mocking. "Celia, Celia. Let it go. Give yourself a break."

Cecelia managed to lay her forearm alongside the young man's flank, forming a long seam between them. What was happening had the feel of being both nearer and more distant than she knew it to be.

"You're wasting what little time you have left. Not everything's a moral choice, you know." Concern now, as if this were the last chance to save her from the lifelong error of her ways, and Cecelia allowed herself to relax a bit.

Luc was afraid. He couldn't remember a time when he hadn't been afraid; fear wasn't his only reality, but all other reality was viewed through fear, which made everything else seem both impossibly immediate and several times removed. He was afraid of losing this beloved old woman, his sentinel and beacon. He was afraid of coming this close to death himself though he knew he had come much closer before and of course would again, afraid he'd say or do the wrong thing and make it worse for her, *afraid.*

A smell took shape in the room with them, not body odors or the stench of bodily fluids, not the caretaking fragrances of powder and fresh flowers, but a bittersweet aroma without a readily discernible source. For a long time afterward, Luc would, wrongly, associate the smell with death.

His head cleared. It came into his mind to say to her, "Don't talk like that, Grandma. You'll outlive us all." Or he could kiss her and softly leave the room; anybody else would say he'd handled a difficult situation very well, and even if she sensed what he'd done—his failure of nerve, his perfidy—she wouldn't be around much longer to reproach him. He could, easily and without consequence, take himself out of the presence of death.

What would Grandma Cecelia do?

She was the person he most admired, and now he knew why. She had long practiced doing the hard thing when it was the right thing; she had made it a habit not to take the easy way out; she had considered, every time, what she ought to do. She had believed in the importance of details, and lived her life accordingly.

So, trembling, Luc eased himself into a position beside her that he could maintain, stroked her straight gray hair and mottled papery skin, watched her labored breathing and the spaces between breaths. "I'm here," he promised, though he was no less afraid.

Cecelia couldn't speak and had no interest in doing so. But she managed to make a shaky circle of her thumb and forefinger and raise it a few inches off the bed, an "OK" signal. Luc saw it and, weeping, smiled. Through the open window above the bed, a breeze filled the space they occupied, smelling of itself and nothing else, and another layer of dimensionality was added to this world.